Nellie

An Historic love story of heartache and betrayal

Sue Towler

To Joanne, thank you for your undying support throughout my writing journey these past few years.

Contents

OTHER BOOKS BY THIS AUTHOR

Elizabeth's Diaries

Brigit

Isolation

Sounds Bad

Tess's Tours – NZ's Wild West Coast

Tess's Tours – Aussie Outback

Deadly Reunion

Chapter One

London, 1843

Nellie covered her ears to block out the overwhelming noise of high-pitched screaming and people shouting. Choking black acrid smoke burned in her throat and stung her eyes. Desperate for escape, she turned and ran, she didn't want to watch the men straining to push down the levers on the water box, pumping water through the hose to spray on the flames devouring her home. She was frightened by the antics of the horse that drew the carriage, as it reared up against its handler who was trying desperately to un-tether it from the water wagon. She couldn't see Mama, Papa or Emilyn. Where were they? Fear gripped her and she kept running. She ran as far and as fast as her bare feet, wafting nightgown, and heavy winter overcoat would allow. When she was exhausted and everything was quiet, she allowed herself to slump down on the cobblestones with her back against the cold stone wall fronting a large, darkened house. Everywhere was dark, except for the small pools of yellow light under the streetlamps. She buried her head on her bent knees and started to sob, great wracking sobs of fear and anguish. A soft female voice and a gentle hand on her shoulder startled her and caused her to look up. There in the dim light was a smiling face full of warmth and comfort.

'My dear girl, what is it? What has gotten you so upset?' The woman scrunched down beside Nellie, placing a comforting arm around her shoulders. 'What has happened?'

Nellie gulped back a sob and fighting to stem the flow of tears tried haltingly to impart her story to this kindly stranger.

'My, my house is burning down,' she pointed in the direction she had come from, 'I can't find my Mama and Papa, and my sister Emilyn,' she sobbed.

'I can see the smoke from here,' sighed the woman sadly. 'I'm sure there will be people looking for you, neighbours and the like.'

Nellie nodded. The lady stood, and gently taking Nellie's hands, pulled her to her feet. Slowly they headed back to the cacophony surrounding the inferno that was once Nellie's home.

'Nellie,' shrieked Mrs Garreth, one of the neighbours. 'Thank God you are safe. Where are the rest of them?'

'I don't know?' Nellie cried desperately, 'I haven't seen them.'

Mrs Garreth looked at the woman standing beside Nellie still clutching the tearful child's hand in her own. 'Where was she? Where did you find her?'

'She was sitting on the street outside my house. I was watching the smoke from my front window when I saw her come running down the street. I could tell something was terribly wrong.'

'Thank you,' said Mrs Garreth taking Nellie's other hand, 'I can take her from here, I will take the poor child home with me.'

Mrs Garreth gathered the child into a firm embrace and held her there, tightly, letting her know she was safe and not alone, her own tears forming and spilling over, running down her cheeks unchecked.

****

'Mrs Garreth, come in, come in.'

The newly appointed Bank Manager ushered her into his dark office, indicating a brown leather seat in front of his sprawling leather topped desk. Sunlight streamed in through the single window lighting up the dust mites otherwise invisible to the naked eye.

'This is a terrible business,' he continued, 'thank you for taking care of young Miss Abernathy. Her father was much loved and revered here at the Bank, I am sure we have never had such a dedicated and hard-working manager. How is the poor child doing?'

Mrs Garreth pulled a handkerchief from her pocket and blew her nose.

'Not well I'm afraid Mr Snodgrass, she has hardly spoken a word since the day of the fire and eats very little. She just sits and stares into space as if she is in a world of her own.' Mrs Garreth sniffled into her handkerchief in a show of despair.

'Mrs Garreth, I have called you in because we have tracked down Miss Abernathy's Uncle, Silas Abernathy.'

Mr Snodgrass settled himself into his chair behind the desk and leaned forward, his forearms resting on his desk.

'He is her only living relative I believe, a Ship's Captain. His ship docked two days ago and I have had a brief discussion with him. As he spends most of his time at sea, he can see no way of taking on the care of his brother's child. The poor man is reeling from the shock of losing his brother and he is most concerned for his niece and asked if I could find someone suitable to take care of her on his behalf. There is a sum of money put aside to assist with her upbringing, might that someone be you Mrs Garreth? The reason I ask is that she is living with you at present, and you have known the girl most of her life. Are you able to take the girl on until she is old enough to fend for herself?

'You say there would be financial support?' Mrs Garreth leaned forward eagerly, her eyes lighting up at the prospect.

'Yes Mrs Garreth, there is. Enough to last for the next four or five years I would say.'

'Well then,' Mrs Garreth said decidedly, 'of course I am prepared to offer the dear girl a place in my home.'

Mr Snodgrass smiled to himself, he could see right through people like Mrs Garreth, but he hoped she would at least provide a comfortable home for Cordelia. There were not many options for a young orphaned twelve-year-old girl.

'Thank you, that is most kind of you, I will let Mr Abernathy know the matter has been settled then. Once the papers have been drawn up, I will send word for you to come and sign them.'

He stood and guided her to the door. 'Thank you for coming in Mrs Gareth, good day to you.'

Mr Snodgrass was more than a little concerned for his former boss's daughter. 'What would George have made of the situation?' he wondered. He made a mental note to keep an eye on young Miss Abernathy, for her sake as well as a show of respect for her dear departed father. Lord knows Mr Silas Abernathy was not in a position to do so, him being away at sea for months at a time.

Silas Abernathy was only too willing to allow the Garreth's to take on his niece. He barely knew the girl, and the fact that she was obviously troubled and grieving for her lost family would have been an added dilemma for a seafaring bachelor. He had liked Nellie on the odd occasion he had seen her, when he went to visit with his brother, her father. He thought she was a nice young lass, a little shy perhaps but polite and obedient. His heart went out to her, what would become of the poor girl? He would make sure he checked in on her every time he returned to port. He knew his brother would have wanted him to do that much at least.

'Boys, where is Nellie, I have something I want to tell you all.'

Enid Garreth bustled into the kitchen with an armload of food items crammed into paper bags which she dumped on the kitchen table.

'Dunno Mum, said the eldest, Richard. Last I saw, she was standing outside her burnt down house again. Why does she do that? Doesn't she know they ain't comin back?'

Enid Garreth sighed. She was becoming impatient with having to constantly go and drag Nellie away from the burnt-out shell of her old home. The poor girl would just stand there, mesmerised, staring into the ruins. Nellie squirmed and fought whenever one of the Garreth's tried to get her to come back to their home.

'I'm going to have to lock that girl in her room if this carries on,' she sighed. She threw open the door and was about to step across the stoop and head up the street when a large figure loomed in front of her.

'Might you be Mrs Garreth by any chance?' he boomed. He was a tall man, quite imposing, with a full beard and long greying hair tied back at the nape of his neck with a leather thong.

'I am,' replied Enid defensively. 'And who might you be?'

'Silas Abernathy at your service ma'am. I understand my niece is staying here with you.'

'She is, Mr Abernathy, yes.' Enid was a little shaken to suddenly come face to face with, until then, the mythical Silas Abernathy. She stood and stared at the man until he spoke again.

'May I come in and have a word with her then?'

Enid hesitated a moment longer, then leaning out so she could see up the street, pointed to the forlorn little figure staring at what was once a happy home full of love and hope.

'That's her, she stands there like that every chance she gets I'm afraid. There's just no getting through to her.'

Silas's heart melted. He strode quickly over to the girl and stood quietly behind her, not wanting to startle her.

'Nellie,' he whispered softly, 'Nellie, it's me, your Uncle Silas. You remember me, don't you?'

Nellie slowly turned around to look at the man calling her name. He crouched down so he could look into her eyes and placed his big gentle hands on her shoulders.

'Nellie, my dear sweet child, I have no idea what you must be going through. This is a dreadful business is it not?'

Nellie nodded.

Silas continued, he had the girl's attention, that was a good start.

'What happened Nellie, can you tell me what happened? Your father, my brother, I miss him too. Can we talk about him for a bit do you think?'

Nellie nodded again. Silas led Nellie over to the remains of a stone fence and sat her down beside him. He turned to face her and took both her hands in his.

'Tell me what happened Nellie, is it alright for you to talk about it?'

Nellie nodded as a tear trickled down her pale cheek.

'Papa said,' she started.

'That's good Nellie, what did your Papa say?'

Nellie cleared her throat; she hadn't spoken in so long her throat felt dry and husky.

'He said if I was ever to see fire or smell smoke when I was in my room, I was to jump out of my window and run to the other side of the road and wait for everyone else to come out.'

'You did well then Nellie, you did exactly what your Papa told you to do, that was very good.'

'But,' her bottom lip trembled, 'they didn't come out, I kept waiting but they didn't come out.'

Silas allowed a tear to roll down his own cheek.

'I know my lovely, I know. They just weren't able to get out in time because they were in the rooms upstairs and yours was downstairs. Your Mama and Papa would have been so proud of you for doing what you did.'

'I don't want to be here without them Uncle Silas. I am all alone now, I want to be with them, I don't want to be here on my own.'

'But you are here Nellie, and you need to make the best of it now. You are a strong wee lass, just like your Mama, she was strong too. Do you think you can make your Mama proud Nellie?'

'How can she be proud Uncle Silas, she is not here to see me.'

'She will know because she will be watching down on you from Heaven, sending you lots of love and encouragement, so will your Papa and Emilyn. They will be looking down from heaven saying, come on Nellie, you can do it, be a big brave girl now and get on with your life. We will watch over you.'

'Do you really think so?'

'I know so Nellie. A man doesn't spend as much time at sea as I have done, and not know that these things are true, believe me.'

He drew Nellie to him and hugged her close. She melted into his big strong arms, relaxing into the comfort and smell of him.

'I like you Uncle Silas, I am glad you are here, and I am glad you are my uncle. Are we the only ones left in our family now?'

'Yes my lass, we are, we are the only family we have left.'

'Can I come and live with you then?'

Silas's heart broke. 'Nellie I am a ship's Captain; I spend more time at sea than I do on land. It just wouldn't be right to leave you here all on your own while I am away. I will come and see you every time I am in port though, and I will bring you lots of lovely presents. Would you like that?

Nellie nodded.

'In the meantime, you are to stay with the Garreth's and continue with your education.'

Nellie was sad, she had hoped to escape from the Garreth's. Living with Uncle Silas would be much better.

'Nellie,' Silas crouched down in front of her again. 'Please, this is the best we can do for you right now. I am sure the Garreth's will take good care of you, and if they don't you can tell me about it next time I come home. How would that be, will you be a good girl for the Garreth's, for me?'

Silas's heart was softening towards this young girl, his niece. He walked Nellie back to the Garreth's house where they found Mrs Garreth waiting on the doorstep, pretending to sweep it while she kept an eye on proceedings.

'I think Nellie will be alright now Mrs Garreth, we have had a good long talk, haven't we Nellie?'

Nellie nodded obediently.

'I will look in on her next time I am in port to make sure all is going well.'

'Will you stop for a cup of tea Mr Abernathy?'

'Not this time I'm afraid, my ship awaits me at the dock. Next time I will though, and I promise I will come bearing gifts for you all from the West Indies.'

'The West Indies Mr Abernathy?' Mrs Garreth's eyes were alight. 'My my, such exotic places you must visit on your travels.'

'I do indeed Mrs Garreth.' He kissed Nellie on the top of her head and smiled and waved as he walked off down the street to the dock.

Nellie settled down after Silas's visit and started to come out of her shell and become more involved with the family. She liked the Garreth's well enough, Mr Garreth was a quiet man, tall, lean, and gruff looking, but Nellie soon learned that beneath the gruff exterior Mr Garreth had a big warm heart, she liked him. Mrs Garreth was a motherly sort, she took care of all the household doings as well as the money side of things. Nellie was not aware of the financial dealings that went on between the Garreth's and the bank. She thought the Garreth's had taken her in out of the goodness of their hearts and she was very grateful. She offered to leave school and go to work to help pay her way, but Mrs Garreth said she would have none of it.

'Nellie you are a clever young lass with a good brain in your head, I will not have you leaving off your education. Me and Mr Garreth will take care of you, for now.'

Nellie was relieved, she enjoyed school and consistently gained good marks. She settled into a comfortable routine within the family and did her best to help out where she could. Being the eldest child in the household she helped to take care of the two Garreth children, Richard, ten, and Alfred, eight. They walked to and from school together under Nellie's watchful eye. Although they could be rambunctious at times Nellie liked the boys, she had never lived with young boys before, just her younger sister Emilyn. She grieved deeply for Emilyn, the two were only a year apart in age and were best friends as well as sisters.

Normal everyday life continued in the Garreth household for the next two years, with the promised visits of Silas Abernathy, who never failed to bring delightful exotic gifts from faraway places. Just shy of Nellie's fourteenth birthday her life underwent another upheaval. Mr Garreth had been feeling unwell and had taken to his bed, which was most unlike him, he had always been strong and healthy with seldom a sick day off work. His health continued to get worse over the next few weeks. One night there was a quiet knock on Nellie's bedroom door.

'Nellie, are you awake dear?'

Nellie sat up in her bed. 'Yes.'

Mrs Garreth came and stood by the bed. Nellie shifted over to allow her to sit down.

'Nellie, there are going to be a lot of changes happening here soon and they will concern you. Mr Garreth has the Consumption and the Doctor has suggested we take him to the country, the fresh air will help him breathe easier. I have written to my sister in the Cotswolds asking if we might go and live there with her and her husband. They have two children of their own, but they have offered us two rooms, one for Mr Garreth and me and one for the boys.' She hesitated for a moment. 'What I am trying to say Nellie is that I'm afraid we won't be able to take you with us.'

Nellie's blood ran cold. 'But, what, what will happen to me?' she wailed.

'Please don't fret my dear, we will do everything we can to get you settled somewhere else.'

Nellie flung her arms around Mrs Garreth's neck. 'Please,' she cried, 'Please take me with you, I couldn't bear to lose my family again.'

'I am very sorry Nellie, there is nothing I can do, I would very much like to take you with us, but I'm afraid I just can't.'

Mrs Garreth pulled Nellie's arms from around her neck and hurriedly left the room before Nellie saw the tears streaming down her own cheeks. She was fond of the girl but there simply was not going to be any room for her at her sister's house.

Chapter Two

Orphanage – London 1845-1847

Clutching the small brown suitcase with all her worldly possessions neatly packed inside, Nellie tentatively opened the door and stepped across the threshold of the main entrance to the orphanage. The bright red brick exterior with its freshly painted white windowsills did nothing to allay Nellie's fears. Her life was starting all over again for the second time in just two years. Tears welled up in her eyes as she looked around the large, dark foyer with doors leading off in all directions, and a wide sweeping staircase leading up to the second floor.

'Hello, you must be Cordelia Abernathy.'

Nellie swung around to see a short, ample bosomed woman with a bright cheerful smile extending her hand in greeting.

Nellie took the warm outstretched hand. 'Yes,' she replied.

'Well, welcome to Knightsbridge Orphanage,' she said, 'let's go in here where we can have a cup of tea and get acquainted.'

Nellie followed the woman into a warm sitting room featuring deep red cushions on two large comfortable lounge chairs and a fire roaring away in the open fireplace, topped by a beautifully carved mantle covered in photographs.

'Sit down here by the fire my dear, you must be quite chilled.'

'Yes, I am a bit cold,' confessed Nellie removing her plain brown felt hat and matching gloves.

The woman poured strong black tea into two fine china cups.

'My name is Mrs Bell but you are welcome to call me Bella, most people do,' she smiled warmly. 'I much prefer Bella to the alternative, Mrs Ding-a-ling.'

Her smile was contagious and it was all Nellie could do not to laugh out loud. She smiled back at Bella and took the cup offered to her.

'Now then young lady, you are a bit of an anomaly for us. Normally we only take in children who are orphaned and under the age of twelve, but you are not exactly an orphan are you, and you are certainly not a child. How old are you, fourteen did they say?'

'Yes,' replied Nellie settling her cup back in the matching saucer. I turned fourteen three weeks ago. Is that a problem?'

'The children's dormitories are almost at capacity, but I have talked with the other members of staff and, considering your age and the fact that you are apparently good with children, we have decided to make an exception in your case. We have a bed for you in the staff quarters, you will be rooming with Jean, she is one of our kitchen gals, a lovely lass not much older than yourself. Now the stipend from your father's estate will cover some of your expenses but you will be expected to do your share of the work in the laundry and the kitchen.

'Stipend? What stipend please?' asked Nellie, confused.

'The money paid for your keep, did you not know of this? It was paid to your former carers, the Garreth's and now that money will come to us.'

Nellie was shocked. 'They were paid to take me in?'

'Yes my dear, they were,' Bella said bluntly.

'I, I didn't know that,' mumbled Nellie over the lump in her throat. 'Is it a lot of money?'

'It's not a fortune by any means but it will cover your accommodation, the rest you will have to work for.

Before Nellie could dwell any further on the situation, Bella picked up Nellie's suitcase and beckoned for her to follow.

'I understand you can read quite well, is that correct Miss Abernathy?'

'Yes I like to read.'

'Very well, you can help teach the children to read, and in the evenings you can assist Miss Murtagh with the mending. Mrs

Garreth tells me you helped her with the mending.'

'Yes I did,' responded Nellie eagerly, 'Mrs Garreth taught me to sew, I like needlework.'

'Good, that's settled then. Breakfast is at 6 o'clock sharp, if you are late you will miss out. This is your bed, and this is Jean's bed. Jean will be in the kitchen helping with dinner preparations no doubt. Dinner is at 5.30. I suggest you unpack your things then get down to the kitchen and see if there is anything you can do to help.'

Nellie hated the orphanage right from the very start, it was nothing like living with the Garreth's. The rules were very strict and she could not come and go as she pleased. Mrs Garreth had always trusted Nellie to do as she was told and allowed her to go off by herself to visit with school friends during the weekends and sometimes after school, before dinner. So long as she did her chores, Nellie could spend her time as she chose. Now though, her every waking moment was taken up with chores. There was no more schooling, no learning, just long endless days of chores and helping with the younger children.

'How many hours does it take to pay for my food and keep if my accommodation is already taken care of?' Nellie asked Jean one evening as they were getting ready for bed.

'If you live here under their roof Nellie, you will always be put to work no matter what your circumstances,' sighed Jean as she dropped exhausted, on to her bed.

Nellie lay awake for some time trying to figure out if there was some way she could escape from the orphanage. Where could she go, what would she do?

It took Nellie a few weeks to get used to the noise and the hustle and bustle of the orphanage. The only quiet time was in the evenings when the children were asleep, or were meant to be, and she and Miss Murtagh would sit by the glowing embers of the fire and mend the children's clothes. Katherine Murtagh was an excellent seamstress and Nellie was eager to learn from her. Whenever the time and opportunity arose, Katherine taught Nellie how to make a pattern and cut cloth to make dresses, trousers and shirts for the children. Nellie was in her element; she was fascinated by the whole process and gradually became bold enough to make designs and patterns of her own. Katherine was impressed with the speed with which Nellie was progressing.

'You are such a quick learner Nellie, you should think about becoming a seamstress.'

'Do you really think so? Do you think I could ever be that good?' asked Nellie eagerly.

'Yes of course I do, you are already very good you know. If I was you, I would learn all I could about fabrics and the way they are made and where they come from? Learn about haberdashery too.'

'What is haberdashery?'

'Ribbons, laces, buttons, embellishments, trimming for garments, things like that,' smiled Katherine.

By the time Katherine had finished talking, Nellie's mind was made up.

'Yes,' she enthused, 'yes that is exactly what I will do, I am going to become a world-famous fashion designer and create fancy clothes for high society ladies,' she laughed as she danced around the room holding up an imaginary gown.

The seed had been sown in Nellie's mind, she worked tirelessly alongside Katherine from then on, learning everything Katherine was able to teach her. The evenings spent with Katherine were the only times Nellie enjoyed being at the orphanage. The children were unruly and difficult a lot of the time and when she wasn't helping in the classroom, she was scrubbing clothes in the laundry or cleaning and helping out with chores in the kitchen. Even though she was exhausted by the end of the day, she would still find the energy to help Katherine with the mending. She didn't consider this work though, she enjoyed it.

The next time Silas Abernathy arrived back in port, he was

disturbed to find that the Garreth's had moved, and even more mortified to find that Nellie was now living in an orphanage. He felt guilty, but he didn't know what to do about it. He wasn't about to give up his life at sea to take care of a child, besides, he wouldn't know what to do with himself if he had to stay on shore for any length of time.

Nellie was thrilled to see her uncle strolling up the path to the front door of the orphanage one day. It had been more than six months since she had last seen him.

'Children,' she called out above the hubbub, 'come and meet my Uncle Silas, he's just arrived back from the high seas.'

The children peered eagerly out the window. Uncle Silas was wearing his colourful uniform of red jacket with gold buttons, white trousers with knee length hose, and black shoes with shiny gold buckles. His black tri cornered hat was tucked firmly under his arm. As soon as he spotted Nellie running towards him, he tossed the hat down and picked her up in his arms, swinging her around as she giggled. The children squealed and clapped their hands with delight.

'What on earth is all this racket about,' boomed Bella from her room across the hall. Oh, I do beg your pardon sir, I didn't realise we had company.' She glared at Nellie. 'What on earth are you doing girl, get back into the classroom immediately.'

'But this is…,' began Nellie.

'Now,' boomed Bella. She turned to Silas Abernathy. 'I do apologise for the unruly outbreak sir; how may I help you?'

'I have come to see my niece, Miss Abernathy, if you please. I am Silas Abernathy at your service ma'am,' he bowed deeply hiding his grin.

'Oh, dear me, my apologies Mr Abernathy, do forgive me. Nellie! Come here my dear,' called Bella placatingly.

'Yes Miss Bella?' called Nellie, feigning innocence.

'Please take your uncle into the parlour and I will arrange for someone to bring you tea.'

She hurried off, obviously embarrassed by her outburst.

Silas spent the next hour telling Nellie about his latest trip.

Nellie was a bit sceptical about some of the tales he told but she wasn't about to interject, she hung on his every word.

'I wish I had known about you being in the orphanage,' he said later as they walked arm in arm around the grounds, I would have brought the children some presents for one thing.'

'Good heavens Uncle, there are almost thirty children here, you couldn't possibly buy presents for all of them, it would cost a fortune.'

Nellie,' he stopped and looked down at her fresh upturned face, 'your father left his stocks and bonds to me and I am well paid for what I do, I can certainly afford to buy gifts besides, I have nobody else to buy for. I love going to the colourful markets and looking at all the beautiful things on display.'

'What about fabrics Uncle Silas, do you get to see lots of satins and silks and laces and ribbons and things.'

'Why yes I do, I have seen some very fine fabrics in my time. Do you like fabrics lass? I could certainly get some for you on my next trip, I'm off to France in a few days. A good acquaintance of mine might be able to source some fine fabrics for me, his wife always seems to be dressed in the finest of cloth and trim, how would that be?'

Nellie was bursting with excitement, 'Oooh yes please Uncle Silas, I am learning to sew, I am going to be a seamstress one day.'

'Are you now, well good for you, I will certainly keep an eye out then, now that I know what you are about. Now tell me, are they looking after you here? I hope you are not being taken advantage of, you know they are being well paid to take care of you, don't you?'

Nellie hung her head. 'I don't like it here Uncle Silas, I really don't like it at all. I only found out about the stipend when I came here, Mrs Garreth never said anything to me about it.'

'Aaah,' he said, 'I thought that might have been the case. Did they treat you well though Nellie? You never complained when I came to see you.'

'Yes Uncle, they did, the Garreth's treated me very well, better than they treat me here. I have to work hard every hour of the day,' she said petulantly.

'I am sorry to hear that Nellie, do you want me to have a word with...?'

'No, please don't say anything, it will only make things worse.'

Silas was not so sure about that but he reluctantly agreed to let things ride for now. 'If things haven't improved by the time I come back from France I will see if there is something else we might be able to do for you Nellie. Will you be alright until then?'

Nellie nodded. She knew nothing would change but she was at least fed and had a warm bed to sleep in, and she certainly didn't want to incur anyone's wrath and end up on the street. Besides, she had a dear friend in Katherine now.

Nellie was sad to see her uncle head off to sea again. She only saw him once or twice a year, it was not nearly enough for her, but he was not about to give up his life on the ocean, not even for her. He had never married and had no children, Nellie was all he had, he didn't like to leave her either but what was he to do? He recalled a conversation he'd had with Nellie on one of his visits when she was still with the Garreth's.

'Maybe I will let you look after me in my old age, when I am too old to put to sea,' he'd offered her.

'I would like that Uncle Silas, I really would. We could live in a nice little house in the country.'

'That sounds grand, as long as it has a view of the ocean though. I must be able to at least see the sea, even if I am no longer able to sail on it.' He'd smiled down at her upturned face and affectionately kissed her on the nose.

Chapter Three

London, 1847

Five months after Silas's visit, Nellie got a visit from Mr Snodgrass, the Bank manager. He called to see her at the orphanage and was shown into Bella's front room. Bella stood up and left as Nellie came in.

'Hello Miss Abernathy, Nellie, how are you my dear?'

'I am well, thank you Mr Snodgrass. What do you want to see me for?'

'Sit down Nellie, we need to have a discussion. I will get straight to the point,' he said avoiding eye contact with her.

'Your Father's funds are running out I'm afraid. We predicted that we thought they would last until you were sixteen, that is six months away is it not?'

Nellie nodded.

'I will speak to your Uncle Silas on his return, I am sure he will be able to help you financially in the future.'

Nellie sat stock still, hardly daring to breathe. 'So, I will be penniless?' she squeaked.

'Almost, I'm afraid. There is enough to last another two or three months and that is all. I suggest you find work where you can so that you can look after yourself.'

He rose abruptly, feeling decidedly uncomfortable with the conversation. The stricken look on Nellie's face was more than he could bear.

'I wish you well Miss Abernathy, I wish you well indeed. Please do not hesitate to come and see me if there is anything I can help you with.' He coughed back the lump in his throat and walked out the door.

Bella came back into the room as soon as Mr Snodgrass left.

'Well girl, I suppose that is that. If there's no more money coming in then we have no further use for you here,' she said cruelly.

'But what about the work I have been doing? Won't that be enough to pay my board and keep?' she pleaded.

'No child. We are fully staffed, we have no further need of your services, you will need to make other arrangements.'

Bella stormed out of the room. She was annoyed that the money coming in for Nellie's upkeep was running out. She had kept the payments to herself and had been putting it all away in an account of her own without telling anyone else about it.

Nellie tearfully poured her heart out to Katherine that evening.

'What am I going to do Katherine, where am I to go, I am only fifteen. I have never lived on my own before.'

Katherine gathered Nellie into her arms and hugged her tightly.

'My poor dear child, what a terrible situation you are in. I am sorry Bella has not agreed to keep you on, I don't understand why she is asking you to leave all of a sudden.'

'The stipend that was coming from my father's estate to pay for my board and keep has almost run out, I will no longer be able to pay my way,' she sniffled.

'Pay your way? Good heavens, I thought you were here like the rest of us, working to pay for board and keep, and all this time Bella was being paid as well? This is not right Nellie, this is simply not right at all. When is your uncle due back in port?'

"I never know when he is coming home, he just turns up. He's been gone for a long time now so he can't be too far away.'

'Where does your uncle stay when he comes home Nellie?'

Nellie's eyes lit up. 'Of course. He has rooms above the shipping office, I could stay there.'

'Oh I don't think you should stay there on your own, it might not be safe, besides, what would you do for money?'

'I will find work,' said Nellie defiantly. 'I will find work and I will keep house for Uncle Silas, I'm all the family he has you know.'

Katherine was sympathetic, 'Yes I do know,' she sighed, 'but I still don't think you should be there alone.'

'Then why don't you come with me?' Nellie challenged Katherine.

'What? I, I couldn't.'

'Why not, we could take in sewing. Yes, why don't we do that Katherine, you and I, we could take in mending and sew ladies' dresses and men's shirts.' Nellie was becoming excited.

'Well, I suppose it's worth thinking about. When do you have to leave?'

Mr Snodgrass said there is about three months' worth of payments left.'

'If I left now, then Mr Snodgrass might let me have that money instead of paying it to Bella,'

'Yes, yes he might,' pondered Katherine.

'Come with me Katherine, please?' Nellie begged.

'I will think about it and let you know tomorrow,' smiled Katherine, but in truth she had already made up her mind. She was almost twenty-one, she had been at the orphanage for five years and was ready to try something, anything, new.

Early next morning the two girls left notes on their beds saying they were leaving and walked out of the orphanage with their suitcases. They walked briskly down to the bank and sat on a seat outside waiting for it to open. Mr Snodgrass was surprised to see them when he arrived to unlock the door. He invited them in and after hearing what they had to say, was more than happy to transfer the funds to Nellie. Nellie was shocked to discover how sizeable the stipend had been and she was angry that she had been treated like a slave at the orphanage. She considered telling Mr Snodgrass about the way she had been treated but decided it was best left alone, she didn't want to cause any trouble.

They left the bank and walked straight down to the shipping

office.

'Leave the talking to me,' offered Katherine, 'I will try and convince them that you are my sister and that we are Silas Abernathy's kin and he has invited us to make use of his lodgings while he is away.'

Katherine played her part so well that the clerk in the shipping office went out of his way to assist them. He showed them up to Silas's rooms above the shipping office and made sure they had everything they needed. They were to let him know if he could help them further. As soon as he shut the door behind him, the girls fell about laughing.

'We did it Katherine, we are here, in Uncle Silas's rooms, I can hardly believe it.'

'Well don't get too comfortable Nellie, we don't know what your uncle is going to think about this when he gets back.'

The girls spent the next two days cleaning and tidying up the two adjoining rooms making them more like a home than a rarely used bachelor pad.

'I do hope Uncle Silas likes what we have done,' Nellie said a little fearfully.

They didn't have to wait long to find out. As they sat by the fire sewing one evening a week later, they heard loud voices then heavy footsteps coming up the stairs. The door flew open and there in all his glory stood Uncle Silas.

'What the dickens is going on here?' He glared at the two girls.

'Uncle Silas, please don't be angry, we had nowhere else to go.'

'What do you mean Nellie, why aren't you back at the orphanage. And you,' he addressed Katherine,' what are you doing here?'

'I didn't want to be on my own so I begged Katherine to come with me. I'm sorry Uncle Silas but the orphanage didn't want me anymore because the money ran out.'

Silas was stunned for a moment. 'Money? Your father's money has run out? Good heavens. I figured there would be enough money in his account to last much longer than this, I'm sure there was. I'm sorry lass, I didn't mean to fire off at you, I was just surprised to see you here that's all. Katherine I am pleased you are here to keep an eye on Nellie, but you can't stay here, it just wouldn't be right. This is not the best of places to live, too many rough characters hanging around these parts so close to the docks.'

'Uncle Silas, please, I am sure we will be fine, we will be very careful and only go out during daylight hours. We thought we could take in mending and perhaps make dresses and shirts for people. We just have to earn some money to buy the fabrics first.'

Silas slumped down on his chair and rested his head in his hands.

'Good Lord, this is the last thing I expected to find when I came home,' he said, his lips curling in a reluctant smile. He looked up at the girls then looked around at his now clean and tidy lodgings.

'Well, you haven't wasted any time cleaning up around here have you, thank you, it looks grand.'

'Would you like a small ale or something to eat?' asked Katherine.

'How about I take you both down to the Old Bell for a pork pie. They know me well there; I can introduce you to the proprietor and ask him to keep an eye on you while I am away.'

"You mean we can stay?' squealed Nellie.

'Yes lass, I guess there isn't much of an option is there.' Silas couldn't help but smile back at the girls' delighted faces.

Silas took a room at the Inn just down the road from his shipping office until he was able to purchase another bed. The girls were happy to share a bed when he was home but he would make sure they had a bed each while he was away. By the end of the week the rooms had been turned from basic accommodation into a warm and inviting home with new curtains, lace tablecloth, flowers in a vase on the table and new bedding and pillows. Katherine and Nellie had even found a lovely painting of a ship at sea, to hang on the wall. Silas loved it.

'Now then ladies, I have a surprise for you too, one I am sure will please you mightily.'

'What is it Uncle Silas?' asked Nellie impatiently.

'Well, by my reckoning it should be here directly, it is being brought up from the ship as we speak. I wanted to wait until we had everything sorted out in here first.'

A short time later there was a lot of noise and banging coming from downstairs and eventually a knock on the door.

'Answer that would you Nellie?' called Silas from the back room, 'it will be for you.'

Nellie opened the door to see two sailors struggling to hold on to a large wooden chest.

She stood back, opening the door wide. As they dropped the trunk to the floor Silas emerged from his room.

'Thankee' lads, I am much obliged. Here, take this for your troubles,' he handed them a coin each.

Nellie was fidgeting excitedly. 'If this is what I think it is Uncle Silas, I am bursting at the seams to see it.'

'Can't have you doin that lass,' he laughed. He took a key from his pocket, unlocked the trunk and threw the lid back with a great flourish. 'Take a look at this my girl,' he smiled proudly.

Nellie squealed with delight. Katherine peering over her shoulder let out an audible 'ooooh'. There, stacked to the brim, were mounds of beautiful fabrics the likes of which Katherine and Nellie had never seen. The girls pulled the bolts of colour out one by one, stroking them admiringly. Near the bottom of the box they were delighted to find ribbons, laces, threads and trim of every colour. Nellie leapt to her feet and threw her arms around her beloved uncle's neck.

'Uncle Silas, thank you so much, you have no idea how much this means to us. We will be able to make beautiful gowns for the ladies and fine shirts for the men.'

Silas was pleased. He loved to peruse the markets and more than that, he loved to buy gifts. He had formed useful acquaintances in France and was pleased with what he had managed to acquire for his niece, he knew she would make good use of it. At least it would give her something to do and give her some income of her own while he was at sea. He would cover all her expenses, leaving her to put aside her own earnings to purchase whatever else she might need. He was a wealthy man and he would offer to set her up so that she didn't have to work, but he didn't think she would be comfortable with that idea, she was an independent young woman and he wanted to encourage that in her. He was also pleased Katherine was there. Being a little older, she had a level head on her shoulders and was proving to be an ideal companion for Nellie.

Chapter Four

London 1848

By the time Silas Abernathy returned from sea seven months later, the women had successfully established themselves as reputable seamstresses. He was very proud of them, although his rooms now looked more like a lady's haberdashery than accommodation rooms.

'Maybe we should consider finding somewhere more suitable for you to set yourselves up,' he suggested. 'I'm heading off to the West Indies on Monday but I hope to be back in about four or five months. Why don't you see if you can find something while I am away and we can sort out a lease when I get back,' he suggested.

Nellie and Katherine were excited at the prospect and spent the next two weeks walking around the streets looking for suitable rooms in which to set up a small sewing and haberdashery business. Eventually they found the perfect solution. They had told Mr Hicks, in the shipping office downstairs, what they were looking for, and when they returned home one afternoon he called out to them.

'Have you found anything suitable yet ladies?'

'No nothing yet Mr Hicks,' said Nellie forlornly. 'We have looked everywhere within walking distance.'

'Well then, I may have a solution for you, come with me.'

Mr Hicks ushered them out the front door, locking it behind him. He marched straight across the street and stopped outside the delightful little confectionery store. It had big bay-windows on either side of the door welcoming the morning sun and a tiny bell that jangled brightly as they entered.

'Mr Hicks, what is it your sweet tooth desires today?' asked the smiling, portly woman behind the counter.

'As a matter of fact, I am not here to purchase your delectable treats today Mildred. You mentioned last week that you were thinking of letting go your lease on this store and moving closer to town. Is that still the case?'

It might be Mr Hicks, it might be, why do you ask?' she was eyeing Katherine and Nellie curiously as she spoke.

'May I introduce Miss Murtagh and Miss Abernathy.'

'I know you,' smiled Mildred, 'I seen you come and go from them shipping offices of yours Mr Hicks.'

'Yes you have Mildred. Miss Abernathy is Silas Abernathy's niece and this is her friend Miss Katherine Murtagh. Miss Abernathy has no other family than Mr Abernathy so she is staying here with him.'

'Hmmmph,' responded Mildred crossing her arms across her ample bosom. 'I did wonder what was going on across there, now I know. So, what has my moving got to do with you?'

'Well,' Mr Hicks placed his hands on the counter and leaned forward. 'These ladies are looking for somewhere to set up their haberdashery.'

'Haberdashery you say? Well,' Mildred cast her eyes around the room, 'I suppose it could do well as a haberdashery. I will have a word with the owner Mr Hicks, and if he is interested I will let you know. I'm not sure he would wish to deal with two young women though, are you going to vouch for them?'

'I will vouch for them Mildred, but Mr Abernathy will no doubt be dealing with the paperwork.'

'Very well then,' she said.

Katherine and Nellie beamed at Mildred. 'Oh, this place will be perfect ma'am,' Nellie said politely. 'Thank you.'

Mildred softened, 'I ain't seen you two in my shop before, are ye not liking sweeties then?'

'We love sweets,' said Katherine, 'but it is a luxury we haven't

25

yet afforded ourselves.'

'Well, because this is a special occasion, let me fill a wee bag for you to take and have with your tea, and be sure to tell that uncle of yours where you got them.'

Nellie smiled and took the package. 'I will certainly do that, thank you.'

'This place looks perfect,' Katherine whispered to Nellie as they left the shop. 'I'm sure Silas will approve, don't you?

'I do, yes. Thank you Mr Hicks, I believe you have found us the perfect place.'

They were so excited with their find they decided to treat themselves to a pie and a pint at the Old Bell to celebrate. As they waited for the owner, Mr Croxley, to bring their order, Katherine leaned close to Nellie and whispered in her ear.

'Look over there Nellie, that young man keeps looking this way, I think he is looking at you.'

Nellie turned to see where Katherine was indicating and found herself locking eyes with the most handsome young man she had ever seen in her life. He had dark red hair, bright blue eyes and a smile that lit up his whole face, Nellie couldn't stop herself from smiling back. That was enough encouragement for the man to leave his seat and come over to their table. Nellie felt her face flush red hot, she had never had anything to do with men before, other than family members. She had no idea what to say to him so she left the talking to Katherine, although Katherine wasn't any more confident talking with men than Nellie was.

'Good evening ladies. Nickolas O'Rourke at your service,' he bowed deeply causing the women to giggle. 'Might I join ye then?'

Katherine and Nellie looked at each other and giggled again, not sure whether to allow him to sit or not. Katherine glanced around the room; nobody seemed to be taking any notice so she indicated the vacant chair between them.

'Thank you ladies, mighty kind of ye. Now what are you two lovely lasses doing out alone?'

'We, um, we,' began Nellie.

'We have been looking for business premises for our guardian,' Katherine said quickly.

'Is that so? And what sort of business might that be then?'

'I'm not sure we wish to discuss this with you Mr O'Rourke, we don't know you and we haven't yet discussed it with our guardian.'

'Who is this guardian you speak of?' he asked.

'You are very inquisitive Mr O'Rourke.' Katherine was becoming a bit miffed at his questioning.

'Sorry,' he said hanging his head, 'I just wanted to know more about you, you seem to be mighty fine ladies. These streets aren't very safe, I would be happy to escort you home if you would allow me,' he offered.

'I am sure we will be just fine Mr O'Rourke but thank you for your kind offer. Mr Croxley turned up at the table just then, with two steaming pies and two mugs of small ale perched on his wooden tray.

'I hope this young man isn't bothering you ladies,' he eyed Nick with a grin.

'Not at all,' lied Katherine. She could see that Nellie was very much bothered, but not in a bad way. She barely ate her pie and seeing it lying neglected on her plate getting cold, Nick dared to ask if he could finish it for her. Nellie merely nodded, her mouth open in awe.

When they had finished their drinks, Katherine shoved her chair back and took Nellie's arm. Nellie, still staring at Nick, seemed oblivious to Katherine speaking to her.

'Nellie!'

Nellie clicked out of her reverie. 'Oh yes, um thank you Mr O'Rourke for your offer to walk us home but we will be just fine.'

They left the pub and made their way hurriedly to their rooms shutting the door behind them before letting out their held-in breaths. They looked at each other and started laughing.

'Well, that was interesting wasn't it,' laughed Katherine.

'He was a very good-looking man, don't you think?' Nellie

sighed, all glassy eyed.

'Goodness Nellie you are quite smitten aren't you.'

Nellie smiled shyly. 'I've never had a man take any notice of me before.'

'Well don't go throwing yourself at the first man who comes along Nellie Abernathy, there will be plenty more suitors I'm sure.'

'But I am nearly seventeen Katherine, I'm practically ancient.'

'Well, if you are ancient what does that make me, I'm twenty-three.'

'Sorry.' So why have you never married? You know everything about me but I fear I have never asked you much about your past life.'

'I was in love with a lovely young man once but he died of influenza. We were at school together, we grew up together. When my parents got sick and died his family took me in. I loved him so much Nellie, he was such a lovely young man. The pain I went through when he died was so dreadful, I decided then and there that I would never allow myself to go through such heartache again.' A tear ran down Katherine's cheek.

Nellie knelt down beside Katherine's chair resting her head on her friend's shoulder, placing a comforting arm around her.

'I am so sorry Katherine, I had no idea.'

'I don't talk about it so how could you have known. Maybe one day I will meet a nice man who will change my mind, but I won't hold my breath.'

The women worked hard over the next few weeks, sewing garments to display in their new premises. One evening they decided to treat themselves to another meal at the Old Bell.

'Good evening ladies, nice to see you again, is everything going well for you?'

'Yes, thank you Mr Croxley,' replied Nellie. 'We thought we might have some dinner here tonight.'

'Excellent idea. Did you walk here alone?'

'Yes we did, but nobody bothered us.'

'There are two ship loads of sailors docked at the wharf at the moment, they have been at sea for many months and I'm sure some of them will be looking for trouble. I would prefer that someone escort you home when you are ready to leave. Silas would never forgive me if I let anything happen to you.'

'I'm sure we will be fine,' said Nellie.

'Thank you Mr Croxley,' Katherine jumped in, 'We gladly accept your kind offer.'

When they finished their dinner Mr Croxley beckoned them over and introduced them to a man he considered would be able to see them safely to their door. None other than Nick O'Rourke.

'Why Mr O'Rourke, we meet again,' smiled Nellie, her face flushing.

'Oh yes of course, I forgot, you have already met Mr O'Rourke?' Mr Croxley smiled.

'We have,' responded Katherine.

'Good. Nick, I want you to stay close and take special care of these two young ladies, they are under the guardianship of a very good friend of mine.'

'I will not let them out of my sight sir,' replied Nick politely, winking at Nellie, causing her to go all weak at the knees.

When the women were ready to leave, Nick joined them and they walked down the cobble-stone streets together in silence. There was a lot of activity going on around them. Girls of the night leaned provocatively against the stone walls of their establishments inviting sex-starved sailors in for some light relief while pick pockets mingled among the crowds taking advantage of anyone who wasn't paying attention. Hawkers offered baked goods and flowers from their baskets while the local lads stood around their fire pits glaring at the sailors invading their patch. Nick's eyes were constantly scanning, watching for any sign of trouble, he was very relieved when they finally arrived at the Shipping Office door unscathed.

'Thank you Nick, that was most kind of you.'

Katherine extended her hand to shake Nick's. Instead, Nick

took her hand and put it to his lips, kissing her knuckles. She smiled coquettishly at him. He then turned to Nellie and did the same.

'I thought I would faint,' Nellie said dreamily once they were safely inside and out of earshot. 'He makes my heart go all of a flutter,' she sighed.

'So I've noticed, you really are quite taken with him aren't you. I suppose we shall just have to frequent Mr Croxley's premises again soon then,' laughed Katherine.

And that's exactly what they did. Every Sunday the women treated themselves to dinner at Mr Croxley's establishment, knowing full well that Mr O'Rourke would be hanging around eager to walk them home. The next time he escorted them back to their lodgings, the conversation flowed a little more freely and by the fourth week they were becoming more and more relaxed and open with each other. Then one evening Nick asked Nellie if he could take her out on a picnic to the beach the following Sunday afternoon.

Nellie looked to Katherine for approval and received it.

'Go ahead Nellie, enjoy your day out, goodness knows you deserve a break. You have done nothing but sew your fingers to the bone since we moved here.'

'So have you Katherine. Why don't you come too?'

'No, not this time, I will enjoy the peace and quiet while you are gone,' she laughed.

'That's a bit cheeky Katherine,' Nellie responded with a pout.

Katherine laughed. 'Don't try that pout on me Nellie, I know you don't mean it,' she was giggling fit to burst.

Nellie was so nervous waiting for Nick to arrive to pick her up for the picnic, Katherine considered giving her some Brandy to calm her down.

'For goodness sake Nellie, it's just a picnic by the beach, not a grand ball.' Katherine was becoming exasperated. 'Take some big deep breaths and let them out slowly, there you go. Just remember, if you feel uncomfortable ask Nick to bring you home. Here he is now, off you go and enjoy yourself and leave me to my peace and quiet,' she said, pushing Nellie out the door towards Nick.

'Hello Nick, please look after Nellie, she hasn't ventured out with a man alone before.'

'I will take extra special care of Miss Abernathy, don't you worry about that,' he said flashing his winning smile at Katherine.

When Nellie and Nick arrived back three hours later, Nellie was glowing from head to toe.

'I'm in love,' she sighed twirling around the room after Nick said his goodbyes.

'Nellie you hardly know the man.'

'I know but I just feel so, oh I don't know, I just feel so special and warm and, in love. My heart melts when I see him, that is, when it's not fluttering madly in my chest. And I go weak at the knees when he touches me.'

'Touches you? What do you mean, he touches you?'

'Oh, just if our hands brush against each other or he puts a hand out to help me up, that sort of thing.'

Katherine breathed a sigh of relief. Nellie was so naïve about life, maybe it was time they had a woman to woman talk about the facts of life.

By the time Silas came home, Nellie and Nick had been seeing each other for several weeks and were getting along famously. Katherine was delighted to see the sparkle in Nellie's eyes, the pink in her cheeks and a smile on her face that just did not fade. Silas noticed it at once.

'Nellie lass, what's up with ye. You look like the cat what's got the cream,' he laughed.

'I'm in love Uncle Silas.'

'Is that so? And who might the lucky young man be?'

'His name is Nick O'Rourke, he works at Mr Croxley's. He has been looking out for us.'

'And taking young Nellie on outings too,' added Katherine

with a smile.

'I would like to meet this young man, I need to make sure he is treating you right and I want to know what his intentions are. I sincerely hope there is more to him than just working for Croxley.'

Nellie's heart froze. 'Please Uncle Silas, don't make a fuss, don't frighten him away.'

'Don't worry lass, if he's genuinely fond of ye then nothing I can say will frighten him off I can assure you. Now tell me, have you found a place to set up your haberdashery yet?'

'Yes we have,' said Nellie excitedly. 'We are sure you will approve Uncle Silas, will you come and have a look at it tomorrow? We told the owner we wanted to wait for your approval before we signed the lease.'

'Very wise my dear, yes I would very much like to see it. Tomorrow it is then.'

'Actually, we don't have to wait until tomorrow to see the outside,' Nellie laughed, 'come over to the window, you can see the shop front from here.'

Silas was curious. 'Which one is it then?' he asked.

'The sweet shop, the white one with the bay windows.'

'Mildred's sweet store, she's never selling up?'

'Oh no she's just moving closer into town. Mr Hicks heard she was thinking of moving and he took us to see her.'

'Well now, I think that's perfect, I will have to thank Mr Hicks.'

Silas was delighted. It was right across the street and close to their lodgings, and they could keep an eye on the premises from the window after hours.

Mildred had asked Nellie and Katherine if they could wait a few weeks to allow her time to set up her new premises and move in and they had agreed, they were in no hurry. In the meantime, they had their work cut out for them making more garments for the shop from the latest trunk full of treasures Uncle Silas had brought back with him on his latest trip.

Chapter Five

The Haberdashery

When Silas first met Nicholas O'Rourke, he was not at all sure he liked the lad, there was something about him that didn't feel quite right. He wasn't keen on him courting his niece but there was nothing much he could do about it while he was at sea. He just hoped that Nellie would continue to be the sensible girl he knew her to be, and not allow the man to take advantage of her good nature.

Nellie and Nick stepped out together twice a week. On Friday nights they would find a dance hall or dine at a pub or tea shop, then on Sundays, Nellie's favourite day of the week, they would picnic down by the beach if the weather allowed. If it was inclement, they would spend their time in Silas's rooms in front of the fire playing card games, with Katherine.

'Do you like him?' Nellie asked Katherine one Sunday evening after Nick left.

'I do Nellie, but I suspect he could be a little hot headed if provoked.'

'Yes, I thought that too, but I don't think he would ever hurt me, do you?'

'Why do you ask Nellie, has something happened?'

'Well no, not exactly. It's just that one night at a dance I saw him grab a man by his collar and hold him up against the wall threatening to punch him. It frightened me a little.'

'As I said, I suspected he could be fiery, what with that red hair and Irish blood running through his veins,' she smiled. So, what happened, what did he say?'

'He didn't know I saw him. He asked me to wait for him inside the dance hall and when he seemed to be taking a long time, I went outside to see what was keeping him. That's when I saw him, he was fighting with another man.'

'So, what did you do?'

'I stepped back inside out of sight. I didn't say anything to him, but it did upset me to see him like that.'

'I'm not surprised you were upset. Nellie, if he ever raises a hand to you, walk away, do you understand? Please do not allow a man, any man, to raise his hand to you. My father did that to my mother on many occasions and I promised myself I would never allow any man to do that to me. And that goes for you too.'

'I won't,' Nellie said softly, shocked at the harshness of Katherine's words. 'Now can we change the conversation to something more pleasant please?'

Silas returned two months later with more trunks full of trinkets, laces, ribbons and fabrics, this time from France. He hoped it would be enough to set the women up in their new store. They were so excited, they questioned Silas endlessly about where and how he had found such wonderful treasures.

'I tell you what ladies,' he said finally, 'Why don't I take you with me next time I go to France so you can see for yourselves. It's not such a long trip and it will give you a chance to see the designs and creations the French excel at. We can purchase what you need and bring it all back with us.'

Nellie and Katherine stared at him with their mouths hanging open.

'Really Uncle Silas? You would truly take us with you?'

'Why not,' he responded. 'My next sojourn is to the West Indies, I will be home in about four months, all going well, then I am off to France again. You can come with me then, if it suits.'

'If it suits? Of course it will suit Uncle Silas, thank you,' Nellie squealed throwing her arms around Silas's neck.

When Nellie told Nick about it, he was not at all happy with the idea.

'But how long will you be gone Nellie? What will I do while you are away? I'm not sure I want you to go, please, don't leave me here on my own without you, I couldn't bear it.'

Nellie was mortified. 'But I really want to go Nick, I really would love to visit France. Uncle Silas said...'

'Uncle Silas, all I ever hear about is your Uncle Silas.' Nick was clearly annoyed.

'Please don't be upset Nick.'

'Well, I suppose it's up to you Nellie. If the trip to France means more to you than being here with me then you should go.'

'But it doesn't mean more than you Nick, I love you. I would only be gone a few weeks.'

'A few weeks? Well don't expect me to wait for you Nellie.'

'Nick, please.'

'Please what?' he spat at her.

'Please don't be like this. Please don't be angry.'

'What did you expect me to say Nellie. That I would be happy to see you sail off across the sea. That I would wait for you to come back when you were damn good and ready? Well, I won't wait Nellie. If you loved me, you would stay here with me, but if you don't then we may as well say goodbye now. What is it to be Nellie?'

Nellie was in torment. She was so looking forward to going on the trip but if it meant losing Nick, then she wouldn't go, how could she. She was desperately in love with him and she couldn't bear the thought of him being with someone else.

'I won't go then,' Nellie said quietly scuffing the toe of her shoe on the ground. 'If it will upset you so much, then I won't go.'

'That's my girl,' smiled Nick broadly. 'Come on, let me buy you a drink.'

Nellie you must come to France please!' begged Katherine. How can I go if you don't come with me?' Katherine was disappointed to hear Nellie say she didn't want to go to France after all.

'Uncle Silas will look after you,' Nellie hung her head. 'I really want to go Katherine but Nick would be so upset. He said he wouldn't wait for me to come back. I couldn't bear to see him with someone else.'

'Nick should not be making such demands on you Nellie.'

'I just don't want to upset him. I couldn't bear to lose him it would break my heart,' she said sadly.

'Well, I won't be able to go either, I can't leave you here on your own,' sighed Katherine resignedly.

'Nick said he would look out for me. I feel safe with him Katherine, I know he will take good care of me.'

Silas wasn't so sure when Nellie broke the news to him.

'I'm not happy about leaving you here on your own either Nellie. I know you trust your young man, but I am not so sure I do.'

'Please Uncle Silas, I promise I won't come to any harm. Katherine, you should go and bring back some wonderful fabrics and patterns. Please I would love for you to go.'

Katherine looked across at Silas. 'What do you think Silas, would you mind taking me with you?'

'It won't be a long trip I suppose,' he mused, 'perhaps just this once. And Nellie I will be having words with Mr Hicks downstairs. If you have any concerns whatsoever you are to take them to him, is that clear?'

'Yes Uncle Silas,' Nellie responded. She was deeply upset at not being able to go with them, but she did her best not to show it.

Chapter Six

Cobbled

Nellie waved Uncle Silas and Katherine off as they set sail for France, a tear trickling down her cheek.

'Come on Nellie,' said Nick as he put his arm around her shoulders, 'as you said, they are only going to be gone for a few weeks.'

'It's not that, it's just that I would love to have gone to France, I hear the fashions are quite extraordinary.'

'Extraordinary eh, well then, perhaps I will take you there myself one day, how's about that?' he laughed leading her away from the dock.

Nick took advantage of Katherine and Silas's absence and spent every moment he could with Nellie, ingratiating himself into her life. One evening as they sat in the Old Bell supping light ale, Nellie noticed Nick seemed a little nervous and distracted.

'One day Nellie, you and I will have a home of our own, and as many children as you want. Would you like that? A home and family of your own to make up for the family you lost all those years ago?'

'I wouldn't say my family was replaceable Nick, but yes I would very much like to have a family of my own someday.'

'Well then,' he said taking her hand in his, 'how about we make it official then. Miss Abernathy, would you do me the great honour of becoming my wife?'

Nellie's heart soared; she was speechless.

'Why Nicholas O'Rourke this is a surprise. Are you sure you want to marry me? We have only known each other for a short time.'

'Do you want to marry me or not?' demanded Nick.

'Yes of course I do.'

'Well that's settled then, we are now officially betrothed to one another. Mr Croxley, more drinks over here if you please, come and drink to the health of my bride to be.'

'Have you talked this over with Mr Abernathy Nick? It would be the proper thing to do.' Mr Croxley did not appear to be as enthusiastic about the idea as Nick had hoped.

'I will approach him when he returns from France,' Nick said confidently, 'I am sure he will be pleased.'

But Silas was not pleased. 'You have not known the lass for very long Mr O'Rourke. If you insist on going through with this plan to marry my niece, then I ask that you please wait for one year.'

'Mr Abernathy, Nellie is nearly eighteen, surely she is old enough to make her own decisions,' Nick said defiantly.

'Yes she is. All I am asking is that you wait for a while before you wed, just to be certain this is what you both want. Nellie has had a difficult time of things these past few years, I don't want her rushing into anything until she is sure it is what she really wants.'

'If that will make you happy Mr Abernathy then we will wait, so long as Nellie agrees.'

Nick was disappointed but he would need to keep on the right side of Silas Abernathy if he wanted to wed his niece, the only heir to his fortune.

Nellie was oblivious to the conversation going on downstairs between Nick and her uncle, she was upstairs with Katherine talking about the trip to France. By the time Silas returned to his rooms, beautiful fabrics had been laid out all over the furniture and Katherine and Nellie were admiring each other in the stunning expensive gowns Silas had bought for them. Nellie ran across the room and threw her arms around her uncle's neck.

'Uncle Silas this is the most beautiful gown I have ever seen, thank you so much.'

'Don't thank me lass, Katherine had a great deal to do with the selection of the gowns, thank her. Here, stand back and let me get a good look at you both. Ah, now you must be the most beautiful young ladies in London. Where are you planning on wearing these gowns may I ask?'

'How about my engagement party,' said Nellie excitedly.

'Engagement? Has Nick proposed to you Nellie?' asked Katherine.

'Yes, he has.'

Silas cleared his throat. 'I have been downstairs talking to Nick just now Nellie, and I have asked him to wait for a year until you wed, I hope that sits well with you. I just want to make sure you are making the right decision, I owe that much to your father.'

Nellie was surprised to hear that Silas had been speaking to Nick, but after giving it some thought she nodded in agreement.

'I am happy to wait Uncle Silas, if you think that is best.' Then she smiled with sadness in her eyes, 'I suspect Papa would have said the same thing.'

'There's not a doubt in my mind about that,' he agreed, 'I knew my brother well enough to know that's exactly what he would have said. Now, let's have another look at these gowns on you.'

Nellie let out a sigh, 'I must admit, I am relieved to know that I have a whole year to plan my wedding, we have so much else to do now with our new store to set up. Perhaps we could wear our new gowns to the opening of our new store,' Nellie suggested to Katherine, 'then we could put them on display in the windows. Uncle Silas, when are you due to go back to sea, we would very much like to have you at our grand opening.'

'Grand opening is it, I can hardly miss that now can I. My next trip will be to India, we have to wait until our trading supplies come in, which I am informed will take at least two more months, does that give you enough time?'

Katherine looked at Nellie and nodded. 'We will make sure we have everything in order before you go Silas, come Nellie, we have much to do.'

The next six weeks flew by in a flurry of activity as the women set up their new business. Silas signed the lease and made shelves and display cabinets for them. The backyard where the privy was, had a high secure fence all around it with a back gate which he secured with a sturdy lock.

'I doubt you will have any need to go into that back alley,' he told the women as he came in from fixing the lock. 'I would rather have someone come in through the front door where that infernal tinkling bell will at least alert you to someone's arrival.'

The women giggled, they knew the bell annoyed Uncle Silas but it didn't bother them, they rather liked it. Besides, it meant impending business. Silas, with the help of a couple of his strong, muscled crew, hefted trunks of fabrics upstairs to the storeroom. It had taken the women the best part of a day to clean the attic room out, it obviously hadn't been used for several years, but they were satisfied with the result. Now it held four trunks and some wooden shop fittings left behind by the previous tenant.

The window dressing took a lot of time and deliberation, but finally the women were satisfied with the effect. In the main body of the shop some of the fabrics were displayed to their best advantage, while others were kept out the back or upstairs to be brought out as required. These were the more expensive, delicate fabrics, and some of the flamboyantly coloured fabrics perhaps not suited to the general enquirer. The most elaborate and stunning laces, trims and baubles were prettily displayed under the glass-topped counter where the previous owner had shown off her expensive handmade chocolates. Cottons, buttons, and a variety of other haberdashery items were kept in drawers in a large cabinet behind the counter with samples pinned to the front of each drawer. The drawers were brought to the counter on request, to be examined under a watchful eye.

They didn't want to run the risk of items becoming damaged or soiled by unclean fingers.

The 'grand opening' was a relatively low-key affair, but it did draw in the local merchants and neighbouring store owners from around the area, all wanting to know about the new shop and its wares. Some high society women from the wealthy side of town also arrived, by horse and carriage. The women had heard about these promising new seamstresses and their exotic fabrics and modern designs and they were most curious. The women gushed over the beautiful, modern gowns Nellie and Katherine wore for the opening.

'You have a very fine hand, ladies,' enthused one of the women inspecting their needlework. 'And I do love these designs, the fabrics and the colours are exquisite. Where do you source your supplies?'

Katherine jumped in before Nellie could open her mouth.

'Our fabrics are imported, mostly from France and the West Indies. We travel to France to hand select our preferred styles and fabrics,' she beamed with pride.

The women seemed impressed.

'You may be seeing more of us then, thank you Miss Abernathy, Miss Murtagh, lovely to meet you. Come ladies it's time to move on.'

Another woman arrived with her two daughters in tow.

'My girls are going to be wanting 'coming out' gowns. Show me your fabrics and if I approve, I will commission you to make them,' she instructed.

Katherine brought out what she considered would be the most suitable fabrics and spread them out across the counter.

'What do you think of these, madam?'

The woman picked up the corners of the fabrics to feel their texture then called her girls over to do the same. The girls eventually settled on the fabrics and designs of their choice and the deal was done.

By the end of the day Nellie and Katherine were exhausted but happy. They had orders for four gowns, two men's working shirts and a request to shorten a pair of trousers.

'Not bad for our first day,' smiled Katherine.

Silas left for India the following week; he would be gone for several months.

I am sure you two will have plenty to do while I am away, and I am counting on Nick, Mr Hicks, and Mr Croxley to keep an eye on you both.'

'We will be fine Uncle Silas, honestly,' Nellie gave him a big hug.

Silas had an uneasy feeling in the pit of his stomach. He'd left the women alone before, but this time he just couldn't put his finger on it, something didn't feel right.

The women on the other hand, had no such forebodings instead they immersed themselves in their new business, often working late into the night. The room at the back of the shop housed a large pattern making and cutting table as well as a small kitchen table where Nellie and Katherine sat to do their stitching. It was a labour of love and they never tired of it. At one end of the room stood an iron wood stove which kept them warm in the icy cold winter months and it was also where they would cook themselves a meal when they were working late. The wall opposite was bedecked with floor to ceiling shelves, thanks to Uncle Silas's handywork. The women would chat away about everything and anything as they sat and stitched, but on occasions, they would simply sit in comfortable silence concentrating on their work.

Now that the shop was open, Nellie and Nick didn't have as much time together as they had previously, their courting was limited to Saturdays or Sundays when the shop was closed. After a busy week Nellie did not feel like going out dancing on a Friday night, which didn't sit well with Nick. He was not happy about having to share 'his' Nellie with the shop. Occasionally Nellie would ask Katherine to join them for a walk along the promenade or skip barefoot along the beach paddling in the lapping waves. They would sometimes dine at Mr Croxley's or take tea at one of the tea houses.

Nick indulged the women when they wanted to go shopping in the city, he would stand outside leaning against the doorway smoking a cigarette. The women would study the different dress styles and fabrics displayed in the bigger stores, then rush home and begin drawing up their own versions of the designs. They created as many gowns as they could from the fabrics they had, then they would hang them on dress racks in the shop, rotating them through the window displays on a regular basis. Other designs went into a book for their customers to choose from.

'We haven't made a wedding gown yet, I just wish someone would put in an order for one so we could practice,' Katherine laughed.

'Perhaps we could just make a start on mine,' Nellie said shyly.

'That's a lovely idea Nellie, perhaps we should wait and see what Silas brings us in the next shipment though, there might be some fabric you like better than what we already have.'

'Yes, and if there is nothing suitable, we could go into the city and see what we can find.'

One evening as they were walking home from dinner at the Old Bell, Nick seemed a little on edge.

'Nick, what is it? Why do you keep looking behind you, are we being followed?' Nellie was becoming anxious.

'No, don't be silly, I just thought I saw someone I knew that's all. It's getting a bit chilly we should hurry home and get the fire going.'

Nellie didn't think it was cold at all but she didn't argue as they quickened their pace. They walked quickly through the narrow streets, their footsteps resounding on the cobbles. They rounded a corner and walked past an alley where three men stood beside a fire pit, talking quietly amongst themselves. The talking stopped when Nick and the women appeared.

'Well, if it isn't Mr O'Rourke himself,' called out one of the men. 'Got yourself a couple of fine ladies have ya Nicky boy? You don't need both of 'em now do ya, perhaps we could take one off ya hands for ya.'

Nick pushed the women ahead of him and urged them to run. He turned to face the men.

'This has nothing to do with them,' he snarled, you leave the women out of it.'

'Is that right Mr O'Rourke, well I don't tend to agree with you, get after them Jakey,' said the leader aggressively.

'No,' screamed Nick lunging for the man. Grabbing him by his coat collar he held him up against the stone wall, 'You leave them alone or I'll feckin kill the lot of ye.'

He was fired up and fighting for all he was worth. When he heard a woman scream the blood rushed to his head and he flew into a fiery rage fighting and kicking for all he was worth as the screaming continued. He saw that two men had hold of Katherine and they were dragging her into the alley trying to stifle her screams. They threw her to the ground and held her down. While he was distracted Nick's attacker grabbed him by the throat. Katherine's muffled screams eventually gave way to tortured groans and gut wrenching sobs. Nick could hear the sound of fabric being torn, he was incensed as he tried to breathe past the crushing hold on his throat. He threw his head back hitting his aggressor hard on the nose. When the man groaned and loosened his grip, Nick fell to his knees. His aggressor took this opportunity to kick Nick in the head, he fell face forward on the cobbles, unmoving. When his senses returned he brought himself to his knees and dragged himself across to check on Katherine, she wasn't moving and her eyes were closed. Bruising was beginning to appear around her throat and she was bleeding, he shook her, yelling her name.

'Katherine, Katherine, please, wake up.'

Nick rose slowly to his feet and turned around to look at the men who stood by defiantly, watching him with triumphant grins on their faces.

'You bloody bastards,' he growled. 'What have you done? What did you want to go and do that for?'

He lunged at the nearest man causing him to fall onto the fire which then toppled over spilling its contents across the ground. The man staggered and fell onto the burning embers and screamed in agony as his clothes caught alight quickly burning through to his flesh. One of the other men took to his scrapers and while the third one tried to pull his friend up out of the fire. Nick grabbed at him, pulled him away and started laying into him in a blind fury. He grappled the man to the ground and began punching him in the face, over and over and over, turning it into a bloody pulp. He continued to rain blows down on the man long after he had stopped struggling. The rest of the men who had been standing around watching and cheering them on from a safe distance, suddenly disappeared. Nick felt himself being lifted up and set on his feet. He swayed unsteadily feeling a hand roughly grabbing his arm.

'What have we here then,' a gruff voice sounded in Nick's ear.

He turned to see a policeman standing beside him, another one was kneeling down to check on the body Nick had just been punching.

'This one looks in a pretty bad way and the other chap ain't lookin' too good either,' he said glancing across to the man lying beside the fire still screaming in pain. 'I think you might have some explaining to do sir.'

'They attacked Katherine,' snarled Nick, still seething and defiant, trying to pull himself away from the constable's tightening grip.

One of the policemen followed Nick's gaze to where Katherine lay in a pool of blood.

'Better call for an ambulance,' he said to his off-sider. 'Looks like we've got three victims here.'

Earlier, when the men had made a grab for Katherine, she had yelled at Nellie to run. Nellie took heed and had run like the devil, hoping Katherine was keeping up behind her. She didn't stop running until she got to the shipping office doorway leading up to their rooms. She turned and looked behind her and was horrified to find that the street was empty; Katherine was nowhere to be seen. Nellie started to make her way back but as she got closer to where she last saw Katherine, she could hear raised voices and a lot of screaming and shouting. She didn't know whether to run back home again, lock the door and wait for Nick and Katherine, or to carry on towards the noise. She had waited once before, for her family to come out of the burning house and they hadn't come. She was not going to sit around and wait again; she had to find Nick and Katherine, she had to know that they were safe. She crept down the streets keeping herself hidden within the dark shadows of the cold stone walls taking care to walk lightly on her toes so as not to make a noise on the damp cobbles. As she got closer to the disturbance, she could see a group of people standing around someone lying on the ground. She crept closer and gasped when she recognised Katherine's clothing. She held her hand across her mouth so as not to draw attention to herself. She tried to get as close as she could and then she spotted Nick being dragged away by two policemen, it was all she could do not to call out to him. She stood frozen to the spot not knowing what to do. She watched in horror as someone came along with a stretcher and lifted Katherine on to it. Nellie took the chance to run across to check on Katherine before they took her away.

'How is she?' she demanded of one of the stretcher bearers.

'We won't know 'til we get er to 'ospital,' he said coldly and hurried off up the street.

Nellie could feel her knees buckle beneath her.

'You awright lovey?' asked a kindly voice, 'ere, come and sit down for a minute. Can't take the sight of blood eh,' she said as she sat beside Nellie on a nearby door stoop.

'Did ya know the poor lass what was attacked then?'

Nellie didn't respond. Everything was a blur; she wasn't quite sure what was happening. Everything seemed to be moving in slow motion, voices sounded like they were coming from inside a tunnel, far away. She staggered to her feet and vomited. The woman rushed forward and held Nellie's arm to steady her and offered to walk with her. Nellie pushed her away and using the walls of the buildings managed to get herself back to the shipping offices where she crawled her way up the stairs to their rooms. She leaned against the door as she unlatched it and fell forward onto the floor. She lay there for quite some time, before rousing herself up and staggering over to the fireplace. Despite her shaking hands she was able to get the fire going and she sat back in one of the chairs, trembling from head to foot staring mindlessly at the flickering flames. The door to their rooms was still standing wide open.

Mr Hicks found Nellie the next morning. He had heard about the attack and was most concerned for the women Silas had left in his care.

'Nellie,' he called as he rushed to her side.

The room was cold, the fire was out and Nellie was lying in the chair with her eyes closed. Mr Hicks gently shook her shoulder. Her eyes sprung open and she glared up at him in fright.

'Mr Hicks, what are you doing here?'

She looked around her, then down at her clothes. Then the reality of the previous night's events hit her. She sprang to her feet.

'Mr Hicks. Katherine, Nick, they...'

'Yes Miss Abernathy I've heard all about it. Is there anything I can do?'

'Yes, you can take me to the hospital to see Katherine, please, and then I need to go and find Nick.'

Katherine was lying pale and unmoving in her hospital bed when Nellie eventually tracked her down. A doctor was checking her pulse, taking her temperature.

'Doctor, is my friend going to be alright?'

'She has suffered severe bruising and has a few cuts and abrasions but no broken bones. She should heal well physically. She hasn't spoken or eaten since we brought her in, you will need to be patient with her, she will come right when she is ready. If she doesn't, then we will need to reassess the situation.'

'What does that mean, reassess the situation?' Nellie didn't understand what the Doctor was saying.

'We don't need to go into that for now, but if Miss Murtagh does not regain her mental well-being she may need to go into an asylum. It does happen sometimes in these cases when women are attacked like this. But let's just wait and see, shall we?' he said encouragingly.

Nellie was mortified. She sat with Katherine, stroking her face and talking to her for well over an hour, until the hospital staff asked her to leave.

Mr Hicks had been waiting patiently outside for Nellie and took her straight to the Police Station when she came out to join him.

'Are you sure you feel up to this Nellie?'

'Yes, I won't be able to sleep until I know what is happening with Nick.'

The constable stared down at Nellie when she asked about Nicholas O'Rourke.

'The magistrate will decide his fate at court on the morrow,' he boomed.

'What is he charged with?' asked Nellie, her knees shaking in fear.

'Disturbing the peace and assault causing grievous bodily 'arm,' he grinned meanly. 'We don't take kindly to the likes of 'im, causing trouble on our streets, likely 'e will be sent away this time.'

'Sent away where?' asked Nellie weakly, not sure she wanted to know the answer.'

'Why don't you come along to the court t'morra and find out for yerself. Now off with ye, I have more important things to deal with.'

Nellie was distraught. She turned to Mr Hicks.

'Will you come with me to court tomorrow, Mr Hicks, please?' Nellie begged.

'Yes of course I will,' he replied taking her arm and leading her quickly back towards home. He was worried about her, she hadn't eaten all day.

'How's about we get something to eat at Mr Croxley's before we head home, eh?'

Nellie nodded and allowed herself to be led to the Old Bell. Mr Croxley was most upset to hear about Katherine's attack, but not so surprised to hear that Nick had landed himself in trouble, this wasn't the first time.

'How is Katherine?' he asked. 'Perhaps I could go and see her, take her one of her favourite pies,' he said hopefully.

'That might help Mr Croxley, she hasn't eaten anything, perhaps one of your delicious pies might tempt her. She's in a bit of a bad way physically with cuts and bruises but thankfully no broken bones. She didn't seem to know I was there, she didn't respond to anything I said. The doctor said something about taking her to an asylum if she didn't get better. I don't want her going to an asylum Mr Croxley, I couldn't bear that.

Mr Croxley hurried away to get his best pies for Nellie and Mr Hicks and came back with a pot of steaming hot tea.

'Do you think it would be fitting for me to go and see Miss Katherine tomorrow, Mr Hicks?'

'Don't see why not, they allow visitors in after the midday meal,' Mr Hicks replied.

'Thank you, thank you,' mumbled Mr Croxley as he hurried back to the kitchen.

Nellie hardly touched her pie, so Mr Croxley put it in a paper bag and gave it to Mr Hicks as they were leaving.

'Make sure she eats something,' Mr Croxley implored, 'she needs to keep her strength up for Miss Katherine.'

Mr Hicks nodded and taking Nellie's arm he gently but firmly guided her back to the shipping office. Nellie spent a restless night alone in her rooms that night, she tried to sleep but eventually gave up. She got up, rekindled the fire and sat in the armchair cuddled up in a blanket. She must have dozed off in the early hours because she was startled awake by a knock on the door.

'Miss Nellie, do you still wish me to take you to the Court. We need to hurry, it will be starting soon.'

Nellie leapt to her feet and swung the door open.

'Oh my Lord is it that time already. Yes, yes of course, please wait for me Mr Hicks, I just need to get dressed and freshen up a bit.'

As soon as Nellie got to the door of the shipping office Mr Hicks appeared and they walked briskly down to the courthouse. By the time they got there the room was filled to overflowing with noisy people all talking and yelling at once. They managed to squeeze their way in and find somewhere to stand where they could watch the proceedings. The magistrate's voice boomed out for order and the place eventually quietened down. Nick was the sixth prisoner to be brought out. The magistrate listened to what he had to say about the attack on Katherine and his reaction to it.

'Mr O'Rourke,' the magistrate stared down at Nick, 'this is not the first time I have seen you in this 'ere court for fighting, is it?'

'No sir,' mumbled Nick, his head down.

'I take into account why you attacked these men, but it is for the law to mete out justice Mr O'Rourke, not the likes of you. Because of your previous misdemeanours and the serious nature of your victims' injuries, I am sentencing you to seven years in the colonies.'

He banged his gavel down and that was that. Nellie felt faint and started to buckle at the knees so Mr Hicks steered her to a wooden bench just outside the courtroom.

'Seven years,' she gasped, 'seven years. How am I going to survive seven years until he comes back? What if he never comes back?'

She was in tears now and becoming hysterical. An embarrassed Mr Hicks pulled her to her feet and quickly led her outside.

'I want to see him,' she demanded. 'I must see him, I need to tell him I will wait for him, forever if that's what it takes.'

Mr Hicks reluctantly led Nellie around the back of the building to a narrow lane behind the courthouse where the prisoners were being held. He had a quick conversation with the gaoler who agreed to let Nellie in, but only for a quick visit. 'A few minutes and no more' were his instructions as he pocketed the coin Mr Hicks had surreptitiously dropped into his hand. He led them both down into a cold, damp, dark dungeon where the prisoners were crammed into dirty, stinking cells. Nellie searched through the cells until she found Nick. He was surprised to see her, he looked beaten and forlorn and nothing like his usual cheery self.

'Nellie,' you shouldn't be down here in a place like this,' he said, feeling ashamed at her seeing him like this.

'I wanted to see you Nick. I understand why you attacked those men, I truly do, and I thank you for it.' She didn't try to stop the tears that began streaming down her cheeks, her heart was breaking.

'How is Katherine?' he asked quietly, putting his hands through the bars to hold hers.

'She will recover from her injuries, but we don't yet know whether she will ever be the same in her head.'

'I am deeply sorry this has happened Nell, it was just a wild fit of rage, and now it has ruined everything for us. My father always said I would wind up in trouble one day, I guess he was right, he always said I had a short fuse,' Nick attempted a smile.

'I still can't believe this is really happening,' she cried, 'I feel like I am in a dreadful nightmare hoping I will wake up soon.'

'Do you know where they will take you?' asked Mr Hicks.

'I hear tell the next lot of prisoners will be going to Norfolk Island,' Nick said fearfully.

'I have the shipping schedules Nick, I will bring Nellie down to see you off. You will be below decks but at least you will know we are there.'

'Thank you Mr Hicks.'

The gaoler came to take Nellie and Mr Hicks back upstairs.

'Come on you two, time's up.'

Nellie held on tightly to Nick's hands. They pressed their heads together through the gap in the bars and kissed. Nellie's resolve gave way and she started to sob uncontrollably.

'I will wait for you Nick,' she wailed, 'I will wait until you come home. Please promise me you will come back.'

'I will Nellie, I promise. I love you.'

The gaoler grabbed one of Nellie's arms and pulled her towards the stairs. The other arm outstretched towards Nick, Nellie called, 'I love you too Nick.'

Once out in the fresh air Nellie collapsed beside the doorway in a crumpled heap. Poor Mr Hicks didn't know what to do with her. Being a bachelor, he had never had much to do with women. Fortunately for him an older woman, whose man had also been sent down, stopped to lend a hand.

'C'mon dearie up ye come, let's get you something to drink eh. Looks like we are both in the same boat.'

Mr Hicks trotted along behind as the woman half dragged Nellie along to the nearest pub. They sat in a quiet dark corner and sipped on brandies. Nellie coughed and spluttered on her first sip but the woman encouraged her to drink until she had finished the whole glass. Mr Hicks kindly paid for the drinks.

'It'll help settle ye a little lass. I've been in your shoes afore, and now 'ere I am again. If the silly beggars would just keep their darn fool fists to their selves, we'd all be much better off. They needs their bums whopping.'

Nellie giggled at the woman's remarks.

'That's ma girl,' she smiled.

Looking to Mr Hicks she said, 'I gotta get back to me young 'uns, tell em their pa is off to sea again, poor little mites. He is good wi' em and they love the old coot, but he does love a good fight.' Turning back to Nellie she said, 'I wish ye well lass.'

'Thank you.' Nellie took the woman's hand. 'I hope things work out for you too.'

Nellie looked across at Mr Hicks sitting quietly with his light ale.

'Mr Hicks, I would like to go and see Katherine this

afternoon, I know I have taken up much of your time already.'

'Of course I will take you,' Mr Hicks cut in. I have instructed my clerk to take over the running of the office for the foreseeable. I am at your service whenever you need me.'

As they stood to leave Nellie gave Mr Hicks a hug. He was embarrassed and a little taken aback, but also thrilled at the first human contact he'd had in a very long time.

Nellie visited Katherine every day over the next three weeks. She was making progress and her wounds were healing nicely, the doctor had said, but she still wasn't her bright cheerful self. Every time Nellie went to the hospital Mr Croxley seemed to be there. He would step outside and let Nellie visit then he would go back in again when she left.

'Mr Croxley seems to be visiting a lot, he obviously cares a great deal for you Katherine?' Nellie commented one day.

Katherine smiled shyly. 'He does, doesn't he. He comes every day with food and sweets and treats, I really don't know what to make of it. I ask him if he shouldn't be getting back to the pub, but he insists that he would rather be here with me and that Mrs Beasley has stepped in to help when he is not there.'

'Well, it certainly sounds like he is enamoured of you, how exciting. It would be good for you to have a lovely stable man like Mr Croxley to take care of you, wouldn't it? Do you like him?'

Katherine blushed and lowered her eyes, dark lashes fluttering on her cheeks. 'I think I might, yes,' she whispered. 'But after all this time, why would he suddenly show some interest in me now? I have to admit I am surprised by his attention, especially now that I am a damaged woman.'

'Damaged! Katherine this wasn't your fault, you were brutally attacked,' Nellie said angrily.

'I know, it's just that I.., I feel kind of soiled now,' she said sadly.

'Katherine please don't think like that, Mr Croxley knows what happened to you, he has known you for some time. If he is keen on you, then he feels that way despite what has happened to you.'

Katherine smiled through her tears and squeezed her friend's hand.

'Thank you,' she smiled.

'When will they let you out of here do you think?' Nellie asked, looking around the ward.

'The doctor said perhaps Wednesday.'

'Good, I can't wait to get you home, I don't like being there on my own and, with Nick away,' she faltered on her words.

'Oh, my poor dear Nellie, has there been any news about when Nick is due to sail?'

'He sailed last week, I didn't want to say anything while you were still in hospital.'

'I am so sorry Nellie, that must have been very difficult for you. Right, I have been here for long enough, I think it is time I came home,' Katherine decided determinedly, 'we need each other now more than ever'.

'The doctor told me that you were recovering well from your cuts and bruises, but he wasn't sure if your mind would recover from the effects of the attack.'

'I don't want to talk about it Nellie, really I don't. It was terrifying and I still have nightmares about it, but I don't want it to take over my life. If Mr Croxley is still keen to court me, then I have something good to look forward to.'

'You are never going to encourage Mr Croxley just because he knows what happened to you and doesn't judge you, are you?'

Katherine smiled, 'He is the first man to pay me any attention in a very long time Nellie. I like him, he is a kind and considerate man, and I would be a fool to let him slip away. So, let's just wait and see if he continues to call on me once I am home, or whether he was just visiting me here at the hospital out of pity. Now, tell me all about the shop, what have I missed, how is our new assistant Evelyn doing?'

Chapter Seven

Courting and marriage

Mr Croxley continued to call on Katherine after she was discharged from the hospital and within three months, he got down on one knee and proposed. She didn't accept right away, she wanted to make sure this was not going to upset Nellie. It wasn't long ago that Nellie was planning her own wedding, now the attention would all turn to Katherine.

She needn't have worried, Nellie was delighted with the news. She admitted to feeling sad about not having her own wedding to plan for any longer but thrilled that at least one of them would be getting married, and soon. Mr Croxley, Benjamin, was a good deal older than Katherine but she wasn't perturbed.

'He is stable, well established in his business, and a good, kind man,' said Katherine. 'I know he will not make too many demands on me other than to be his companion.'

'Do you not want to have babies then?' asked Nellie.

'I think we will just let things develop the way they are meant to,' responded Katherine.

Mr Croxley had been secretly in love with Katherine from the first moment he laid eyes on her. He had admired her from afar but was well aware of their age difference and didn't have the confidence to approach such a beautiful young woman. It was the vicious attack on her that spurred him into action. He was appalled and heartbroken by it and the thought of not seeing her again, or worse, seeing her admitted to an asylum, encouraged him to take his fears in hand and spend as much time as he could with her, willing her to return to her old self.

Heartened by her recovery and her welcoming response to his visits, he finally found the courage to propose.

Since Katherine had accepted his proposal, Benjamin became a changed man, he had a spring in his step and a permanent smile on his face. All his customers commented on it, some of them chiding him for being such a soppy old fool. He didn't take offence, he was far too happy to allow anyone to bring him down.

Nellie and Katherine threw themselves into planning the wedding and making Katherine's gown.

'Goodness you haven't given us much time Katherine,' wailed Nellie one afternoon as they rushed around town looking for suitable trimmings.

'I just hope Silas arrives back in time,' said Katherine, 'Mr Hicks seems to think he will, provided they don't get held up by bad weather. Mr Croxley, Benjamin,' she blushed, 'said we could wait for Silas to come home if I wanted to. I told him if Silas wasn't home before the wedding then yes, I would like to wait. Silas has been like a beloved uncle to me too.'

The next few weeks became a whirlwind of activity and excitement as the day of the nuptials grew nearer. Silas did arrive home in time, they didn't have to wait, everything was all set.

Silas proudly walked Katherine down the aisle to her waiting groom. Mr Croxley looked fit to bursting with happiness and Katherine simply glowed. She had become very fond of her soon-to-be husband over the ensuing weeks and the night before the wedding she had shyly admitted to Nellie that she truly did love Benjamin.

'I now pronounce you husband and wife,' declared the Minister. There wasn't a dry eye in the house as the happy couple kissed and turned to face the congregation.

'You are all invited back to the Old Bell for the reception,' announced Benjamin Croxley proudly as he led his wife down the aisle.

'You are a very lucky man Croxley,' Silas boomed, shaking Benjamin's hand. 'You treat her well mind, else you will have me to deal with,' he laughed heartily.

'You have no need to worry on that score Silas,' he responded, 'I will love this woman with all my heart for the rest of my life.' His smile could have lit up the whole of London.

'I'm just sorry it wasn't you this time,' Silas said as he sat down beside Nellie at the reception table.

'I am too Uncle Silas, but I am very happy for Katherine, doesn't she make a pretty bride.'

'She does indeed lass, she does indeed.'

The reception room was filled with laughter and good cheer with the celebrations looking to continue on into the wee small hours. That is, until Benjamin Croxley kicked everybody out, locked the doors and took his wife upstairs to bed. They would be leaving for their honeymoon in the morning, two glorious, peaceful weeks in the Cotswolds.

Chapter Eight

Tragedy at Sea

Silas and Mr Hicks were talking quietly in the doorway of the shipping offices the day after Nellie waved Katherine off on her honeymoon. She had locked up the shop and was walking across the street when she saw the two of them huddled together looking decidedly upset. They looked up when they saw Nellie coming and she watched curiously as Mr Hicks ducked back into his office. Silas waited for Nellie to reach the doorway then took her arm and led her up the stairs.

'I have some news for you Nellie, it's not good news I'm afraid, you might need to sit down.'

Nellie was stunned, she sat down and glanced anxiously up at her uncle.

'What is it Uncle Silas? What's happened.?'

'It's Nick. Nellie, his ship went aground on rocks in high seas as they were approaching Norfolk Island.'

Nellie stared at Silas dumbfounded, saying nothing.

'The ship sank Nellie, I haven't heard if there were any survivors but with the prisoners being below decks, they wouldn't have stood a chance.'

Nellie's mind was reeling as the news sunk in. 'Nick's dead? No, he can't be, not my Nick. He promised he would come back to me.'

Nellie started wailing loudly. Silas knelt beside her chair and pulled her into his arms.

'I'm sorry lass, this is yet another cruel blow in your young life, it just doesn't seem fair,' he whispered softly. He stayed there cradling her in his arms, rocking her gently, as she gave way to despair and grief. Eventually she became quiet. Silas let her go, stood up and picking up her limp body, laid her gently on the bed.

For the next few days Nellie lay on the bed facing the wall, barely moving. Silas was becoming quite concerned for her, she wouldn't eat and she hadn't spoken a word since the night he'd broken the news to her. He decided it was time to call the doctor in.

'She is in a state of severe melancholy Mr Abernathy. If she doesn't snap out of it soon you might consider sending her to the asylum.'

Silas was furious. 'I'll be damned if I am sending my niece to any asylum doctor. Despite the losses she has suffered in her short life I have every hope that she will recover. Now what can I do to keep her alive in the meantime, she refuses to eat.'

'We could take her to the hospital and force feed her,' he offered.

'Force feed her? Is that the only option?'

'Well, it's up to you Mr Abernathy, you either get some sustenance down her throat yourself or we force feed her, or...' he hesitated.

'Or what?' asked Silas.

'Or she dies Mr Abernathy,' he said bluntly.

Silas was distraught. 'I will let you know how she progresses,' he said, knowing that he would be doing everything in his power to prevent her from dying, or having to go to any hospital for that matter. He couldn't stand the thought of people holding Nellie down while they forced rubber hoses down her throat, and he certainly wasn't going to allow her to be sent to any asylum. He decided he would try to get her to eat one way or another. He went to the Old Bell and got Mrs Beasley to make up some delicious smelling broths and sweet liquids to try and tempt Nellie with. He would take them home and, placing a pillow behind her head, he would attempt to pour liquid into her mouth from a spoon. The first attempts were futile, the liquid would run down the sides of her mouth and onto her dress, the same one she had been wearing when Silas had told her the news about Nick. After several attempts he gave up and went back to the 'Old Bell'.

'Mrs Beasley,' Silas leaned across the counter and whispered in her ear, 'might I have a word?'

They walked out the back of the hotel into a quiet corner outside the back door.

'What is it Silas?' Mrs Beasley was concerned at the despair written all over Silas's face.

'I wonder if I might call on your services further,' he pleaded. 'Nellie is still in the same clothes, it's been six days now, I need to get her out of that dress and into a nightgown. She desperately needs a wash down and the bed linens changing. And for the life of me, I can't get her to eat anything.'

'Say no more Silas, I will be around as soon as I have locked up at the pub. Have some hot water, a tub, and a couple of towels ready. I will bring some nice soap and sweet-smelling oils with me.'

Three hours later, Silas was very grateful to see Mrs Beasley arrive with wash cloths, lotions, potions and a beautiful, lace trimmed, nightgown.

'I thought a nice new nightgown might be just the ticket,' she said as she placed her wares on the table. I got one of the lasses in her store to pick one out for me, I'm sure she wouldn't mind me doing that.'

'No of course she wouldn't Mrs Beasley, that was very thoughtful of you. By the way, how are the women getting on in the shop?'

'Very well by all accounts. They miss Mrs Croxley and Nellie of course but they have had some good sales and are comfortable with how everything is progressing.'

'That is a relief,' he sighed.

'Right then, let's see what we have here. Oh my, the poor mite, she really is in a bad way isn't she. Come on lassie, let's be 'avin ya, up we go. Silas, can you grab her legs and swing them over the side of the bed for me, that's it.'

Silas started to move away as Mrs Beasley began removing Nellie's stained and smelly dress.

'No need to move away Silas, I need you to hold her up. Just avert your eyes if you need to, no need to be embarrassed, this lass's needs are way more important than your embarrassment,' she said forcefully.

They placed Nellie gently into the tub and Mrs Beasley set to work washing her body and her dry matted hair. Nellie's eyes stared straight ahead, unfocused, her body completely limp.

'At least she isn't resisting,' said Mrs Beasley gratefully. 'Right, now let's dry her off, get her into the nightgown and sit her by the fire. Perhaps you might like to try her on some of that broth while I change these sheets on the bed,' she instructed.

Silas pulled up a chair and sat in front of Nellie with a bowl of steaming broth and a spoon in his hands.

'Nellie, my beautiful girl, you need to eat. Please, you must eat.' His voice faltered. 'Nellie, I couldn't bear it if you left me, you are the only family I have.'

Nellie slowly lifted her head, focused on her uncle, and watched as a tear rolled down his cheek. He smiled when he saw she was looking directly at him then he gave way to sobs as he saw tears begin to form in her own eyes. He put the bowl and spoon down and reached out to give her a hug. He held her gently, murmuring to her not to leave him. He told her how much he loved her, how much everyone loved her.

'Katherine will be home tomorrow,' he said, 'she will be upset to see how thin you have become. They need you in the shop too, the ladies are missing you and your beautiful smile. They say it is just not the same there without you Nellie.'

Nellie let out a sob, drew in a big breath and started to cry. Mrs Beasley looked up from her bed-making and smiled across at Silas. At last, a breakthrough.

Nellie continued to regain her strength over the next few weeks but she was far from being her old self, she had become withdrawn and distant. Katherine asked one of the ladies who had watched the store for them, to stay on for a while so she could spend more time with Nellie. The woman wasn't near as good a seamstress as Nellie was, but she had a pleasant disposition and she was good with the customers. Mr Croxley was very understanding when it came to Katherine spending time with Nellie.

'Take all the time you need Katherine. Both of you have suffered dreadful tragedies, she needs you more now than ever.'

Katherine resisted the urge to talk about her honeymoon and the lovely man who was now her husband. Instead, she focused on Nellie and talked about fabrics and designs in an effort to keep Nellie's thoughts away from Nick. It would work for a while, then Nellie would stare out the window and drift off, seemingly oblivious to everything around her.

Nellie hadn't left the rooms now for over two months. Silas had let his last ship leave without him, they would be away for a good six months and he decided he couldn't leave Nellie for that length of time. He wanted to see her well and back to her old self, if that was possible, before he felt comfortable about going to sea for any longer than a few weeks.

One bright summer's day Katherine breezed in with a basket of delicious smelling pies and sandwiches, Benjamin came bustling in behind her.

'We are all going on a picnic,' she announced. 'Nellie, I have brought one of my new gowns from the shop for you to wear, come, let's go and try it on.'

Nellie allowed herself to be led into the other room to dress.

'Goodness girl, you are like a ragdoll. Come on, let's get this shift off you and put a fresh clean one on. There, that must feel better.'

Once the gown was on and Katherine had brushed Nellie's hair, she turned her around to face the mirror. As Nellie stared at her reflection, her eyes grew large and she brought her hands up to her mouth.

'Is that me?'

'Yes it is my dear. Don't you look a picture.'

'No, I look awful, look how thin I am. The gown is beautiful but I look so pale and thin,' she gasped.

'Yes you do,' said Katherine, hoping shock tactics might work. 'That's why I am taking you out for some sunlight, fresh air and good food.'

'Thank you Katherine. I am sorry I have been so, so...'

'So nothing my darling girl, so nothing. Come on let's not keep these hungry men waiting.'

Benjamin and Silas watched Nellie as she walked into the room.

'That gown is beautiful on you Nellie,' gushed Silas, walking over to kiss her on the cheek. 'Now let's get outside and put some pink in those pretty cheeks of yours.'

Nellie's recovery took a big step forward from that day on. Eventually she felt confident enough to venture down to the shop to visit Katherine and the shop assistants who had been helping out in her absence.

'Nellie, it is so good to see you here, we have missed you,' cried Katherine, drawing her into a warm hug.

'I'm not sure I am ready to come back to work in the store just yet Katherine, but I would like to see how you are all getting along.'

Much to Katherine's despair Nellie showed no desire to return to the shop in her former capacity as Katherine's business partner. She would wander in from time to time to sit at the table and go over some designs and patterns or talk about fabrics and trims, but then she would just get up and leave. Katherine spotted Silas walking by one day and called out to him.

'I'm worried about Nellie, Silas, she's still not herself. Physically she is fine, but mentally, I am not so sure. I was lucky enough to have Benjamin there to pull me out of my mental state, but I fear Nellie has nothing strong enough to pull her out of hers.'

'I agree,' said Silas sadly, 'but I don't know what else I can do for her. I worry about what will become of her when I head back to sea.'

'Benjamin and I will take care of her, you know that. Perhaps she could move in with us, we have a spare room above the pub.'

'Thank you Katherine, that is most kind of you.'

When Katherine broached the subject with Benjamin, he countered with another idea.

'I wonder if getting away from here altogether might not be a better idea for Nellie,' he said quietly.

'Where do you suppose she might go?' Katherine was surprised at Benjamin's suggestion.

'New Zealand.'

'New Zealand? But that's such a long way away, isn't it? How long would it take to get there and why New Zealand of all places?'

'I have thought about going to New Zealand ever since I received a letter from my brother who moved there a couple of years ago.'

'You never said you had a brother living in New Zealand.'

'We've never had much to do with each other. He is quite a bit younger than me and I left home to go to boarding school when he was still very young. He wrote and invited me to visit him and see what I thought about emigrating there. He tells me it is a land of opportunities, especially for an Inn Keeper like myself. I must admit I was tempted to at least go and have a look.'

'So why didn't you?' asked Katherine, surprised at this revelation.

'Because the letter came when you were in the hospital and I never gave it another thought, until now.'

Katherine was quiet for a moment. 'Perhaps we could all go together,' she suggested.

Benjamin was surprised but excited by Katherine's response. He thought she might reject the idea outright.

'We would be under no obligation to stay,' he said hopefully, 'we can always come back again and just call it a trip abroad. The distraction and the sea air might do Nellie the world of good.'

'I have an idea,' said Katherine.

She invited Silas and Nellie to have dinner with them at the Old Bell. As they walked in the door Nellie stopped and looked around as if she was looking for someone. Katherine saw the stricken look on Nellie's face and realised she hadn't stepped foot in the Old Bell since Nick left. She felt awful about not considering how Nellie might feel about being back in the place where she first met him. She grabbed Nellie's hand.

'Nellie dear, I'm sorry I didn't think. This was a mistake, shall we go someplace else?'

'No,' said Nellie quietly, 'I need to get over this. I know Nick is not coming back, I just need to get used to the idea. I see him around every corner, I even call out to people who look like him sometimes.' Tears spilled over onto her cheeks and made their way down to drop on the bodice of her gown.

Benjamin handed her a brandy and sat down beside her.

'We all miss him very much Nellie, but you know Nick would want you to carry on without him don't you. He would be heartbroken to see you grieving like this.'

Nellie glanced up at Benjamin and nodded, not daring herself to speak. Katherine began talking to Silas about New Zealand. Nellie seemed distant and disinterested for a while then as the discussion progressed to descriptions of the beautiful countryside, as described by Benjamin's brother in his letters, Nellie began to tune into the conversation.

Benjamin and I thought we might go to New Zealand and see it for ourselves, and if it is to our liking, we thought we might stay,' Katherine was telling Silas.

'Katherine,' shrieked Nellie, 'you can't leave me, please. What would I do without you?'

'Why don't you come with us then,' she smiled mischievously. Her plan was working.

'Come with you, to New Zealand?' she said disbelievingly.

'Yes, why not. Benjamin and I have discussed it and we would love to take you with us. It could be a whole new adventure for us Nellie. We could set up shop anywhere, so why not New Zealand. Women there must wear gowns and have a need for laces and trims too. I'm sure Silas will be able to send supplies to us in New Zealand from time to time, could you Silas?'

'I believe I could arrange something, yes,' he said enthusiastically, realising that Katherine had set the whole evening up for Nellie, hoping she would warm to the idea of leaving England.

'There are a lot of good memories for us here Nellie, but there are a lot of unpleasant ones too. Perhaps we could leave them behind and start afresh.'

'But Uncle Silas, what about you, would you come too?'

'Nay Lass,' he smiled, 'I won't be going with you but there's nothing says I can't come and visit you, is there? Besides, it will be good for me to start writing letters.'

'We don't have to make a decision now, we can take as long as we like,' cut in Benjamin. 'Let's get together and talk about it some more before Silas heads off again. There are many things to consider.'

Over the next two weeks the four of them got together almost every day to talk about the idea of sailing to New Zealand. Silas was able to tell them what to expect on the trip and Benjamin sourced information and advice about what would be expected of them as immigrants, and what they would need to take to start a new life, if they decided to do so.

'It won't be an easy trip all the way, Silas had advised them, there will be times when there are storms and there will be times when there is no wind and you will be becalmed. It will most likely take you around three months to get there, all going well. I will check the schedules and see which ships are travelling down there and when, so I can advise you on the best ship to book passage on.'

Finally, the decision was made. Benjamin, Katherine and Nellie would sail to New Zealand. Benjamin wasted no time filing papers and getting things in order. Nellie and Katherine packed up the shop, cancelled the lease and stowed the goods into storage trunks to be left at the shipping office until they were either sent for, or to be collected if they returned to England.

'I will miss this wee shop,' sighed Katherine as she turned the key in the lock for the last time. 'It seems like only yesterday that we first opened, doesn't it?'

'I am sorry I let you down Katherine,' Nellie said as she placed her hand through her friend's arm.'

'Don't be silly Nellie, you have been through so much, I am surprised you are doing as well as you have been. You are doing well, aren't you Nellie? You do want to go on this trip, don't you?'

'Yes of course I do. I have to admit that ever since we talked at the 'Old Bell' that first night, I have thought of little else. It has stopped me dwelling constantly on Nick, and my nightmares have finally stopped. This is a good thing, we will make it a good thing. You and I have both had a lot to deal with health wise this past year, this is exactly what we both need.'

She kissed her friend on the cheek and they walked back to the shipping office to find Silas and Benjamin hunched over a desk tying up loose ends.

Chapter Nine

New Zealand Bound - 1850

The three travellers planned to leave London in June, hoping to arrive in New Zealand during the Springtime so they could begin to acclimatise before experiencing their first New Zealand summer.

According to my brother Harry, the summers there can be pretty hot,' said Benjamin cautiously. 'We will need to make sure we have some lighter clothing with us. I hear also that the winters can bring snow and strong winds, especially where Harry lives. He is in a place called Christchurch, lots of flat land edged by very high mountain ranges.'

'It sounds interesting,' said Katherine. 'Do they have cities like London there?'

'Heaven's no,' said Benjamin, it is a newly established colony. We will be early settlers; you need to understand that my dear. As we have talked about before, this will not be the easy life we have had here. It might be a better life of course but the living will be a lot more basic. I have no idea about the stores there, Harry didn't elaborate. He is very excited about our impending visit and has bought a large house for all of us to live in.'

'He sounds like a well-made man if he can afford to buy a large house,' mused Nellie.

'I do believe he has done alright for himself, yes,' said Benjamin.

The women had been over and over the instruction leaflets and read everything they could about what they might be greeted with when they arrived in New Zealand.

'Where is that list of provisions that we are advised to take?' asked Nellie. 'There doesn't seem to be much there, what are we going to do with all our other clothes?' she wailed.

'We will still be able to stow our trunks on board the ship,' explained Katherine. 'These instructions are only a guideline and they have set out the minimum things required to start a new life there. I am sure Silas has made all the necessary arrangements for our extra luggage to be taken aboard and paid for, that is his line of work after all. We have been over and over this Nellie, please don't fret. Now, let's go over that list again.

Katherine read aloud:

2 gowns or 18 yards of printed cotton
2 petticoats or 6 yards of calico
12 shifts or 30 yards of longcloth
2 ditto flannel or 6 yards flannel
6 caps or 3 yards muslin
6 handkerchiefs
6 aprons or 6 yards check
6 neckerchiefs
1 pair stay
6 pairs black worsted stockings
2 pairs shoes
1 bonnet

Nellie sat looking forlornly at Katherine.

'What are you looking at me like that for?' demanded Katherine.

'It seems like an awfully dull wardrobe doesn't it.'

'Well, we do have some pretty coloured cottons and fine muslin to hand, why don't we make ourselves some dresses and shifts while we are on the trip. That way we can embellish them with trims and laces from our collection.'

'Nellie brightened up immediately. 'That is a wonderful idea Katherine. Yes, we could use some of those lovely French patterns and add our own trimmings.'

Katherine sat back, pleased with her idea and relieved that

Nellie accepted it so readily.

Finally, the day of departure arrived. Katherine, Benjamin and Nellie climbed into the lighter that would take them out to the ship sitting at anchor in the deepest waters of the harbour. God Bless, called Mrs Beasley. She would take over the running of the Old Bell until Benjamin was certain he really wanted to live in New Zealand.

'God Speed,' called Mr Hicks, waving enthusiastically. 'Don't forget to write to me and your uncle, Nellie. I'm going to miss not seeing you coming and going every day. Travel safe,' he said wiping a tear from his eye.

Nellie didn't trust herself to speak, her throat was tight with unshed tears, she waved vigorously instead. But once they were out of sight, she turned away to face the open sea and allowed the tears to roll unchecked down her cheeks and onto her hands, wringing them together in her lap. She had already had a very tearful farewell with Uncle Silas when he left on his latest voyage and now that was all coming back to the surface again. Katherine was trying desperately not to cry but when she saw Nellie give way to tears, she followed suit.

'Goodness me, look at you two,' smiled Benjamin, 'anyone would think you were going to your deaths not starting a new adventure.'

The women smiled through their tears then laughed, breaking the tension.

It was a long three-month journey and not without its share of drama. As Silas predicted, there were wild storms and gales which tossed the great ship around mercilessly at times, pitching everyone from their bunks and tossing them about like rag dolls if they happened to let go of their handholds. Nellie and Katherine suffered some bruising but fortunately nothing worse, like broken bones. Although Katherine was a little seasick to begin with, she soon found her sea legs. Nellie and Benjamin were both lucky enough not to succumb to the dreaded sea sickness but once or twice during heavy seas they admitted to feeling unwell.

The two women spent as much time as they could working on their shifts and gowns but made time to walk around the deck twice a day to stretch their legs, rest their eyes, and get some fresh air.

Then, as Silas predicted, they found themselves becalmed for several days causing the passengers and crew to become unsettled and out of sorts.

'Oh the irritability of some people,' growled Katherine one day in a rare show of anger, 'I have just been accosted by Mrs Longbottom over there. I have to admit though, she does have a right to be irritable.'

'Why is that?' asked Benjamin, amused.

'Because she has six small unruly children. I am sure I would not have the patience to deal with such little tykes as those.'

Benjamin roared. 'Why Mrs Croxley, I don't think I have ever heard you speak so against another person. You must be feeling the pressure of our situation. I have to admit it is rather tiresome and I am fed up with playing games and walking around on deck. I just wish we could pick up some wind and get moving again.'

No sooner were the words out of his mouth than the ship moved ever so slightly. Katherine looked at Benjamin.

'My word husband, are you some kind of magician? Perhaps you have summoned up the Gods of wind. Well done.'

The three of them climbed quickly up the wooden ladder to the deck, giggling as they went. It seems they weren't the only ones to feel the shift. All of a sudden there were sailors running around everywhere, the captain and his mate were shouting orders, orderly chaos ensued. The three of them remained on deck, trying desperately to stay out of the way of the sailors as they readied the sails to catch the coming wind. At last, they were on their way again.

They saw a variety of sea and birdlife from time to time and even hove-to off some small exotic looking islands, all of which Nellie noted in her diary, the one Uncle Silas had bought her.

It was a farewell gift, leather bound with fine gold-edged pages. Nellie had been thrilled with it and promised she would write in it every day.

'Do that lass and I will have to buy ye another one next year,' he laughed.

On a beautiful blue-sky day, they had finally arrived at Lyttleton Harbour on the east coast of the South Island of New Zealand.

'I can't believe we are finally here,' laughed Nellie as she leaned over the side of the ship watching the activity on the crowded wharf below. She watched the people jostling for position, no doubt hoping to see whoever it was they had come to meet. She felt Benjamin move in closer to the rail and leaning over as far as he could, hailed his brother, Harry. Harry waved back enthusiastically.

'Welcome brother, it is good to see you here safe and well,' he called through cupped hands.

Finally, they were allowed to disembark and they greeted Harry with much excitement.

'You will feel a tad unsteady on your feet for a while,' he laughed. 'It's going to take some time for the crew to unload the ship and may even take until tomorrow to get it all off, so I have booked us into a small lodging house while we wait. I have taken the liberty of reserving a table at the eating house as well.'

'Thank you brother,' said Benjamin gratefully, 'I'm not sure we would have known what to do if it wasn't for you.'

Harry laughed. 'You would be among the majority of people who arrive here totally bewildered and lost Benjamin, but there are plenty of people on the wharf happy to guide you along, never fear. Now, let's get ourselves off to the tea house, I am sure the ladies would love a nice cup of tea.'

'Bit parched myself,' said Benjamin. 'I hope they serve a nicer brew than what we have been subjected to for the past three months.'

Chapter Ten

Settling in – New Zealand 1850

It was a long and arduous trek up and over the hills from Lyttleton Harbour to the flat land on the other side the following morning. Rising up in the distance on the far side of the flat plains was a mountain range the likes of which none of the travellers had ever seen before. Nellie, hand at her throat, squealed with delight.

'Oh my word Katherine, have you ever seen anything as beautiful as this? Is that snow on the top of those mountains?'

'It surely is Nellie,' smiled Harry 'but it will be gone before too long. In the middle of winter that snow comes right down to the bottom of the hills and sometimes covers the whole of these plains for a brief time. It's quite magnificent, that's if you don't mind the cold.'

Katherine and Benjamin were equally enthralled at the scene spreading out before them.

'You didn't say the landscape was this breath-taking Harry,' admonished Benjamin.

'Thought I would just let you see it for yourselves,' he smiled. 'Knew you'd be impressed.'

They were tired and hungry by the time they reached Harry's home. Benjamin was impressed when he saw the size of the house.

'Harry, you have done well for yourself, our parents would be very proud of you.'

'Thank you Benjamin, yes I have worked hard. I hope someday to impress a young lady enough to want to share it with me and be my wife.'

Benjamin smiled at his brother. 'Are there many eligible women to choose from around here?'

'Not that I have come across, but then I have spent most of my time working rather than socialising,' he laughed.

By the time the setting sun was casting its apricot glow up from behind the mountains in the west, Harry had everyone settled into their rooms, the fire was roaring in the living room and roast mutton was cooking in the kitchen, the delicious aroma permeating the whole house.

'What's for dinner?' asked Katherine as she took the sherry Harry offered her.

'Roast mutton, the likes I guarantee you have never tasted before,' he said proudly.

'Surely it can't be any better than my mutton pies, brother, I am well known for my mutton pies back home,' Benjamin chipped in.

'Sorry Benjamin but this meal is going to be hard to beat.'

By the end of the evening all three visitors had to agree that they hadn't tasted anything quite like the roast meal Harry and his young servant girl had served up. The hogget was melt-in-the mouth tender, the potatoes and kumara were baked crisp on the outside and soft in the middle, and the carrots and peas were fresh out of Harry's vegetable garden that morning. To top it all off, they had a rich brown gravy and mint sauce.

'Harry,' Benjamin said as he pushed his chair back and stood up with his glass of port in hand, 'I have to admit you were right. That was by far one of the most delicious meals I think I have ever had. And I would like to take this opportunity to thank you for inviting us to come down here and for sharing your lovely home with us.' He raised his glass to his brother and the others followed suit, echoing Benjamin's sentiments.

The following weeks became a whirl of social engagements and visits to various business offices around town. Benjamin was eager to investigate opportunities that might give him and

Katherine a reason to remain in a country he was becoming more and more impressed with.

Katherine and Nellie spent their days wandering up and down the streets taking in all the newly established stores and businesses, comparing them to those back in London.

'It seems so fresh and new,' remarked Nellie one afternoon. The skies were a clear deep blue and the sun was so warm the women wore light clothing and carried parasols.

'I know what you mean Nellie, but I must admit I do love the history of our beloved England, the old established buildings and all that.'

'Do you think you might decide to go back then?' Nellie was concerned that they might not want to stay. She was enjoying her new surroundings; they were exciting and they awakened a pioneering spirit in her young soul.

'I don't know,' she sighed, it will be up to Benjamin, he needs to be able to open a business here and get settled if we are to stay.'

That evening over dinner Benjamin excitedly announced that he had been successful in securing a small building in which to set up a bakery business. Katherine was caught by surprise, he hadn't said anything to her about it.

'Do you not think we should have discussed this first, husband,' she said a little coolly.

'I'm sorry my love, if I didn't sign up for it straight away it would have been snapped up by the man waiting in line behind me.'

'Well maybe you should have let it go then and looked around for something else,' she snapped as she got up and left the table and went upstairs to their room.

Benjamin was mortified. 'Excuse me,' he said rising from the table, 'I think I may have some apologising to do.'

Benjamin and Katherine did not appear for the rest of the night but at breakfast the next morning they appeared to have settled their differences and were in good humour. Nellie took Katherine aside after breakfast to make sure.

'Katherine, have you and Benjamin sorted things between

you? I have never seen you quite so upset as you were last night.'

Katherine smiled at her friend, 'Yes, I am alright now Nellie. I am still not sure I want to stay and settle here but Benjamin has taken that choice out of my hands,' she explained. 'He has promised that we will give it one year and if we both don't enjoy being here, we will make the decision together as to whether we will stay or go. I am content with that, for now.'

'I don't know what I would do if you were to go back to England,' cried Nellie. 'I couldn't imagine staying here without you and I really don't want to go back to England, at least not for a while yet.'

'Then we shall just have to see if we can get you well settled before we go then shan't we.' Katherine smiled confidently hoping to allay Nellie's fears.

By the end of their second month in New Zealand, Benjamin had established his bakery and Katherine had set up their accommodation in the rooms above the shop. Nellie moved in with them despite Harry's assurances that she was most welcome to stay at his residence.

'I appreciate your kind offer Harry, but I don't think it would be quite proper for me to be staying here with an unmarried man,' she explained.

Harry laughed, 'Well my maid lives here with me and as far as I know there has never been talk of anything untoward between us. However, I do see your point and I beg your pardon. If I ever get married you would be welcome to come and stay with us. Nellie thanked him for his kind offer and decided to keep it in mind just in case Benjamin and Katherine should decide to return to England.

Nellie and Katherine rolled up their sleeves and went to work for Benjamin in the bakery. His meat pies became very popular in a short space of time. They were an improvement on the pies he made back in London as he had the advantage now of good supplies of fresh beef and mutton. Nellie and Katherine loved working together again, although rolling dough was a far cry from needles and thread, but they settled into a comfortable routine as the weeks and months ticked by.

One afternoon a young man entered the shop and it was Nellie's turn to serve at the counter.

'How can I help you today sir?' she enquired.

The young man took off his hat and nodded at Nellie. 'Good afternoon ma'am,' he said shyly, 'I have heard about your delicious meat pies and would like to take some home for our tea.'

'Mutton or beef?' enquired Nellie.

'Pardon me?' said the man, a quizzical crease appearing on his forehead.

'Would you prefer a mutton pie or a beef pie?' responded Nellie patiently.

'Oh, ahh, make it one of each please.' He dove into his pocket for change.

'Nellie selected the pies and handed him the paper bag. He handed her the money.

'Thank you sir,' said Nellie brightly, 'I hope you enjoy them.'

'I'm sure I will,' he said taking a long look at Nellie before turning on his heel, almost knocking over another customer as he bolted out the door.

Katherine appeared behind her after the next customer had left the shop.

'I wonder who that young man was, he seemed to take an interest in you Nellie.'

'Well, that would be too bad because I am not sure I am ready to start courting again just yet.'

'I understand,' said Katherine reassuringly, 'but Nellie if a nice young man comes along and wants to spend some time getting to know you, it would be wise to at least try, wouldn't it? You are under no obligation to marry the first man who comes along, you know that. At least give it some thought.'

Nellie wasn't at all comfortable about courting again so soon after losing Nick, but she nodded in agreement just to call a halt to the conversation.

The young man turned up at the bakery once or twice a week after his first visit. He bought pastries and cakes and couldn't take his eyes off Nellie as she went about her work behind the counter. If Katherine or Benjamin happened to be serving, he would be straining his neck to see if he could see her out the back. Katherine very boldly asked him outright one day if he was interested in courting Nellie. The young man blushed to the very roots of his hair, he was so embarrassed.

'I, well, that is…' he stammered, 'yes as a matter of fact I would like to get to know her,' he replied.

'Good, then why don't you come to tea this evening and I shall introduce you,' announced Katherine.

'Ahh, this evening, yes, aah that would be capital, yes capital indeed,' he said as he stumbled out the door.

'We will see you at five o'clock then,' called Katherine. The young man turned and waved his acceptance.

Nellie was not pleased when Katherine told her what she had done.

'You had no right to set this up without asking me. What makes you think I want to get to know this man anyway?'

Katherine and Benjamin smiled at each other. 'Nellie darling it is written all over your face every time he comes in.'

Nellie blushed. 'Well, what time is he coming then?'

'Soon after we close, at five o'clock.'

Nellie became flustered at the thought and mentally went through her wardrobe trying to decide what she might wear. She was annoyed that Katherine hadn't given her much notice but underneath it all she was feeling a little excited, if a bit nervous. She hadn't felt like this in a very long time, not since… She forced herself not to dwell on Nick and instead focused on the young man she was about to share dinner with.

There was a knock at the door of the bakery promptly at five.

'Well, he's punctual, that's a good start,' smiled Benjamin.

After the awkward introductions and long silences, which Katherine tried valiantly to fill, Benjamin brought out a bottle of Port, which helped to break the tension.

'So, Mr Fitzgerald, Albert,' Benjamin began, 'what brought you here to New Zealand?'

'My father was a Major in the army. We went to India when I was fifteen,' he explained, 'I joined the army myself when I turned seventeen, that was ten years ago.' He blushed and looked down at his feet wondering if he was giving too much away at their first meeting.

'Go on, urged Nellie,' finding herself interested in what he had to say.

'We went back to England when my father retired but we found everything so changed that my parents felt they didn't want to stay, so they brought us to New Zealand. My parents live in Wellington, my father is a politician there. I live here with my sister Felicity now.'

'Do you work here in Christchurch?' asked Benjamin.

'Yes, I am the manager of the farm supply store on East Street, perhaps you've seen it? Mr Gould is the owner.

'Well,' said Benjamin with a smile, 'that's a far cry from being a soldier is it not?'

Albert laughed, 'It is, but I always loved the academic side of business, my father is an excellent academic with a good business head, perhaps I inherited that from him,' he said shyly. Albert looked across the table to Nellie.

'So how long have you been in New Zealand and what brings you all here?' he enquired.

Nellie looked to Katherine for support, not sure how much she wanted to tell this man at this stage.

Katherine started.

'We were living in London until quite recently, we only arrived here a few months ago. We had some unpleasant experiences back home and thought it a good idea to perhaps leave England and do some travelling for a while. Benjamin has a brother here and his glowing letters encouraged us to venture down to this new land to see it for ourselves.'

'And how do you find it?'

'I like it well enough,' admitted Benjamin, 'but I fear my

lovely wife might not love it as much as I do.'

Katherine smiled at her husband, 'I like it well enough but perhaps I'm not so comfortable as my husband is. As for Nellie,' she turned to her friend, 'you have never really said how you feel about living here.'

'No, I suppose I haven't really thought too much about it,' Nellie said hesitantly, 'so much has been going on in such a short time. I like it well enough, I enjoy the warm sunny weather very much, and I do like the clean fresh air. We haven't ventured too far from town at this stage but from what I have seen it is a very pretty country.'

'If you would allow me then,' ventured Albert, 'I would very much like to take you on a trip out to the country if you would permit me.' His offer was aimed squarely at Nellie.

She hesitated for a moment looking for approval from Katherine.

'Nellie, I think that's a wonderful opportunity, why don't you go. Benjamin and I could use some time to ourselves while the shop is closed for the day.

It was settled. Benjamin arrived the following Sunday morning as promised, his horse and buggy standing patiently outside waiting while he cleared his throat and knocked on the door. Nellie was a bundle of nerves, just as she had been when she first walked out with Nick. Katherine answered the door and showed the young man to the kitchen out the back where Nellie stood nervously wringing her hands.

'Are you ready to go Miss Abernathy,' he smiled warmly.

Nellie's heart shifted a little, she let out the breath she didn't realise she had been holding, and nodded her head. 'I am ready Mr Fitzgerald.'

Chapter Eleven

Farm visit – 1851

During the summer months and into early Autumn, Nellie and Albert went out every Sunday, whatever the weather. They were becoming more and more comfortable in each other's company, and although Nellie admitted to herself that she didn't feel the tingles and thrills she had when she was with Nick, her feelings for Albert were growing stronger each time she saw him.

'I met Albert's sister, Felicity, today,' Nellie told Katherine at dinner one evening. 'I don't think she likes me, I suspect she might be jealous of me taking up with her brother.'

'Nellie, don't over think things, just give yourselves time to get to know each other, she might just be shy.'

'Perhaps you are right,' said Nellie thoughtfully, but she wasn't so sure that was the case.

A week later Albert arrived at the bakery with an offer none of them could refuse.

'I have friends who own a sheep station up in the high country and we have all been invited to stay with them any time we choose. Would you like to go?'

It was a collective yes! from everyone.

'I have always wanted to visit a farm, I love animals,' enthused Nellie, 'but I have only ever seen them in books or from a distance. It would be wonderful to see them up close. What animals can we expect to see Albert?'

Albert smiled at Nellie's childish enthusiasm.

'Why don't we wait and see,' he said kissing her tenderly on the cheek.

'What does one wear on a sheep farm?' asked Katherine.

'Why don't you pop into the store later on this afternoon,' suggested Albert, 'no doubt we will have something suitable for you to wear.'

Nellie and Katherine gladly accepted Albert's invitation. Nellie had never visited Albert at his work before and he was eager to show her around. 'It's generally quiet around two o'clock if you would like to stop by then, we can have a cup of tea in the staffroom afterwards.'

The women tried on anything remotely suitable for a foray in the country, despite the fact that most of the items were designed for men. When they had finally made their selections, with Albert's help, they were ready for their promised cup of tea. Albert went through all of their purchases piece by piece and noted them down in a sales book. He would be paying for the goods and was delighted to do so. There were two pairs of sturdy boots, two pairs of men's woollen trousers, two waterproof coats and slouch hats and two pairs of thick merino wool socks.

'Not very flattering I'm afraid but it will keep you warm and dry if it rains or we run into snow?' said Albert as he put the money in the drawer.

My goodness,' exclaimed Katherine, 'are we likely to run into snow?'

'It is possible, yes,' smiled Albert. 'We sometimes get early snow falls on the mountains at this time of the year, that's why, if we are going to go before winter, we are best to go sooner rather than later. How does next week suit everyone? We could start out first thing on Friday morning, stay Saturday and Sunday then travel back on Monday. Could you find someone to run the bakery for you Mr Croxley?

'No, I think I will just close up shop on Thursday night and put a sign up to say we are closed until Wednesday and leave it at that,' smiled Benjamin. I've barely taken a day off in my life, I am feeling a little bit rebellious.' Katherine laughed, she was enjoying seeing this more relaxed and jovial side of her husband, New Zealand was definitely agreeing with him.

Nellie was beside herself with excitement. 'I don't think I can wait nine more days,' she exclaimed, clutching Katherine's arm enthusiastically.

The women packed, repacked and packed again before they were satisfied that they had every potential situation covered. Benjamin laughed when he saw what they had packed on their first attempt and suggested they might like to consider the poor horses who would be pulling the wagon.

Finally, the much-anticipated day arrived. It was clear from the outset that Albert would be the planner and Katherine the organiser, leaving Nellie and Benjamin content to just follow along. Albert had planned the trip down to the last detail and was pleased to find that Nellie and Katherine hadn't over-packed, as his sister Felicity tended to do whenever they travelled. He suspected Benjamin might have had some input in that regard.

At last they were all ready to go. It was still very early in the morning but Albert had insisted on an early start, it was going to be a very long day. There was a distinct biting chill in the air as they loaded the wagon, the horses breath hung in small clouds around their heads. The sky was a deep clear blue with hardly any clouds.

'It's a beautiful day,' breathed Katherine.

'Couldn't be better for travelling,' replied Albert.

'There seems to be an awful lot of supplies here for just one weekend Albert,' remarked Benjamin as he made himself and Katherine comfortable in amongst the boxes and sacks of goods on the back of the wagon. Nellie would ride up front on the flat wooden driver's seat with Albert.

'It's not all for us,' explained Albert. 'Simon sent an order through with one of his stockmen earlier in the week and asked if we could bring these supplies with us.'

'Being a city dweller myself, I never really considered the inconvenience of not being able to walk or ride to a store for supplies. Where did you say we will be staying tonight?'

'There is a spot by a lake called Clearwater, we will set up camp there, it's where most people stop when they are heading that way. The days will be long, and at times uncomfortable, but I can guarantee you will sleep well,' smiled Albert.

The four travellers chatted excitedly for the first few miles before settling down to enjoy the scenery. They stopped for something to eat and drink along the way and to ease out their cramped legs and numb bottoms. Nellie stretched her arms up over her head in an effort to ease the ache in her back.

'Are you comfortable up the front Nellie?' asked Katherine. 'I wondered if you might like to sit back here with me for a while, perhaps Benjamin would like to sit up front with Albert and talk about whatever it is that men talk about,' she giggled.

Both parties agreed and swapped seats. The men chatted away quietly while the women alternated between talking and napping until they stopped for lunch. Everyone was hungry and very grateful for the tasty fresh pies and pastries Benjamin had packed for them that morning. Katherine and Nellie had also made big chunky meat sandwiches from the fresh bread straight out of the oven that morning, they were melt-in-the-mouth delicious. They sat around with full stomachs enjoying the breath-taking scenery, reluctant to get up and get going again until Albert urged them on.

'We still have a lot of ground to cover before nightfall,' he reminded them.

They were very quiet for the next part of the journey, the women would doze for a time only to be rudely jolted awake when one of the wagon wheels went over a rock or dropped into a rut, then they would gaze around them again, taking in their surroundings. When they breached a hill to reveal the stunning lake before them there were gasps of delight.

'This is one of the most beautiful places I have ever seen,' exclaimed Nellie.

Streaks of pink, grey and orange rays from the setting sun had begun to appear from behind the snow-topped mountains, the colours reflecting in the clear waters of the lake. It was becoming markedly cooler now, but nobody seemed to notice as they stared at the majestic scene that lay before them.

Within an hour they had set up camp beside the lake. The women would sleep under the wagon while the men rigged up a canvas lean-to beside the wagon for themselves. They sat around the fire enjoying a hot meal of baked beans and bacon, they would leave the rest of the pies and sandwiches for the journey the next day. The fire pit had been dug several years ago and was well used by passing travellers. Metal rods had been set into the ground on either side of the fire pit, supporting another metal rod across the top where pots could be hung over the flames.

Once the women were settled in for the night the men sat on a log by the lake and smoked their pipes.

'Have you ever thought of trying your hand at farming Albert? You sell farm supplies, I just wondered if that might have been something you'd ever considered?' asked Benjamin.

'Yes, I have thought about it, but I'm afraid I don't think I'm quite cut out for the harshness of high-country living.'

'I know what you mean,' nodded Benjamin, 'I doubt I could survive too far away from town, it's all I've ever known.'

The four travellers were rudely awakened early next morning by large drops of icy cold water falling on them. The clouds had rolled in and were building into a menacing looking storm.

'Let's get packed up and on the move,' Albert said, his words taking on a concerned tone. 'No time for breakfast, we can eat along the way.'

He was moving quickly and anxiously, causing the others to follow suit. Within a few minutes they had packed everything onto the back of the wagon and shrugged themselves into their wet-weather gear. The men covered the women and supplies with a canvas sheet and tied it down securely, leaving them a gap for air and light to get in, then they set off with haste. The horses were skittish and reluctant to move until Albert cracked the whip. He hated using the whip but this was not a time to molly-coddle them. He had been alarmed to see the cloud build up in the south, it was not a good omen, bad weather was on the way.

They managed to ford the next river crossing they came to, but Albert knew there was an even wider one ahead before they reached the homestead, and if the rain came down in torrents, as he feared it might, they may not get across and they would become trapped between the two rivers. They forged on at a steady pace, Albert was reluctant to put any further stress on the horses, they might have to ride them if they had to ditch the wagon.

The rain got heavier over the next couple of hours and didn't appear to be letting up. The women rummaged around and found the sandwiches and pies left over from the day before and handed some to the grateful men. There would be no warming tea to wash it down, just ice-cold water drawn from the lake before they left. The temperature continued to drop the closer they got to the mountains. When they reached the second river, Albert was relieved to find that although it was flowing quite fast, it didn't appear to be too deep for them to cross. He jumped off the wagon and, taking his walking pole, ventured out to test the depth. It was still within a reasonably safe depth so he swung back onto the wooden seat and taking the reins, urged the horses gently into the river. They were hesitant and threatened to bolt but Albert urged them on with strong confident commands which kept them stepping nervously forward. The water came up to the horses' bellies and they almost lost their footing at one point, which would have spelled disaster, but when they reached shallower water and gained sturdier footing, their confidence grew. Once they reached the banks of the river Albert got down and urged the horses to pull forward with all their might to bring the wagon up out of the gravel and on to firmer ground. He guided them up under some trees on the outskirts of a thicket of bush where he unhitched them from the wagon took them down to the water for a drink then tied them to a fallen log where they could graze for a while. Walking deeper into the bush he found a clearing with a bit of cover from some high-topped trees.

'Let's see if we can build a fire,' Albert said, 'I could murder a nice hot cup of tea.'

He was visibly shaken and he noticed he wasn't the only one. Both the women were quite pale and Benjamin was eager to get down off the wagon and do something constructive before anyone could see his hands shaking. They managed to get a small fire going to boil some water and huddled together to keep warm as they sipped on the nourishing hot liquid. They had something to eat and sat quietly for a while before settling back onto the wagon to continue their journey. At one point Albert leaned back to address the women, his face wore a grim expression.

'Ladies, it looks like it might snow before too long if those blue-grey clouds are anything to go by, so snuggle down and try and stay as warm and as dry as you can, I hope to have us at the homestead before dark.'

They hadn't gone far before the first snowflake splattered itself on Benjamin's knee.

'Oh,' he said, 'I do believe that was a snowflake.' He looked up then smiled across at Albert, but his smile soon disappeared when he saw the concern on Albert's face.

'If it snows heavily this far from the homestead, we may not make it there tonight,' Albert whispered to Benjamin and held a finger to his lips tilting his head back towards the women in the back. 'I don't want to alarm them at this point.'

Benjamin nodded in agreement but concern showed on his face now too. They ploughed on steadily, watching anxiously as the snow settled on the ground and began to get deeper with each passing mile. The men were huddled down in their coats, their hats pulled down so low over their faces, they didn't see a rider approaching until he called out to them. Albert looked up startled.

'Albert, Albert,' called the rider. 'Thank goodness, Millicent was getting worried and begged me to come look for you.'

'Simon, I am very pleased to see you my friend. I must

admit I was getting concerned about our ability to reach the homestead before dark too.'

'That's why I am here Albert, I've decided it would be best if we spend the night in the shepherds' hut, it's just a short distance up this way,' he indicated to his left. 'It's too risky to try and make it to the homestead tonight, there is still a reasonable distance to cover and the hut is much closer. Follow me if you will.'

They made their way across to the foot of the nearest mountain range and got down from the wagon. They unhitched the horses and left them and the wagon in a sheltered spot taking only the barest of essentials with them. They followed Simon's footprints in the snow as they climbed their way up to the hut. Benjamin, being the eldest, struggled a little so Simon found him a sturdy stick to serve as a walking aid. It worked well, Benjamin was most grateful. Eventually, drenched and exhausted, they were relieved to hear Simon announce that they were almost there.

The hut was a modest dwelling, but once they got a fire roaring in the hearth and a hearty stew, courtesy of Millicent, bubbling away in the pot overhanging the flames, it felt like a welcoming hotel to the weary travellers. There were two sets of bunks so the women decided they would share one bunk to allow the men to have a bunk each. The women were able to warm their chilled bodies and with the heat from the fire and full bellies, they slept soundly until they were awakened by Simon putting the billy on to make a cup of tea.

'Gosh is it morning already?' asked Katherine as she stretched and looked across at Simon.

'Just gone daybreak,' whispered Simon, glancing at the other sleeping forms in the bunks. 'Did you sleep well?'

'I did indeed, the best I've slept in a very long time, must be the mountain air.'

'You'd be right about that,' he smiled at her.

By the time the others had risen and enjoyed a delicious breakfast of oatmeal porridge, toast and tea, the sun was well above the horizon. The sky was clear blue showing no signs of any more snow on the way, at least not for now. The snow that had settled on the ground the previous day was beginning to melt, as the travellers slushed their way back down the hill to the horses and wagon. The horses seemed well rested and a lot more settled this morning. Simon rode alongside them and guided them the rest of the way to the homestead. It was a very relieved and excited Millicent and her three young children who greeted them as they came into the yard.

'Oh I am so relieved you are all here safe and sound,' she breathed. 'You are all safe and sound aren't you?' she was suddenly concerned at not seeing Katherine and Nellie. The two women poked their heads up from their nest in amongst the supplies and smiled. Millicent clutched at her chest and smiled back.

'Good. Let's get you all in by the fire then.

The visitors were ushered into the house to be greeted with the familiar smell of roast mutton cooking. Katherine's tummy rumbled and she giggled. They unwrapped themselves from their outdoor clothing and sank gratefully into the big comfortable fireside chairs which had been vacated for them. Before long they were sipping welcoming hot sweet tea and devouring the tastiest fruit cake Nellie thought she had ever tasted.

'I would love your fruit cake recipe Millicent, that's if it is not a family secret of course. I don't think I have ever tasted anything quite so delicious.'

'Thank you Nellie,' smiled Millicent, beaming at the compliment, 'there's no secret, I use fresh fruit off our trees in the orchard and dry them myself. Our fruit trees and gardens seem to thrive here, so long as we keep the stock and the rabbits and the possums out. I am happy to share the recipe, perhaps you could make some for your bakery Mr Croxley,' she suggested shyly.

'Millicent, I would be delighted to add this cake to our selection, I agree with Nellie, it really is quite delicious.'

Millicent bustled happily off to the kitchen to attend to the midday meal preparations. Four more adult mouths to feed on top of her family of two adults and three children was nothing out of the ordinary for Millicent, she had been cooking for shearers and musterers for as long as she could remember, she was born to it. Her mother had been a very capable farmer's wife and had raised ten children. Millicent, being the second eldest, shared much of the responsibility of cooking, cleaning and washing with her big sister. Cooking was her favourite chore, although she didn't consider it a chore, she loved to cook.

They sat around the warm comfy lounge beside the fire, talking and playing board games with the children, until it was time to prepare the vegetables for dinner. Nellie and Katherine helped with the preparations while the men went for a stroll over to the sheds to have a look around.

'What a wonderful way of life this must be,' sighed Nellie dreamily as she watched Albert out the window.

Millicent smiled. 'It is most of the time,' she said, 'but it can be a difficult and challenging one too. 'There's nothing romantic about being a farmers' wife let me assure you.'

Nellie was disappointed. 'Oh, I suppose I hadn't really thought about the not so good times,' she said thoughtfully. 'I would love to hear about your life here Millicent, it is so very different to what Katherine and I have experienced.'

'Perhaps we could share our stories,' said Millicent brightly, 'I would love to hear what sort of life you have come from in London, and what your plans are for living here in New Zealand.'

The women talked about their lives and experiences right up until it was time for bed. They had much to share, resulting in them all forming a bond of respect for each other.

The travellers slept soundly in the children's soft comfortable beds that night. The children didn't mind vacating their beds for the visitors because it meant they got to make a hut under the table in the small room off the kitchen where they were allowed to make beds on the floor and pretend they were camping somewhere in the mountains.

The sun was well up by the time the four sleepy visitors emerged from their rooms and wandered into the kitchen following the smell of bacon cooking.

'Sit yourselves down at the table,' instructed Millicent as she put out warm plates and began piling them with scrambled eggs, bacon and fresh buttered toast.

'I am starving,' said Nellie as she forked scrambled egg into her mouth.'

'Me too,' agreed Katherine, 'this looks so good Millicent, thank you.'

'You are very welcome, it's lovely to have people to stay, especially at this time of the year. During the winter months we rarely have any visitors.'

Simon burst in the back door slamming it shut to prevent any of the kitchen heat escaping.

'By jingo's it's cold out there,' he said briskly rubbing his hands together before holding them out over the stove to warm up. He turned to look at the four people sitting at his table.

'The sun is out at least, so it should warm up a bit later this morning. I can take you all out and show you around if you like, do any of you ride?'

Albert nodded but the other three shook their heads.

'Not yet,' said Nellie, but I would like to learn one day.'

'I did a bit of riding as a young child,' admitted Benjamin but I think I'm a bit too long in the tooth to be doing it now, how about you Katherine?'

'Not for me. I'm a bit frightened of horses, probably because I have never had anything to do with them. They seem so awfully big and powerful.'

'Not to worry,' smiled Simon, 'we'll go for a walk up the hill where you can get a good view across the valley. It looks mighty spectacular covered in snow, doesn't it my love?' he threw Millicent a warm smile.

She smiled back. 'There is never a day goes by that I don't marvel at the scenery around here,' she gushed. 'The mountains are beautiful at any time of the year, but when they have a blanket of snow on them, well,' she paused, 'there's nothing quite so magnificent.' She smiled at Simon and then at the group. 'We thank God every day that we are fortunate enough to be living here.'

She quickly hurried off to the sound of children squabbling in the lounge. A heated debate ensued between mother and children, followed by a few stern words before peace reined once again. Millicent bustled back into the kitchen, smiled sheepishly, and brought the boiling kettle to the table to top up the teapot.

The second day was spent enjoying the fresh mountain air, walking the lower ranges behind the homestead, checking out the orchard and gardens and meeting the various farm animals. The children had been allowed to select one lamb each at lambing time and were allowed to hand-rear it. Simon explained that it helped to have a couple of tame sheep in the flock when it came to moving them around the farm. Katherine and Nellie were a little hesitant when the children suggested they help bottle feed the lambs, they weren't sure what to expect. Once they were handed the bottles and the lambs greedily latched on to the teat and began sucking, the women relaxed, this was fun.

Another long evening of talking and playing cards followed the perfect day. They were reluctant to go to bed but Albert reminded them that they still had a couple of long days ahead of them to get back home.

The visitors were reluctant to leave the next morning. 'Please come again soon,' pleaded Millicent, 'I have so enjoyed meeting you lovely ladies.'

'We'd love to,' said Katherine. 'Nellie and I have your measurements and colour preferences now so we can make you some new dresses and perhaps we could include a shirt or two for Simon and some clothes for the children, provided you don't grow too quickly,' she grinned at the children. 'Then perhaps we could come and visit you again in the Spring or you could come and stay with us?'

Millicent glanced across at Simon and he nodded saying, 'we will be due a trip to town by then. We like to take the children in at least once or twice a year for health and teeth checks,' he explained.

'We will write and let you know how we are progressing with your garments then we can decide whether we send them to you or give them to you in person if a visit either way is pending,' suggested Katherine.

After hugs and handshakes all round, Albert and Benjamin helped Nellie and Katherine get tucked comfortably into the back of the wagon, then they settled onto their seats up the front. They all waved goodbye as Albert turned the wagon and headed out of the yard back towards home.

They arrived in Christchurch two days later after a long, chilly, but invigorating trip and began to unpack their supplies at the bakery. Katherine and Benjamin thanked Albert profusely and said it had been the most exciting thing either of them had ever done in their lives and they hoped to do it again sometime soon. After they went upstairs to bed, Albert and Nellie sat in the kitchen at the back of the bakery enjoying a cup of tea and some of Millicent's delicious fruit cake.

'Have you ever thought of going farming Albert?' Nellie asked.

'Yes, I've thought about it, but to be honest I don't really think I have what it takes to be a farmer, why, would you like to be a farmer's wife?' he wasn't sure he wanted to hear the answer.

'I did think I might for a while, until I heard Millicent say how hard she works,' she laughed, 'besides I am not sure about living in such isolation.'

Albert was relieved. 'That's good, we are both agreed then, farming is not in our future.'

'Agreed' smiled Nellie.

Chapter Twelve

Proposal – 1852

Six months later Albert Fitzgerald got down on one knee and proposed to Miss Nellie Abernathy. He chose a beautiful sunny day with no clouds in the sky to take her to one of their favourite spots by the sea. They spread out a tartan wool blanket and unpacked the picnic basket Katherine had packed for them. It was full of delectable delights from the bakery as well as delicious fresh fruits Katherine had purchased from the markets first thing that morning. Seagulls swarmed overhead eyeing the tempting food offerings below. They chatted about anything and everything while they ate, finally lying back on the blanket gazing up at the sky.

'Happy?' asked Albert.

'Blissfully,' answered Nellie with a satisfied sigh.

With that, Albert got up, pulled Nellie to a standing position and got down on one knee.

'Nellie, I love you, I think I have loved you from the moment I first saw you in the shop that day. I can't imagine the rest of my life without you in it, would you please do me the great honour of becoming my wife?'

Nellie was stunned, she wasn't expecting this, well not this soon anyway, she hesitated for a moment looking down at Albert and, as her mind cleared, she said, 'yes Albert, yes of course I will marry you.'

Tears formed in her eyes as he stood and took her in his arms kissing her soundly. He suddenly pulled back, causing Nellie to think something was amiss, but he was smiling from ear to ear as he reached into his breast pocket to retrieve a small velvet ring box. He flicked it open to reveal the most beautiful diamond ring Nellie had ever seen.

'Albert, it's gorgeous.' She put her left hand out for him to place the ring on the third finger, it fitted perfectly.

'I love it,' she said, smiling up at him, eyes shining with tears.

'I have to confess,' he said, 'I did have some help. Katherine came with me to help me choose the ring, I had no idea of your ring size or what you might like so she offered to help.'

'She knew all along that you were going to propose, and she didn't say a word? Wait until I get my hands on her,' she said playfully.

From that day on it was all go, Albert had many plans he wanted to implement. First and foremost, he wanted to buy a bigger house, as his sister Felicity would continue to stay on living in the house with them after they were married. Nellie had always been aware that Felicity would be living with them, she didn't like it but she accepted that that's the way it would be. She had come to learn more about Felicity and the scarring on her face and did have sympathy for the girl. Albert had explained to her that as a young child, Felicity had reached up to the stove and pulled a pot of boiling water over herself, causing ugly scars down one side of her body and the left side of her pretty face. Although she had healed reasonably well with the limited medical expertise that was available at the time, the horrible scarring had left her ill-equipped to deal with life on her own. She was convinced she would never marry, she didn't believe she would ever find a man who could love her disfigured body. She shied away from people, men in particular, and clung to the only person she ever trusted, someone she loved dearly her brother and only sibling, Albert. On one of his trips home to visit his parents, Albert was saddened to see Felicity so isolated and alone, that's when he decided to take her back to Christchurch to live with him. He offered her a new life where nobody knew her. He knew she wasn't always easy to get along with and that she had a nasty tongue at times, but he cared about her, she was his sister and only sibling. Felicity couldn't pack her bags quick enough when Albert suggested she might like to go and live with him and take charge of his household. He didn't have time to deal with household and domestic issues, his job kept him busy enough so this seemed like a perfect solution for them both. So, for the past four years Felicity had been in her element running Albert's household, that is, until Nellie Abernathy came along.

'I don't think Felicity likes me very much,' Nellie confided in Albert a couple of days after the engagement.

'Felicity doesn't warm to many people Nellie, just give her time, I'm sure she will come around. Give her a chance to get to know you.'

'Why did she not stay with your parents?'

'She wanted to, but with father being in politics there were always people coming and going and lots of socialising, she just didn't cope well with all of that. She was miserable, so she jumped at the chance to come down and stay with me. I guess I will have her under my roof for the rest of her life now, are you going to be able to live with that?'

Nellie sighed, 'I am sure we will get along in time Albert.'

In an effort to forge a closer bond with Felicity, Nellie asked her to be her bridesmaid. Felicity was taken aback by the offer.

'Oh, I couldn't,' she said nervously raising her hand protectively to the scarred area at the side of her face.

'I am sure you could Felicity. We can arrange your hair to cover your scars and, if you like, you could wear one of those lovely big picture hats we saw at the dress shop last week.'

Felicity was thoughtful for a while. 'Are you sure you want me to be your bridesmaid, what about Katherine?'

'Katherine will be my maid of honour.' When Felicity didn't respond Nellie jumped in. 'Good, that's all settled then. I understand Albert is going to ask his brother Harry to be best man?'

Felicity blushed but said nothing.

Albert was keen to provide Nellie with suitable premises for her to start up a haberdashery shop. She had spoken at length with him about the store she and Katherine had leased back in London and he wanted to give her that same opportunity here in New Zealand. Truth be told, he would have given her the moon and the stars if he could, he was so besotted with her. He knew Nellie didn't feel quite as strongly for him, but he was ever hopeful that one day she might. He knew Nick had stolen her heart and that it would take time for her to get over the tragedy of his death. He finally came across a large two storied house with a piece of land alongside it on which would be the perfect place to build the haberdashery shop. It was down the end of the main street and had other traders such as a milliner, a doll and teddy bear shoppe, a sweet shop, a shoe store, and a wool shop close by. The house had been recently built but the owner had returned to England after the death of his wife during childbirth. Albert opted not to tell Nellie about the former owner's demise, he figured they would put their own positive stamp on the house instead. Nellie was thrilled when he took her to see the house.

'Do you like it my love? See this piece of land here, we can build your shop right next to the house. You and Katherine could pick up where you left off in London, would you like that?' Nellie's head was spinning, she was overwhelmed by Albert's thoughtfulness and generosity.

'I can't believe you would do this for me Albert, thank you.' She reached up and put her arms around his neck and kissed him lovingly on the lips. 'You are the kindest, loveliest man I have ever met Albert Fitzgerald and I love you for it.' Albert's heart fluttered, just the response he was hoping for.

Benjamin took on two new staff members in the bakery to help fill the gap left by Katherine and Nellie once they began building their haberdashery. The first thing Nellie did, after Albert proposed, was send a letter to Uncle Silas telling him the good news, that she was to be married to a lovely businessman and that she and Katherine were once again going to have their very own haberdashery and dress shop. She knew he would be pleased, and relieved too no doubt. She followed this up with a letter to the Shipping Office to get their trunks sent out on the first available ship. It would take several months but it gave them time to work on the plans with the builders, design the interior, and decide what shelving and display units they would need.

The building itself went up quickly with several people offering to help. The local merchants were always keen to assist a new business owner to get established, and Albert's staff at the mercantile store were also a great help with various labouring jobs. They liked Albert, he was an excellent boss and looked after his staff well, they were happy to lend a hand.

Nellie and Katherine stood arm in arm with tears in their eyes when the last dab of white paint went on the exterior of the building. It was a larger replica of the beautiful shop they had leased in London but instead of being joined on both sides by other buildings, this one stood proudly on its own, and being completely white, made quite a statement.

'It's perfect,' breathed Katherine.

Nellie could only nod in agreement. After a pause she said, 'it reminds me so much of our shop back in London that it takes me right back there, back to all we left behind, the good and the bad.' She reached into her pocket and pulled out a small silver heart and kissed it.

'I've seen you take that wee heart out and kiss it a few times over the years Nellie but I didn't like to ask about it. I could see by the expressions on your face each time you did it, that it is something very precious to you.'

Nellie looked down at the trinket in her hand and smiled sadly.

'It was a gift from my mother for my twelfth birthday, the last one I ever had with my family. Mama and I were going to find a chain to put it on so I could wear it but we never got the chance.' Nellie looked up at Katherine with tears streaming down her face. 'It was in the pocket of my nightgown the night of the fire. I picked it up off the nightstand and put it in my pocket, it was the only thing I took when I jumped out the window and ran away from those awful flames.'

Katherine could see the memories of that time were flooding back, she put her arm around Nellie's shoulders and led her into the house away from curious onlookers. Albert rushed over thinking that Nellie was unhappy with the shop.

'No Albert,' Katherine assured him, 'Nellie was just thinking about her parents and how she would love to have shared all this with them, she misses them terribly.'

Nellie nodded and glancing up at Albert through tear filled eyes said, 'Albert the shop really is perfect, it's just the memories of Mama and Papa and Emilyn that have caught me by surprise. I will be fine in a minute; I just need to catch my breath. It has been a busy few months I suppose I am just a bit overwhelmed.'

'Understandably so my love,' said Albert fondly as he leaned down and kissed the top of her head.

'Please let everyone know how thrilled we are,' said Nellie. 'Perhaps we should have a party to celebrate.'

Albert agreed and, reassured that Nellie was happy with the new building, he went back to inform the gathered group that there would indeed be some form of celebration in due course to thank everyone for their efforts.

The display cabinets and shelving took a lot of time and deliberation but the women were determined to have everything just so. The reason the interior and exterior of the building were painted pure white was so the colours of the gowns in the bay windows and the colourful fabrics and haberdashery items on the shelves would stand out.

When the trunks finally arrived from England, there was great excitement. Squeals of delight emanated from the back room as the women brought out item after item, things they had forgotten all about. They tried to encourage Felicity to join in and help them set up and become involved with the shop, but she would have none of it. Her place was in the home, she had told them bluntly. Nellie jumped on this opportunity to try and forge a way ahead for them both.

'Felicity,' she said one morning as the two of them sat at the breakfast table after Albert had gone to work. 'You know I am not very good with the household and domestic side of things, and you are a natural, why don't we come to an agreement that the running of the household will still be your domain and mine will be the shop. Would that be agreeable to you do you think?'

Felicity was thoughtful for a moment then, setting her cup quietly down on the saucer looked up at Nellie and said with a wan smile, 'yes Nellie, that would be agreeable to me.'

With that she stood up, picked up her cup and saucer and went into the kitchen to begin her day.

The opening of the shop and the wedding day all fell in the same month. This created a whirlwind of activity but everyone jumped in to help. The opening day came first and it couldn't have been more different from their 'grand opening' back in London. It was a beautiful warm day, so Albert arranged for a quartet to play in the garden where Benjamin's staff served cups of tea and slices of cake. There was a constant stream of people through the shop the entire day, leaving Nellie and Katherine overwhelmed but thrilled with the number of orders they had taken.

They wasted no time getting down to business the following morning. They worked tirelessly day in and day out to keep up with orders, but neither of them were about to complain, they were in their element, back doing what they loved.

Bit by bit Nellie began to move some of her clothes and meagre possessions into Albert's house. He had bought her a large wardrobe and a chest of drawers and installed them in a small room beside the main bedroom, which was to be her dressing room. He also bought her two full length mirrors, an oval oak wood one matching her new wardrobe and one with painted white surrounds for the shop. Nellie and all her worldly goods would be fully ensconced in her new home by the day of the wedding.

Katherine and Nellie deliberated for hours over the design of Nellie's wedding gown as well as the bridesmaid and matron-of-honour gowns. Katherine felt they needed to show everyone what they were capable of when it came to creating beautiful dresses, for any occasion. They decided that the women in New Zealand shouldn't have to rely on gowns and dresses being homemade or shipped here at great expense, they were here to fill their every need. Nellie finally settled on pastel blue satin for her attendants and soft ivory silk with lace trim for her own gown. A long veil with lace trim would be made to match the gown. Katherine had put some ideas together for the headdress and had shown them to Nellie one afternoon as they took a lunch break, Nellie was impressed.

'Katherine, these are beautiful, we must include them in our range.'

'I hadn't thought of that,' remarked Katherine. 'Yes, I suppose there could be a call for pretty headdresses. Hopefully we will get orders for wedding gowns, I just never thought of making the headdresses as well, I suppose I considered them to be more of a jeweller's line, like a tiara with gems. I don't think anyone else in town is making them so yes, maybe we could do that.'

Nellie picked out an elegant design that would showcase Katherine's artistic talents.

'I'm going to work on the headdress when you are not here,' said Katherine, 'it will be my gift to you on your wedding day.'

Uncle Silas sent a large trunk of fabrics and treasures from France, including some hats, one of which suited Felicity perfectly. She was thrilled to bits with it and even managed to smile and say thank you to Nellie. She also admitted that she was pleased with Nellie's choice of colour for the bridesmaid's dress. she suited pale blue and found the style quite flattering. She would never admit it, but she thought the dresses on display in Nellie and Katherine's shop were the prettiest and most beautifully made gowns she had ever seen. Katherine's gown had to be altered at the last minute to hide the bump that was beginning to appear. She and Benjamin hadn't planned on having children, deciding instead to let God make that plan for them. It appears he did.

When the big day finally arrived, they were once again blessed with a beautiful warm sunny day. They were to be married in the Chaplain's garden, the church not having been completed yet. This would be followed by a lavish wedding reception in the dining room of the largest hotel in town. When Katherine and Felicity went to check on how things were progressing at the hotel on the morning of the wedding, they both stood open-mouthed taking in the magnificent floral displays, crystal chandeliers and beautifully adorned tables laid out with fine china, gleaming silverware and sparkling crystal glasses. The manager came over and asked them if they were happy with what had been done.

'This is wonderful,' gushed Katherine, 'how clever you all are, thank you, Nellie will be delighted.'

As Katherine and Felicity left the reception room Felicity turned to Katherine and asked if she was feeling nervous.

'Excited perhaps,' said Katherine, 'but nervous, no not really. Why, are you feeling nervous Felicity?'

'I am a bit,' Felicity confessed. 'I don't like being in public places and certainly not where there is going to be a lot of people. They will all be staring at my...' she put her hand to the scars on her face.

Katherine's heart went out to the woman. 'All eyes will be on Nellie and Albert today, Felicity, but if it makes you feel any better, I have some cosmetics which might help to cover any of your scars that are not going to be hidden already by your hair or the hat.'

Felicity brightened. 'Cosmetics? 'Do you really think they could cover these hideous scars?' she asked hopefully.

'Let's go and see, shall we.' Katherine linked an arm through

Felicity's and marched her off to the bakery and upstairs to her bedroom. She sat Felicity down in front of the dressing table, opened up a small leather case and took out a stick of product that she hoped would do the job. Katherine worked on Felicity's face for several minutes then turned her around to look in the mirror above the dressing table. Felicity was stunned.

'It's hardly noticeable,' she gasped, leaning closer to the mirror. 'My goodness that really is quite clever, where can I get some of that?' she asked pointing to the stick of paste Katherine was holding.

'You can have this one, I have more, I bought several cosmetic items in France when I went there with Silas. If you like, I can show you how to apply it to your face the way the French women do.'

Felicity's eyes filled with tears. 'Yes,' she nodded, 'yes I would like that very much, thank you.'

Katherine felt sorry for Felicity. She wondered if anyone had ever tried to help her adjust and cope with her disfigurement. Felicity floated out of the room as if she was walking on air, a broad smile on her face. Benjamin saw her leave and asked what magic Katherine had managed to perform in order to achieve such a change in the woman. Katherine explained what she had done and hoped that it might help Felicity's demeanour.

'I doubt that,' muttered Benjamin. He had never warmed to Felicity, 'I think her demeanour is well ingrained, but all credit to you for at least getting her to smile, today of all days.'

It was decided that Nellie, Katherine, and Felicity would get dressed for the wedding and leave from Albert's new home. Their gowns were hidden away at the back of the shop and would be taken across to the house as soon as Albert left to spend the day with his brother Harry. Harry had arranged for the men's suits to be delivered from the tailor's shop to his place. They would be wearing dark pin-striped trousers with grey waistcoats over white shirts, a pale blue cravat and dark tailored jackets. Their black shoes were polished to perfection and their top hats were taken out of their boxes and brushed clean of any dust and lint.

Nellie had broken down in tears at one point during the planning of the wedding.

'Who's going to give me away?' she wailed.

'You leave that to me,' Albert had reassured her, I will arrange all of that, don't you give it a second thought, so she hadn't.

Now, the man who would be walking Nellie down the aisle, was standing in front of a mirror asking Albert if he thought he looked sharp enough to be walking his pretty bride-to-be down the aisle.

'You look perfect for the job,' smiled Albert. 'Now, best you get yourself over to the house, the women should be almost ready,' he said, checking his fob watch.

Felicity and Katherine were both dressed, adorned, and had their lips rouged and were now concentrating on Nellie. Felicity gasped when the cloth covering Nellie's gown was drawn away to reveal her magnificent gown. Katherine had outdone herself. Nellie had helped with the beading and some of the lacework but Katherine had done all the rest herself. The gown was wide at the shoulders with a fine netting fabric running from the top of the shoulders to form a delicate sleeve around the neck with lace trim. Puffed sleeves finished at the elbow with a lace edged frill and the heavily beaded bodice fitted snuggly to accentuate Nellie's trim figure. From the waist the skirt draped to the floor in layer upon layer of fine silk, edged with delicate lace. At various points the layers were ruched up and held in place with bunches of tiny pale blue and white roses. Finally, the veil appeared and Katherine brought the previously unseen headdress out of its hiding place. Nellie burst into tears. She took it gently in her hands and studied every minute detail of the finest piece of millinery artwork she had ever seen. The tiara shaped adornment sparkled as the sunlight streaming in the window, danced across the tiny crystals woven into the bed of tiny white roses that matched the ones on her dress. A small silver heart had been sewn into the centre with a white ribbon.

Nellie's eyes widened.

'I didn't even miss this,' she cried, eyes filling with tears.

'What is that?' asked Felicity curiously.

'It was in my coat pocket the night of the fire when my family all died. My mother had given it to me as a birthday present. Apart from my fading memories, it is the only thing I have from that life all those years ago. Katherine how clever of you to think of this, thank you. Now I know my family will be here with me today, well almost all of them.'

There was a loud knock at the door downstairs.

'I'll go,' said Katherine pushing in front of Felicity. It will be the man who's walking you down the aisle.' She turned at the door and looked back at Nellie. 'Are you ready to go?'

'Almost,' said Nellie, wiping away a tear. Felicity helped Nellie set the headdress in place.

'Are you all set for today Felicity? Not too nervous?'

'Not nervous at all,' said Felicity smiling. 'Katherine has given me some cosmetics to cover my scars, look.'

'What a marvellous job she's done, you can't even see them.' She leaned in and gave Felicity a hug. Felicity hugged her back but quickly pulled away, embarrassed at showing any affection to a woman she secretly despised.

Nellie could hear voices downstairs. She walked out the bedroom door on to the landing and peered over the rail, curious to see who this man was who was going to be giving her away. There in all his glory stood dear old Uncle Silas. Nellie squealed with shock and delight and burst into tears. She couldn't get down the stairs quick enough. She threw herself into his loving arms and sobbed.

'Oh Uncle Silas, I never in my wildest dreams thought you would come all this way just for my wedding.'

'Albert and I have been planning this from the moment I received your letter telling me you were engaged to be married,' he smiled. 'How could I not be here for my beautiful niece's wedding.' He pulled away from her and held her at arm's length. 'My my lass, you have grown into a beautiful young woman.

Your parents would be very proud, and so would Emilyn.'

Nellie burst into tears again. Felicity rushed off to get a moist towel to wipe Nellie's reddening face and hopefully hold off any swelling of her tear-filled eyes.

'Come and sit down for a moment Nellie,' said Katherine handing her a small glass of brandy. 'Perhaps we should have brought Uncle Silas here to see you yesterday.'

'How long have you been here?' asked Nellie.

'I only arrived yesterday, I wasn't sure I was going to get here in time, we struck bad weather off the coast and couldn't land for two days. I was about to dive in and swim to shore but fortunately the weather cleared,' he laughed.

'How long are you staying?'

'I'm here until the ship sails again, two weeks. I'm keen to have a look around while I'm here, Albert said he didn't think you would mind delaying your honeymoon until after I leave.'

'Of course I don't mind. How could I relax and enjoy my honeymoon knowing you are here.'

Katherine introduced Felicity to Uncle Silas. She smiled at him shyly then hurried off to refresh Nellie's face cloth.

Silas and his beautiful entourage arrived at the wedding venue ten minutes late but nobody was worried about that. The guests were all standing around talking amongst themselves until they saw the carriage coming down the street, then they quickly sat in the seats that had been arranged in orderly rows in the garden. The same quartet that had played at the opening of the shop now played the wedding march as Katherine and Felicity preceded Nellie and a beaming Uncle Silas down the flower bedecked walkway between the chairs, to the rose covered archway where the service would be held. There wasn't a dry eye in the garden as Nellie and Albert exchanged vows and promised to love each other – 'Until Death do us part.'

The reception that followed was a poignant affair with all the people attending now living far from their places of birth, most of them missing family back home, wherever that happened to be. Simon and Millicent and their children had all made the trip to town to attend the wedding. Millicent was very excited to see the new haberdashery shop. The toast 'to absent friends' evoked a tear or two among the guests until Uncle Silas stepped in to save the day. He spoke fondly of 'his Nellie' telling the guests how he had watched her grow into the beautiful young woman she is today. He was becoming a bit emotional so he decided to lighten the mood and tell them about some of the more light-hearted moments in Nellie's life. Like the time he had come home from sea ready to fall into his flea ridden bed, only to find Nellie and Katherine had moved in. He had many stories to tell and by the time he finished, everyone had cheered up. After a delicious meal of baked ham, roast mutton, new potatoes, fresh peas and carrots and green salad, the cake was cut. This was Benjamin's gift to the happy couple and he had done himself proud. The white three-layered fruit cake, Millicent's recipe of course, had exquisite lace piping around the edges adorned with the same tiny blue and white roses that were on Nellies gown.

'You have outdone yourself Croxley,' said Silas sincerely. 'You've come a long way since the days of the 'Old Bell', that I can assure you. Your bakery and its delectable delights are a credit to you'

'Guess the ability was always there, Silas, I just didn't have much of an opportunity to use it back at the Bell.' Benjamin was humbled by Silas's words.

The two weeks that followed the wedding flew by. Albert and Nellie spent every chance they got with Silas, showing him as much of their new home as they could. Silas had to admit that it was a beautiful country but he said he wouldn't trade his beloved England and his life on the sea 'for all the tea in China'.

Fittingly it was gloomy and overcast the day they waved Silas off at the wharf in Lyttleton. Nellie sniffled all the way home, she had no idea when she might see her beloved uncle again. Albert took Nellie upstairs as soon as they got home and laid her gently on the bed. He removed her shoes then his own and snuggled in beside her and held her while she gave way to her emotions. It had been a very eventful couple of weeks and he wasn't surprised to find his darling wife becoming so overwhelmed. When she finally dozed off, he slid off the bed and went downstairs, he had a few more arrangements to make before they left on their honeymoon the following day. He was taking her to Wellington to spend a bit of time with his parents. They weren't able to stay on after the wedding, his father had important meetings to attend to back at parliament but they were looking forward to getting to know their new daughter-in-law better. From there they would be going to a secluded beach on the coast where Albert had rented a small cottage by the sea. There would be no-one around for miles, just him and his beautiful Nellie.

Chapter Thirteen

The family grows- 1853

The summer of 1853 had been busy and exciting, with the opening of the new shop and Nellie and Albert's wedding. Autumn, however, was marred by the sad news that Katherine had lost her baby. She and Benjamin were so distraught, they were losing hope of ever having a child. It took Katherine several months to get over losing the baby but Nellie and the cheerful atmosphere at the shop helped pull her through.

One afternoon Nellie was up and down and wandering around restlessly until Katherine made her sit down and tell her what was bothering her.

'I think I am with child Katherine. Because of your recent loss I have been too afraid to tell you because I knew it would upset you,' Nellie was almost in tears.

Katherine smiled. 'Nellie that is wonderful news, if I can't have children of my own then helping you raise yours is the next best thing, I am delighted for you. Albert must be thrilled.'

'I haven't told him yet,' Nellie confessed. 'I wanted to tell you first. I haven't even been to see the doctor yet.'

'Well then, no time like the present,' said Katherine getting to her feet and taking charge. 'Let's close the shop for the afternoon and go for a walk down to the doctor's office and make an appointment, then when your pregnancy is confirmed, you can tell Albert. Maybe wait until he comes over to the shop so you can tell him out of Felicity's earshot. I'm not sure she will take the news well, so best enjoy the moment with Albert before you tell her.'

'Do you really not think Felicity will be happy with the news?'

'To be perfectly honest with you Nellie, I never have any idea which way Felicity is going to go at the best of times, but I can't imagine her being very enthusiastic about having noisy children running around making a mess and leaving toys all over her pristine household.'

'You have a point, but still, you never know with Felicity, she might like the idea of having children around, we've never really talked about it.'

At her doctor's appointment a week later Nellie's pregnancy was confirmed. Katherine and Nellie were so excited they went and celebrated with tea and cakes at Mrs Lansbury's tea house. They talked non-stop about babies and what garments they could make for it and how they would decorate the nursery.

'I had better tell Albert today,' said Nellie, 'I don't think I can hold the news in any longer and I certainly don't want him to hear it from anyone else.' She glanced around to make sure no-one else was sitting close enough to overhear what they were saying.

Nellie waited until Felicity went to bed that night to break the news to Albert. She closed the lounge door and sat in the armchair in front of the cosy warm fire opposite Albert. She stared at him until he looked up from reading his book.

'What is it Nellie? You look like you have something on your mind.'

'I have Albert, something very important.'

'Very well,' he said laying his book aside. 'What is it?'

Nellie hesitated for a moment, choosing her words. 'We're going to have a baby, Albert, you are going to be a father.'

Albert sat stunned for a moment, then a huge grin spread across his face, he rose from his chair and pulled Nellie into his arms and swung her around the room. When he put her back down he looked into her eyes and said, 'my darling this is the most wonderful news, I have longed for this moment ever since I first laid eyes on you. I decided way back then that I wanted you to be the mother of my children and here we are. Thank you Nellie, thank you, thank you, thank you, you have made me the happiest man on earth. This calls for a celebration.'

He went to the cabinet and poured a whiskey for himself and a small brandy for Nellie. They raised their glasses and drank to the health of their unborn child.

Margaret Elizabeth Fitzgerald arrived in February the following year weighing a healthy 7lb 5oz. Albert couldn't wait to get to the newspaper office to put the birth notice in the next edition. Never was there a prouder father than Albert Fitzgerald, the broad smile never left his face, that is until the sleepless nights began to take their toll.

Although Albert didn't get up in the night to attend to Margaret when she cried, the disruption to his sleep pattern did get to him for a while and his grumpiness didn't help with Nellie's lack of sleep disposition either. Enter Felicity.

'Nellie,' she was clearly annoyed, 'why don't I get up every second night and give Margaret a bottle, that way you could get some sleep and maybe we could all have a little peace around here. She had been putting up with the tired niggly couple for the past three weeks since Margaret was brought home from the hospital and now she had had enough.

Nellie and Albert were stunned by her outburst. 'I admit I am tired and yes I suppose I have been grumpy,' said Nellie apologetically, 'I am sorry.' She burst into tears and ran upstairs.

Albert glared at Felicity. 'Now look what you have done. Nellie has not had a full night's sleep in three weeks, of course she is tired, now you've only gone and made things worse.'

'I was only trying to help,' Felicity pleaded, 'and you have been no better than Nellie, Albert. You have been somewhat short-tempered yourself.'

Albert pushed himself away from the table and stomped up the stairs to check on Nellie. He sat down beside her on the bed, wrapped his arms tightly around her and they both cried. It was like a release valve.

'I'm sorry Albert,' Nellie began. Albert hushed her by putting a finger to her lips.

'It's nobody's fault Nellie, from what I have heard from Ted at the store, this is perfectly normal when there is a new baby in the house and he's had four so he would know.' He attempted a smile. 'I wonder if we shouldn't consider Felicity's offer of getting up to Margaret every second night or even just one or two nights in a row so you can get some sleep.'

Nellie looked down at the sodden handkerchief she'd been wringing in her hands and nodded. 'We could give it a try I suppose. She hasn't had much to do with the baby, I'm not sure how Margaret will take to her, she's not exactly a matronly type is she.' Nellie tried to stifle a giggle but Albert laughed out loud.

'Never a truer word spoken,' he said, 'come to think of it I don't even remember her playing with dolls when she was a child, but we can only try.'

Felicity was as thrilled as Felicity could be, to find herself included in the upbringing of the baby. Nellie showed her all the ins and outs of feeding, nappy changing and burping. Margaret took a day or two to get used to the changes but once Felicity felt more confident, so did the baby. Felicity's demeanour slowly changed and in the end she proved to be a lovely nanny.

Once Margaret was off the breast and eating solids, Felicity took over caring for Margaret while Nellie returned to the shop full time. Katherine was more than excited to have Nellie back again, it hadn't been the same without her. Nellie had visited every day when she was out walking the baby but she felt ready now to get back to work.

Marigold Emilyn Fitzgerald arrived in August of 1857, when Margaret was two years old. Once again Albert was delighted to welcome another daughter. He didn't mind one bit that Marigold wasn't a boy, two beautiful daughters was enough for him. They were both healthy and beautiful, 'what more could a man want', he had said to Harry.

Uncle Silas continued to send trunks full of wonderful

supplies and gifts from the countries he visited and now those trunks included toys for the children. He was delighted to hear of the expansion of his family line.

'Now there are four of us with Abernathy blood running through our veins,' he had written in a letter to Nellie. 'You won't find a happier great-uncle in the whole wide world.'

When the girls were two and four years old, Katherine dropped a bombshell. She and Benjamin had decided to return to London.

'Benjamin has been so homesick Nellie, especially since we lost the baby. He has stayed on just for me these past two years, he knows how much I love our shop, but now I feel it is time for me to follow him back home to where his heart truly is, the 'Old Bell'.

Nellie couldn't believe what she was hearing. Her mind swam with the consequences of losing her nearest and dearest friend in all the world. How would she cope without Katherine? She poured out her despair as Katherine held her in a tight embrace.

'I'm terribly sorry to do this to you Nellie but I think deep down we both knew this day would come.'

Nellie nodded, sniffling. 'Yes, maybe you are right but I always hoped and prayed it never would. I can't imagine how life is going to be without you, what about the shop?

'Nellie,' Katherine gripped Nellie firmly by the shoulders and stared her straight in the eye, 'you are more than capable of running the shop and lord knows you certainly have the talent.'

'You have taught me everything I know Katherine, but I will never be as good as you.'

Katherine laughed, 'You are as good as me Nellie, even better at some things. There's nothing I can do that you can't. Come on now, wipe away those tears, we need to make plans for how you are going to continue on with the business. First things first, we need to find you an assistant seamstress and perhaps a girl to help out in the shop and do the cleaning and dusting.'

Within six months Katherine and Benjamin had sold up the bakery business and sailed back to London. Nellie was inconsolable the day she waved them off. Albert arranged for Felicity to look after the children while he took Nellie off to the beach for the rest of the day. They sat on the foreshore digging their toes into the warm sand while Albert encouraged Nellie to talk about her life back in London, hers and Katherine's. Remember all the good times you have shared both here and back in England, take the memories and turn them into your strength Nellie. I know you will do well here despite not having Katherine with you. My family is here to help you, you know that.'

Nellie looked across at Albert, a little alarmed. 'You don't think I want to go back to London too, do you?'

'Well,' hesitated Albert, 'the thought did cross my mind.'

'Heavens no my darling, I couldn't bear to go back to London to live. My life is here with you and our beautiful baby girls, no, England will never be my home again.'

Albert was so relieved he almost cried. 'I was so worried, seeing how much Katherine and Benjamin's departure affected you, I thought you might want to follow them.'

'My family is here now Albert, you and the girls and Felicity and Harry.'

They lay back in the sand holding hands and smiling as they watched light fluffy clouds dance across the sky, both knowing all would be well.

Before she knew it, Nellie was sewing little dresses for Margaret to wear to school. Her first day of school was bittersweet for both Nellie and Felicity. Nellie couldn't believe Margaret was five years old and about to embark on a new stage in her life. Felicity would miss her terribly too, she loved the girls in her own way, she wasn't overly affectionate to them but they knew she loved them all the same. At least she still had Marigold at home to fill her days, but that would only be for two more years, then what was she going to do with her time?

The Fitzgerald household eventually fell into a comfortable rhythm. Felicity would get Marigold up and dressed while Nellie made Margaret's lunch and got her ready for school. They would all sit down to breakfast together before Albert left for the office, then Nellie would walk Margaret to school. When Nellie got back home she would get herself organised and wander across to the shop. Mavis, the young girl Nellie had employed to be the shop assistant and do the cleaning and dusting, would have the shop open and in winter she would light the fire and put the kettle on to boil. Mrs Jackson, the seamstress would arrive an hour later and set to work on whatever Nellie had assigned for her. They worked well together but Nellie still missed the close friendship she had with Katherine. No one would ever fill that gap.

At three o'clock, Nellie would walk down to the school to get Margaret and they would talk all the way home about what she had learned and anything exciting that might have happened at school that day. She would stop in and check on Felicity and Marigold before heading back to the shop to close up and let Mavis and Mrs Jackson go home. Business was steady and reaped a healthy income for Nellie. Albert insisted that the money be put in a separate account at the bank in Nellie's name, to be used to buy goods and pay the shop's expenses. He didn't feel right about using her money to pay the household bills, he was the head of the household and it was up to him to provide for his family.

Nellie would be home in time to give the girls their bath while Felicity started on dinner, if she hadn't already. The girls would be fed early and put to bed leaving the adults to have their meal in peace and discuss the day's events. Rarely were there any arguments or disagreements among the three of them. Nellie and Felicity had not grown any closer over the years, instead they had reached a comfortable truce. Albert was none the wiser, as far as he could tell the two women got along very well together and he was thankful for that.

Chapter Fourteen

Inheritance– 1859

A letter arrived addressed to Nellie, dated the third of May 1859. It was from Mr Hicks at the shipping office, informing Nellie that her dear Uncle Silas had passed away.

'You will be relieved to know that he died in his sleep and in his own bed Nellie. He enjoyed good health till the end. The doctor said his heart just stopped. I have been to the solicitor's office and they asked if I knew how to make contact with you, I hope this is still the correct address. You will no doubt be receiving papers from them in due course. If there is anything I can do for you Nellie please do not hesitate to ask. I have passed the news on to Mr and Mrs Croxley, who are terribly upset by the news as I know you will be. They said they would be writing to you.

I will leave you with my heartfelt condolences now Nellie. Please write and let me know you received this and that all is well. There will no doubt be some things amongst Silas's possessions that you might appreciate having. I will pack up anything I consider appropriate and will ship them to you on receipt of your letter and advice therein.

Sincerely,
Trevor Hicks

Albert wasn't sure how he was going to console Nellie this time. In her short life she had lost both her parents, her sister, her fiancé, her best friend was living halfway around the world and now her only living relative had gone too. How much more could the poor woman take.

In amongst the rest of the mail sitting on the table just inside the front door was a letter from Katherine. Nellie ripped it open, sobbing, unable to read it. She handed it to Albert to read it to her. She was shaking uncontrollably.

'Maybe we should leave Katherine's letter for later my love,' suggested Albert gently. 'I think you have had as much as you can take for now.' Nellie nodded and went upstairs to her bed. She lay down on her side and let the tears and memories flow, her mind going back to the first time she met Uncle Silas when he came to her after the fire. He was so gentle and caring despite the fact that he was such a big bear of a man. She had latched on to him straight away, he was her lifeline, the only link she had to her family.

Albert went to work, leaving Felicity to manage the children and get them off to school. She checked on Nellie from time to time during the day and eventually Nellie cried herself to sleep. She was still asleep when Albert came home that night. When he walked in the girls were playing quietly on the lounge floor in front of the fire and Felicity was in the kitchen cooking dinner.

'How is she?' Albert asked.

'She cried herself to sleep, she hasn't woken up yet,' replied Felicity.

Albert took his shoes off and carried them upstairs so as not to make too much noise. He quietly opened the bedroom door, Nellie was lying on the bed with her back to him. He sat carefully on the bed and reached out a hand to rest it on her shoulder, letting her know he was there. She stirred and turned over giving him a weak smile.

'Hello,' she whispered. 'What time is it?'

'Almost time for dinner my love, you must be hungry, Felicity said you haven't eaten all day.'

Nellie sat up and waited until her head stopped swimming before she swung her feet over the side of the bed.

'Don't get up Nell, I can bring something up to you if you like.'

'No, I want to see the girls, I want to hear about their day, I need the distraction Albert.'

He walked around the bed and pulled her into a loving embrace. They stood there like that for a few minutes until a little voice at the door said, 'are you sad mummy?' It was Marigold.

Nellie brushed the tears from her face, put on the brightest smile she could manage and said, 'yes my darling I am a little sad because my favourite Uncle Silas has died and I will miss him very much.'

'Is that the man who sends us all those lovely presents from faraway places?'

'Yes, it is.'

'Then who's going to send us presents now?' wailed Marigold.

Nellie looked across at Albert and smiled.

Katherine's letter was sitting beside Nellie's plate when she came down for dinner. She picked it up and went over to sit in the fireside armchair to read it.

'My dearest darling Nellie, I don't know what to say. I know you will be reeling from the terribly sad news of your Uncle Silas's death, I just wish I was there to comfort you. Benjamin and I have talked about my coming back for a visit, I so long to see those beautiful babies of yours, but he has not been very well and I don't feel I could leave him just yet. We saw Silas whenever he came home from a trip, he was always well and happy Nellie, there was never any sign of illness. Mr Hicks said the doctor told him Silas died peacefully in his sleep. That's a beautiful way to go, don't you agree?'

The rest of Katherine's letter was bright and cheerful as she wrote about their daily lives and about the people Nellie knew. It seems a lot had changed in London since Nellie left and she shared some of the more interesting bits of news with Albert and Felicity over dinner. The letter lifted Nellie's spirits, Katherine's final words had been encouraging and supportive and they definitely helped.

The solicitors letter arrived on the next ship a month later. It was a large package containing several papers which Nellie and Albert poured over together.

'It seems you are Silas's sole heir,' exclaimed Albert in surprise. 'Do you have any idea what that includes or what he was worth?'

'No idea at all,' said Nellie, 'but I suspect it could be a reasonable amount, depending on what debts he might have. Who knows, I might be inheriting a good deal of nothing,' she laughed. 'I'm not concerned about any of that, but I do think I will have to go back to London to sort it all out, as the Solicitors' have suggested. What do you think, will you come with me? I'd like to show you my old life.'

After much discussion over several days, it was decided that Albert couldn't leave his office for any great length of time so he would stay behind and take care of the girls. Nellie wasn't sure about asking Harry to accompany her but as it turned out he would be up in the North Island on business during that time anyway. That only left Felicity. She and Nellie had been getting along well enough these past couple of years so Nellie asked her if she would like to ccompany her to London. Felicity was stunned to say the least.

'You want to take me with you to London, why?'

'I don't want to travel alone,' explained Nellie, 'Wouldn't you like to see England? You've heard Katherine and I talk about it often enough, are you not curious to see it for yourself?'

'I'll think about it,' said Felicity gruffly. 'I will let you know tomorrow.'

Chapter Fifteen

England revisited– 1859

Felicity and Nellie arrived at the docks in London on the morning of the 15th of November 1859. It had been nine years since Nellie had left this very same port.

'It still looks just the same,' said Nellie as she leaned over the railing. 'The only difference this time is that Uncle Silas is no longer here,' she sniffed.

'It's going to be fine Nellie, I will be here with you and don't forget your friends Katherine and Benjamin are here.

'Yes, I can't wait to see them,' Nellie brightened, 'it's been ages.' She turned to look at Felicity. 'Thank you for coming with me, I know this hasn't been an easy trip for you and I do appreciate your sacrifice, I don't know what I would have done without you. I am not looking forward to the return trip anytime soon.'

'Neither am I,' sighed Felicity, 'but having said that, the sooner we get things tidied up here the sooner we can return home again, I'm beginning to get a little homesick.'

'Me too,' admitted Nellie. 'I am missing Albert and the girls so much. I wish Albert had been able to come with us,' Nellie sighed sadly.

'It was unfortunate that he couldn't leave his work for all these months, but he will be there for the children.'

'Yes, that is a blessing,' Nellie wiped her eyes with her handkerchief.

Their luggage and cabin trunks were carried off the ship and transported to the shipping office rooms where Nellie had once lived with Katherine and Uncle Silas.

'I'm not looking forward to facing all those memories again Felicity.'

'I suppose not, but you are a brave woman Nellie, I know you will get through this. It will be interesting to hear what the Solicitor has to say, won't it?'

'Yes. Do you know I have no idea how much Uncle Silas's estate is even worth; it was hard to tell from the Solicitor's letter. I know Uncle Silas received my father's Stocks and Bonds when he died, but as far as I know, most of that would have been spent on my board and keep over the years. We will just have to wait and see I suppose.'

The two women settled themselves into Silas's rooms after throwing open the windows and dusting off the thick layer of dust that had settled on the furniture.

The next morning they dressed, made themselves a quick cup of tea and headed off to see the Solicitor.

'It's so good to see you again Miss Abernathy, how long has it been?' asked Mr Wellington as he ushered them into his office.

"It's Mrs Fitzgerald now and it has been nine years since I left these shores Mr Wellington. I have two beautiful daughters now. This is their aunt, my sister-in-law, Felicity Fitzgerald. Mr Fitzgerald was unable to make the journey, so Felicity has come as my companion instead.'

'Lovely to meet you Miss Fitzgerald. Right let's get down to business shall we. Your Uncle has left you a wealthy woman Mrs Fitzgerald. There are your late father's stocks and bonds which Mr Abernathy left intact, as well as his own shares and bonds in the shipping company, which, if I might say, are doing extremely well these days. There is a substantial amount of cash in the bank and of course the building which houses the shipping offices and the accommodation rooms upstairs.'

Nellie's mouth dropped open. 'You mean he owned that building?'

'Yes, of course, did he not tell you?'

'No. Come to think of it we never really discussed his financial affairs.'

'And there's his ship of course, he had full ownership of that too. All in all Mrs Fitzgerald, it adds up to a very tidy sum indeed. Now if I may suggest, perhaps you would like to keep ownership of the building and lease it out. I could arrange for the lease monies to be sent to you annually.'

'Mr Wellington,' Nellie held up her hand in exasperation, 'I will need some time to consider all this information. I had no idea buildings and ships were involved.'

'Please take your time Mrs Fitzgerald, this has obviously come as quite a shock. There is no hurry to finalise anything, just let me know when you are ready to take things further. No doubt you will have many questions so please don't hesitate to call in and see me, I will make myself available to you at any hour. Mr Abernathy was one of my biggest clients, I would like to see his affairs settled to a satisfactory conclusion for both of you.' He stood and ushered the ladies to the door. 'Good day ladies.'

Nellie let out a soft whistle as soon as they stepped outside.

'Heavens above, I wasn't expecting that.'

'No, I am sure you weren't.' Felicity was not sure how she felt about Nellie becoming so wealthy. Her own family were reasonably well off, but she was living with her brother, and had no income of her own. Now here was Nellie, married to her brother, a successful businessman, with two beautiful daughters. She had everything that Felicity craved, and to top all that, she had just become a wealthy heiress, it just didn't seem fair. Felicity was becoming extremely jealous.

Nellie didn't notice Felicity's cooling demeanour as they walked down the street.

'I want to call in and see Katherine and Benjamin at the 'Old Bell' Felicity, do you want to come with me?

'Yes of course, it will be lovely to see them again.'

'Wonderful, let's go and get something to eat, I am famished and heartily sick of that terrible slop we were given on board the ship.'

Mr Croxley spotted Nellie the moment she walked through the door and rushed over to gather her in a big hug.

'Nellie, I can't believe you are here, Katherine will be so thrilled to see you. Hello Felicity, lovely to see you too. Wait here while I go and get her.'

He disappeared up the stairs while Nellie and Felicity settled themselves at one of the tables. Katherine came bounding down the stairs and stood staring at Nellie, her eyes filled with tears.

'Nellie Fitzgerald, well if you aren't a sight for sore eyes,' she said as she quickly moved to gather Nellie in a warm embrace.

Nellie was also moved to tears and after a few moments of squeezing the life out of each other, the two women pulled back from their embrace, laughed at themselves and their tears, and hugged again.

'It has been so long. Hello Felicity, it's lovely to see you here as well. How are Albert and the children, oh we have got so much to talk about.'

Nellie, Felicity, Katherine and Benjamin sat around eating, drinking and talking for the next two hours. The 'Old Bell' was beginning to get busy so Benjamin left the women to carry on talking while he went to help out behind the bar. That's when Katherine dropped a bombshell.

'Nellie, there's something I need to tell you,' Katherine looked around the bar then leaned in closer to whisper to Nellie. 'Nick is alive, he is living back here again.'

'What? What are you saying Katherine? Nick… Nick is alive?' The blood drained from Nellie's face, her head started to spin and she felt sick. 'Nick is alive, here?'

'Yes Nellie, Nick is alive. I wrote to let you know, but you must have already sailed by the time the letter reached New Zealand. You know how we all thought he was dead after the ship sank, well he wasn't. He survived and did his time, all seven years of it, then he was transported to Australia where he has spent the past two years trying to get back to England. He has been back here for just over three months.'

Nellie felt as if the room had tilted, then everything went

black.

'Nellie, Nellie, wake up, you look like you've seen a ghost,' cried Felicity.

'Perhaps she has,' muttered Mr Croxley who had come running over when he saw what was happening. He was bending over Nellie's crumpled form.

Nellie opened her eyes to see anxious faces peering down at her, someone was holding smelling salts under her nose. She coughed and tried to sit up, surprised to find herself on the floor.

'What, what happened?' she gazed anxiously around the room.'

'You fainted Nellie, are you alright?' Katherine was fussing.

Nellie looked up at Katherine as her mind cleared.

'Is it true then, what you said? That Nick is still alive.'

'Yes, he is. He doesn't know you are here, I didn't tell him you were coming because I wasn't sure how you would react.

'I did,' confessed Benjamin. 'I told him you were coming to sort out Silas's Estate. He will be in this evening.

'No, no. Please don't tell him I'm here yet, I.. I just need some time to think. Oh my heavens this can't be happening, what am I to do?'

Nellie was shaking like a leaf. 'I, I think I need to go. Katherine, I'm sorry but I have to..., I need to..., I will come back and see you tomorrow,' Nellie was all over the place.

Felicity was concerned, and confused, who was this Nick person and why was Nellie reacting so dramatically?

As they made for the door, Mr Croxley came running out from the kitchen at the back of the pub.

'Here, I have some of your favourite pies,' he said tucking a paper parcel under Felicity's arm.

'Thank you Mr Croxley, that is very sweet of you. Nellie, are you able to walk? Do you need to sit for a while before we go?'

'No, no I need to get back home, now. I need to lie down.' Nellie's voice was no more than a whisper.

When they got back to the shipping office rooms, Felicity set the fire going and sat deep in thought by the window while

Nellie lay on the bed sobbing. After a time, she went and sat on Nellie's bed. She picked up her cold hand and asked, 'Nellie, who is Nick? Why have you never spoken of him?'

Nellie turned to face Felicity, her eyes were red, her cheeks wet with tears.

'Nick was my fiancé,' she said softly. 'I told Albert all about him when we were courting. Nick broke the law and was sent away to a penal colony on Norfolk Island. We were told his ship sank and that none of the prisoners survived. I thought he was... Nellie stumbled on the words, 'I thought he was dead Felicity, it broke my heart. His death was the reason I left England, to start afresh, somewhere new, to forget.'

'Oh dear,' said Felicity, 'No wonder you are so upset. What are you going to do? Are you going to see him? What will you say?'

'I have no idea what I am going to say. I have no idea what I am going to do. There was a time when I was deeply in love with him, but now I have Albert and the girls. I love Albert, Felicity, you know that, I love him very much. But I'm afraid of what I might feel if I see Nick again. I don't think I want to see him.'

'Maybe you do need to see him Nellie, to put that ghost to rest. Otherwise you will never be able to put him out of your thoughts again. You will always wonder what might have been.'

Felicity's mind was buzzing, 'could this be the opportunity she has been waiting for, to get her dratted sister-in-law out of their lives, hers and Alberts and the girls?'

Nellie did not rise from her bed for the rest of the day and slept fitfully through the night. She rose early in the morning and set the fire going to make herself a cup of tea. She found the package with the pies inside and quickly devoured one, cold. The rest she put on a tray beside the fire to heat up. The package was unopened, so Felicity had obviously not eaten anything either.

As the sun came up Nellie pulled the curtains back to let the light in. She was sitting at the table beside the window wrapped up in a blanket sipping her tea when she spotted movement across the street. A man was standing in the doorway of the store across the road. He lit a cigarette, took a deep draw and blew out a cloud of smoke. He glanced up at the window and stiffened. Nellie gasped, 'Nick?' she whispered. 'Oh my Lord, it's Nick.' She quickly drew the curtains back across the window, shutting him out. Her heart was pounding so hard she feared it might push right through her chest. Her hands were shaking so much she couldn't hold her cup steady, she put it down clumsily on the table. She stood up and began to pace the room then sat down again. She peered out from behind the curtain, he was still there, watching. Should she go down and see him or should she try and avoid him. No, she decided, she had to see him, she had to let him go once and for all, cruel as that may be, but for her sanity it needed to be done. After a few more moments of indecision, she pulled herself together, stood up with determination and went to see if Felicity was still sleeping. She was, good.

Nellie changed into her day dress and quietly slipped out of the room. She stopped inside the downstairs door of the shipping office and took a deep breath before slowly opening it. And there he was, standing right in front of her. Nellie's knees buckled beneath her and he quickly reached out and held her up. The strength and warmth of his arms was more than she could bear, she sank into him and allowed him to hold her.

'Nick, my dearest Nick, I had no idea. I thought you were dead,' she pulled back and looked into the depths of his sparkling blue eyes. He had aged somewhat but he was still the good-looking man she had been so madly in love with all those years ago.

'Well clearly I am not,' he laughed, his cheeky smile lighting up his face. 'Nellie did you not get my letters? Perhaps you did not, else you would have known that I survived the ship sinking. Come, let's go and find somewhere to sit and talk, we have a lot of catching up to do.'

The sun was above the horizon, casting its yellow glow across the harbour. They sat on the same stone wall they used to sit on when they were courting.

'I can hardly believe I am sitting here again, in this place, with you.' Nellie felt as if she was dreaming.

'Neither can I,' said Nick. 'I desperately wanted to write and let you know that I had survived the ship wreck Nellie, but the authorities said they would notify our next of kin on our behalf. You were obviously never notified,' he said sadly.

'I never received any letters, Nick. If I had known, I would have waited for you, I promised you I would. What happened, after the ship sank, how did you survive? Uncle Silas said many lost their lives.'

'Yes, sadly many of them did, I was one of the lucky ones, if you can call spending the next seven years on Norfolk lucky,' he glanced down at his feet, remembering. 'Two of us prisoners had been hauled out of the hold to help the sailors with the sails because the winds were so strong and we were getting too close to the rocks. That's probably the only reason we survived. When we saw that the ship was about to hit those rocks, we dived overboard and swam to shore. We tried to make a run for freedom, but there were some constables standing on the shore watching what was happening and we were caught. There wouldn't have been anywhere to run to anyway, it's a very small island. I served my seven years, and when I got to Australia I wrote to you. When I didn't hear back from you, I thought you no longer wanted anything to do with me so I found work for a couple of years until I saved up enough to buy a passage back to London. I've only been back for a few months. Mr Croxley told me you had gone to New Zealand and that you are married with two children. I was hurt Nellie, I really was.'

'Nick I am so sorry,' Nellie took his hand and turned to look him in the eye. I promise you, I did not receive any letters. The last I heard was that the ship went down and the prisoners were all dead. I fell into deep despair, for weeks. That's when Katherine and Benjamin decided to take me to New Zealand, to get me away from here and all the sad memories.'

Nick put his arms around her and held her close. 'My dearest Nellie, what a cruel set of circumstances we have endured.'

They sat in silence for a long time, lost in their own thoughts.

'What are we to do Nellie? Can we pick up where we left off do you think? Do you want to go back to New Zealand, do you like your life there?'

'Nick,' Nellie faltered, 'I am happily married now, I have two beautiful daughters, I even have my own lady's drapery store.'

Nick withdrew his arms from around her and clasped his hands together between his knees, squeezing them tight, teeth clenched.

'So, you had no trouble moving on from me then.' His tone was sharp.

'Nick, I thought you were dead. It's been nearly ten years. What was I supposed to do?'

'How long did you wait until you got married to someone else Nellie, how long?'

'Nick, please don't be angry, I never stopped loving you, I will always love you.'

'Yet you found someone else to love and have children with.' Nick couldn't control his jealousy.

'I love him, yes, but not the way I loved you. You were, and always will be, my first, my dearest love.'

'So, what are we to do then? You don't need to go back you know, you could stay here with me, we could pick up again from where we were before I went away.'

Nellie was stunned. Could she do that? Could she just not go back to Albert and the girls and stay here with Nick?

'I don't know, I don't know,' Nellie stammered. I have a lot to think about, and I have my uncle's affairs to sort through and....'

'Yes, I heard Silas had died, I am sorry to hear that, he was a good man. I suspect his estate is quite sizeable.'

'Yes, it does appear that way, I haven't had a chance to go through it all yet,' said Nellie distractedly.

Nick squeezed her hand. 'I am here to help Nellie, I could take care of all that for you.'

'Benjamin and Katherine have offered their help along with

Mr Hicks so I am sure I will be well taken care of but thank you, I appreciate your offer.'

After a few minutes of silence Nellie stood up and brushed her skirts down, she hadn't noticed the tightening of Nicks' expression.

'I'd best be getting back, Felicity will be wondering where I am,' she said.

'Felicity?'

'Yes, she is my sister-in-law, she travelled here with me.'

They walked slowly back to the shipping offices.

'Why did your husband not come with you?' asked Nick.

'He is a busy businessman and could not afford to leave the company unattended for so long. I am quite capable of dealing with my uncle's estate,' she added defensively.

Nick shrugged. 'You certainly have changed from the shy young girl I fell in love with.'

'Do you love me still?' she asked hesitantly as they reached the front door of the shipping office.

'Before I heard you were back here in London I would have said no,' he said. 'I was angry and upset when I didn't hear back from you, but now that I see you and touch you, my God Nellie I believe I still do.'

He leaned down and kissed her full on the lips. Nellie leaned into him and kissed him back. The familiarity of his kiss stirred up her emotions while her head swam with contradictions.

She quickly pulled away and turned and ran up the stairs. Nick watched her close the door then turned to walk back down the street. A movement in the second-floor window caught his eye. He looked up and saw someone watching him. Felicity smiled to herself, this was perfect. She swung around to face Nellie as she burst breathlessly into the room.

'How dare you, Nellie Fitzgerald. How dare you kiss that, that man,' she blustered. 'I am assuming that was the Nick character you have been swooning over since you heard he was still alive. You are a married woman with children for goodness sake, do you have no shame?' Felicity was pleased with her performance, maybe she should have been an actress.

Nellie was dumbstruck, she wasn't expecting Felicity's onslaught. The woman had obviously been watching out the window and had seen them kissing. Nellie was still reeling from the stirred-up emotions she felt when Nick kissed her and she had no idea how to deal with Felicity right now. Instead, she turned around and walked out the door again slamming it shut behind her. She raced outside and walked briskly towards the river where she paced along the noisy wharves before venturing up a quiet side street that led into a more subdued housing area, not one she had been in before. She wandered around aimlessly deep in thought for some time before realising that she was quite lost. Panic started to set in but she pushed the fear aside and headed in what she hoped was the direction of the river. She was relieved when she finally saw the wharf down at the end of the street and slowly made her way back. She was reluctant to face Felicity's wrath again but she had no choice. She walked slowly up the stairs and quietly opened the door. The room was quiet, too quiet.

'Felicity? She called out. 'Felicity are you here?'

Nellie walked into the bedroom and was shocked to see Felicity's suitcase was gone; her heart skipped a beat. 'Where on earth have you got to Felicity Fitzgerald?' She was relieved that she didn't have to deal with Felicity right now, but also worried about where she might have gone. She was alone in a strange city. Nellie walked back down the stairs, searched up and down the streets and called into the nearest lodging houses to see if Felicity was registered, but to no avail. She didn't know what else to do so she went back to her rooms and decided to wait.

'She will calm down and come back,' Nellie tried to convince herself.

But Felicity did not come back the next day or the day after that. On the third day Nellie ran into Mr Hicks coming out of the shipping office downstairs.

'I see your travelling companion has left for New Zealand without you Mrs Fitzgerald, will you be alright here on your own?'

'Left for New Zealand, when?'

'Yesterday. Did you not know?'

'No Mr Hicks, I did not.' Nellie was flabbergasted, her blood ran cold with foreboding.

'Mr Hicks, when does the next ship leave for New Zealand, please?'

'I'm sorry lass but there isn't another one for several months. You were booked to depart in four weeks I believe.'

'Yes we were, is that not still a possibility?'

'I have just learned today that the ship you were booked to travel on ran aground on its last voyage and has sustained severe damage, it will be out of action for some time. I could however, book you on the Night Star but that doesn't sail for another three months.'

'Three months! What am I going to do now?' she thought.

'When you have a moment, I would like to have a word about the business?' Mr Hicks broke into her thoughts.

'Now is not a good time Mr Hicks, how about tomorrow morning?'

'Yes, tomorrow morning suits me well.'

Nellie left the office in a daze and went upstairs. She sat up all night worrying about what Felicity might say to Albert, and now here she was stranded in London for months before she could return home. The next morning, tired from lack of sleep, Nellie washed, dressed, and went downstairs to see Mr Hicks. She supposed he wanted to know what she intended to do with the building.

'Good morning Mr Hicks.' They sat down in his office while the junior clerk went off to make them a cup of tea. 'I must say first up that I have not yet made any decisions about the future of the building,' Nellie began.

'It is not about the building Mrs Fitzgerald; it is the matter of Mr Abernathy's trading company that I wish to discuss with you. I understand you are Mr Abernathy's sole beneficiary?'

'Yes I am, but I don't recall the solicitor saying anything

about a trading company. Then again there was so much to take in perhaps it did not register. Please, tell me about this trading company,' Nellie sighed, sinking back in her chair.

'Your Uncle had a lucrative trading operation Mrs Fitzgerald, not all of it aah,' he spluttered an embarrassed cough, 'not all of it above-board, shall we say. No one except he and I knew about his side dealings and you will no doubt be pleased to learn that this side of the business has died along with him. However, there are still the other personal trade deals he had with his business contacts abroad, some of which culminated in the trunks of goods he was able to supply to you and Mrs Croxley. I thought about it during the night, Mrs Fitzgerald, and as you are not able to return to New Zealand for a while, why not take the opportunity to travel to France yourself, perhaps you could keep that side of the business going. I know Silas sent trunks of goods from France to you at least twice a year, there is no reason why that should not continue. I can give you a letter of introduction to people who would treat you fairly and I have every confidence in the ship's captain. He grew up under Silas's guidance over the years and has always held him in high regard, almost like a father-figure you might say. I know he would be only too pleased to escort his late boss's niece to France.'

Nellie let out a breath which sounded like a punctured balloon.

'Mr Hicks, I have had more shocks and surprises these past few days than I have had in a lifetime, and that's saying something. I will need time to think things through.'

'Of course, I apologise for laying another burden on you Mrs Fitzgerald.'

'Please, call me Nellie, and don't upset yourself Mr Hicks. I will come back and see you when I have had time to think things through. I need to go and talk to the Croxley's.'

'Don't hesitate to come and see me if you have any questions, I am here to help as much as I can,' he said as he stood and opened the door for her.

Nellie made straight for the 'Old Bell'. She desperately

needed to see Katherine. As she walked in the door, she caught sight of Nick in the back corner by the fire, he was kissing and cuddling a woman sitting on his knee, he hadn't seen her. She was shocked. Nick had said he still loved her, was he lying to her? A myriad of confused thoughts raced through Nellie's mind as she turned around and walked back out of the pub. With everything that had happened these past few days she thought her head would explode. She needed to go somewhere quiet, she needed to be by herself for a while to think things through. She would love to have shared her scrambled thoughts with Katherine but she wasn't up to dealing with Nick just yet. She stepped into the sanctuary of a tea house down by the water's edge and ordered a cup of tea and a piece of Madeira cake. While she was waiting for her order, she watched idly out the window, trying to calm the myriad of thoughts cascading and whirling through her brain. Then, before her very eyes, she spotted Katherine and Benjamin walking along the beach. She raced out to them and threw her arms around Katherine, surprising the life out of her.

'Am I glad to see you,' she gushed. 'Katherine, I need to talk to you, now, everything is such a mess. Come and sit with me, please.' She looked imploringly at Benjamin.

'You two go off and talk,' Benjamin offered, taking in Nellie's obvious distress. 'I will carry on with my walk and catch up with you later.'

Once they were seated at the tea house and Katherine had ordered her own tea and cake, she looked across at her friend and, reaching across the table, took both Nellie's hands in her own.

'Nellie, you're trembling,' exclaimed Katherine, 'is it the business dealings,' she hesitated then said, 'or is it your feelings for Nick that are upsetting you?'

'The business with the estate does have its challenges, but yes, it is Nick. I saw him the day after you told me he was still alive. We came down here to the beach and talked for a while and he told me he still loves me, my heart has been in a turmoil ever since. And then I walk into the pub just now and he is kissing another woman. I know it sounds silly, but it shook me up a bit. I'm a married woman for goodness sake and yes, I do love Albert very much, but seeing Nick with someone else after he had just asked me to stay here with him and not go back to New Zealand, I don't know what to think. Oh Katherine, I am so confused.'

'Nellie, it is only natural your feelings would be all over the place at seeing Nick again, especially after believing he was dead all these years, it's no wonder you are confused.' Katherine smiled at her friend. 'But are you seriously considering not returning to New Zealand? Is that what all this is about?'

Nellie stared blankly at her friend for a moment. 'I, uh, no, oh I don't know.'

'Nellie, I need to talk plainly with you,' said Katherine staring imploringly into Nellie's eyes. 'Nick may well still have feelings for you but since he has been back, I have seen big changes in him. He might have had an eye for the ladies before you two got engaged, but he is even worse now. Every night he is cavorting with one woman or another. He told us that he had been living with a woman in Australia, a former prisoner like him. They were planning on getting married but she got knifed in a brawl and died, that's when he decided to come back to England. Since then, he has bedded more woman than I care to imagine. Nellie he is wild and rough and loose with his tongue. He tells all the girls that he is in love with them, just like he did with you. Oh, I am not saying he doesn't still love you, he probably does, but Nellie he is no longer the man you knew and loved. Prison has changed him, and not for the better. Has he made any attempt to come and see you again?'

'Well, no,' Nellie hesitated, 'I figured he was giving me time to think. He wants me to stay here with him and not to go back to Albert. What do I do? I love Albert and the girls and my life in New Zealand, but my stirred-up feelings for Nick have got me questioning everything. He said he wants to help me with Silas's estate.'

Katherine squeezed Nellie's hands to get her attention.

'Nellie, look at me,' Nellie looked up into Katherines serious face, 'I am so dreadfully sorry to have to tell you this but I feel you need to know before you make what could be the worst decision of your life.'

'What is it Katherine?' Nellie's frayed nerves were about to unravel.

'When Nick came back from seeing you, he was asking a lot of questions about Silas's estate and what it might be worth. Benjamin could see right through him Nellie, he suspected Nick might take advantage of you in order to get to Silas's money. I know this must hurt, I am sorry to have to be the one to tell you all this.'

'Then why hasn't he come to see me again?'

Katherine hung her head, pushing cake crumbs around her plate with her fingers, then looked up and said, 'because Benjamin warned him off. I'm sorry Nellie, we both felt it was for the best. I know it is breaking your heart but...'

Nellie held up her hand. 'No, don't apologise, you are right, I need to let him go, again, and get on with what has to be done. I have a wonderful family back in New Zealand, how could I even consider not going back, what on earth was I thinking. I have allowed my heart to rule my head. Thank you Katherine, heaven knows where I would be if it wasn't for you and Benjamin.'

'So where is Felicity, did she not want to come here with you today?'

Nellie blanched. 'No, that's the other thing I wanted to talk to you about, she has taken herself back off to New Zealand without me. I am furious with her Katherine,' she said through gritted teeth.

'What? Why did she do that?'

'Because she is annoyed with me I suspect. She saw Nick and I kissing and she got very angry and left. I am afraid of what she will tell Albert. I will write and explain everything to him myself but there isn't another sailing to New Zealand for quite some time so I fear Felicity will have done her worst by then.'

'There's absolutely nothing you can do about it Nellie. You

just have to get on with what needs to be done here, then get yourself back home and face whatever greets you when you get there.'

The two women sat in silence as they finished their tea and cake then Nellie leaned forward and taking one of Katherine's hands said, 'come to France with me.'

Chapter Sixteen

Nellie leaves for France - 1860

'The weather looks to be in our favour,' commented the captain as they pulled away from the shore in the lighter. 'Ever been to France before Mrs Fitzgerald?'

'No this is my first trip but Mrs Croxley has been before.'

'Yes I have,' said Katherine, I went once with Silas.'

'I remember,' said the young man, 'I've sailed on every voyage with Captain Silas for the past fifteen years, he was like a father to me, I will never forget him, he taught me everything I know. It is a privilege to be taking you both to France Mrs Fitzgerald, Mrs Croxley. If there is anything you need, you only have to ask.'

Once they were aboard the ship, Nellie leaned against the railing looking out to sea. 'I am so pleased you are able to travel with me Katherine, I can't wait to see France after what you and Uncle Silas told me about it.'

'I am excited to be going back,' said Katherine, 'especially this time when I can share it with you.'

Katherine proved to be the perfect travel companion. With the help of Mr Hicks's letters of introduction, they were soon able to reconnect with Silas's old business contacts. Katherine was thrilled to meet up with some of the people Silas had introduced her to on her previous trip with him all those years ago. Everyone they spoke to was sad to hear of Silas's passing, they held him in high regard and they were more than happy to continue a business relationship with his niece. They were also fascinated to hear about New Zealand, this newly colonised land halfway around the other side of the world.

Trade deals were written up and agreed upon over the next three weeks as Nellie and Katherine immersed themselves in the wonderful world of French fashion and design. Nellie was in her element and couldn't get enough of the new and exciting styles and fabrics that were beginning to appear on the fashion scene. She loaded up several trunks with fabrics, accessories, haberdashery and patterns to send back to her shop in New Zealand. She made arrangements for the crates to be shipped directly from France and also took the time to write to Albert and the girls, hoping her letters would get to them before she got home. She shared her adventures and told them of her plans to return home on the Night Star leaving London in two months' time and explained why she had been delayed.

'I will have to expand the store at this rate,' Nellie laughed as they watched the trunks being loaded aboard the ship.

'Or you could open a second shop,' suggested Katherine.

'I never thought of that, good idea. I must admit that would be a rather daunting option though, I would need to find the right person to manage it.' She hesitated for a moment. 'Don't suppose you would consider coming back to New Zealand with me, would you?' she smiled pleadingly at her friend.

Katherine laughed. 'I would love to Nellie, but unfortunately I doubt very much that Benjamin would ever travel back there again. He enjoyed the experience but he is well settled back here in his beloved 'Old Bell'.'

'Have you ever thought about trying again for another baby?' Nellie asked gently.

Katherine looked sad. 'No, losing our baby back in New Zealand was so traumatic for us, we both agreed not to go through that again. I think that is one of the reasons Benjamin decided to come back here, he needed to be back in familiar surroundings again.'

Nellie spent many hours with Silas's Solicitors', there were three of them dealing with his estate. They were very patient with Nellie and took the time to explain everything in detail. She decided to sign the Shipping Office over to Mr Hicks, it was the least she could do. She left her father's stocks and bonds intact and listed her children as the beneficiaries in the Last Will and Testament the Solicitors had written up for her. A Will was something Nellie hadn't ever considered but being the sole heir of such a large estate, the Solicitor's advised her it would be a wise thing to do. They said they would be happy to continue to manage the estate on her behalf if she so wished. After talking everything over with Katherine and Benjamin, Nellie decided to make Benjamin her Power of Attorney in regards to all her affairs in England.

Finally, Nellie was able to take a deep breath and relax, all that needed to be done had been done. She had recovered from her initial shock encounter with Nick and was certain in her own heart and mind that Albert was the only man she wanted to be with, for the rest of her life. She couldn't wait to get home to tell him so, and she longed desperately to hug her two beautiful daughters.

Mr Hicks had been completely overwhelmed when Nellie handed him the Solicitors' papers giving him outright ownership of the building housing the Shipping Offices. Since that day he had walked around with his shoulders back and his head held high, he was now a proud property owner, he felt like a new man. Nellie loved seeing the positive changes in him, he had been so good to her over the years, she was glad she could finally do something for him in return. He looked quite dapper in his new custom-made suit as he stood alongside Katherine and Benjamin at the wharf. They were there to wave Nellie off as she boarded the ship that would finally take her home. As she leaned over the side of the ship waving down to them, something made her look up. Nick. He stood off at a distance, leaning against an old wooden shed, smoking a cigarette. He realised she'd seen him, flicked his cigarette away and turned and walked off with his hands in his pockets. She realised then that he was probably just making sure she was leaving the country and that he didn't have to avoid her anymore.

'How sad that it all ended this way,' she thought.

Chapter Seventeen

New Zealand – April 1860

It was a glorious summer's day when Nellie arrived back in New Zealand. She hoped the letters she'd sent from France had reached Albert and the girls, in which she confirmed her travel arrangements and the estimated time of arrival of the 'Night Star' in Lyttleton. She expected to see Albert standing on the wharf to greet her, maybe he would bring the girls with him. She hadn't received any letters from home but decided there probably hadn't been enough time for them to write back, although she had been away for more than nine months.

She searched for Albert from the bow of the ship but couldn't see him anywhere, maybe he had been delayed. With a heavy heart she walked down the gangway and headed to the tea house to wait for her luggage to be offloaded. She had four large trunks and two smaller ones. If Albert did not arrive to pick her up, she would need to find someone to transport them for her. Suddenly a familiar face appeared in front of her.

'Harry,' she squealed, 'how wonderful to see you.'

'And you Nellie. What are you doing here?

'I have just arrived back from England.

'Is Albert here to get you?' he asked, looking around the shop.

'No, I am afraid he is not. Perhaps he didn't receive my letter informing him of my arrival.'

'Then may I offer my services ma'am,' he bowed deeply before her, smiling.

Nellie laughed. 'You may kind sir, but I fear you will change your mind when you see what my luggage consists of.'

When the trunks were finally off-loaded Harry let out a long low whistle. 'I see what you mean Nellie. My goodness, you do not travel light do you.'

'Most of this is goods for my shop, only the two smaller trunks contain my personal belongings.'

'Then may I suggest I transport you and the two smaller trunks to your home and put the other four in storage. You can always arrange to get them delivered to you later.'

Nellie accepted Harry's offer with gratitude. When they pulled up outside Nellie and Albert's home it was all very quiet. The first thing Nellie noticed was the empty shop.

'I wonder where everyone is, I hope we haven't missed them at Lyttleton, there were an awful lot of people there.'

She walked up to the house and knocked on the door. Felicity opened the door and stood staring stonily at Nellie.

'Felicity I am so glad to see you, where are Albert and the children? And what has happened to my shop?'

'You no longer live here Nellie. Albert has gone away with the girls, he doesn't want anything to do with you and he has closed up your store and given all your things away,' she said slamming the door in Nellie's face.

Nellie was stunned. Harry, who had stayed seated on the wagon waiting to help unload the trunks, was shocked at what he just witnessed. He stared in horror as Nellie banged on the door crying and screaming at Felicity to open up and talk to her. Finally, she slumped down on the step and sobbed. Harry leapt off the wagon.

'Come Nellie, we have a spare room, come and stay with us until things are sorted out. Clearly there is something amiss here.'

Nellie nodded and allowed Harry to pull her to her feet and get back on the wagon. Nellie looked up at the top floor window to Felicity's room and saw the curtains moving. She could not believe Albert would just walk away from their marriage without talking to her first, but she was not surprised to witness the loathing on Felicity's face. She knew the hatred had always been there, just below the surface, waiting for a chance to be exposed.

Nellie stayed with Harry and his wife Agnes for the next two weeks while she figured out what she was going to do. Every day she would walk down the street and stand in front of the house, hoping and praying for a glimpse of Albert and the girls, but the house was deathly quiet.

'Maybe Felicity is right, maybe Albert doesn't want me anymore,' Nellie confided to Harry and Agnes as they sat across the dinner table.

Agnes reached out and took Nellie's hand. 'If that is the case Nellie, you are welcome to stay here with us for as long as you like,' she offered kindly.

'Thank you Agnes, thank you both, but I have decided that if I am no longer wanted by my family then I cannot stay here in Christchurch. I have enough goods in my trunks to start up another store and I am certainly not short of money, so maybe I should just move away and start over.'

'What happened while you were away Nellie, you've never said.'

'Aggie, maybe Nellie doesn't want to talk about it.' Harry jumped into the conversation. He knew how much Agnes liked to get involved in other people's lives.

'After all your kindness and support the least I can do is try and explain,' sighed Nellie, 'it's been a very difficult time.'

Nellie told Agnes and Harry about her trip to London with Felicity and she told them all about the trip to France, and the endless paperwork she'd had to deal with as she finalised her uncle's estate. Agnes was amazed.

'My my, quite the worldly one aren't you,' she said. 'So, what happened with Felicity, why did she come back early? I know you two have never been close but why is she so hostile?'

Nellie explained what had happened with Nick, how seeing him had thrown her off balance for a while and what Felicity had said when she saw Nellie and Nick kiss.

'Oh?' said Agnes, sitting forward eagerly on the chair. This was much more exciting than hearing about business dealings. She glanced at Harry. 'Has Albert not spoken about any of this with you?'

'Well no, not exactly. He said there had been some disagreement between Felicity and Nellie and that Felicity had come home earlier than expected, but he didn't say much more than that.'

'Felicity was so angry with me, she boarded the next ship back to New Zealand. No doubt she has poisoned Albert with her stories of my betrayal.' Nellie buried her head in her hands and let the tears flow.

Agnes emerged from the bedroom after getting Nellie settled and into bed.

'What's going to become of that poor girl Harry, surely Albert wouldn't treat her this way. At least she has money, but that's not a substitute for a loving husband is it.' She sat on Harry's knee and snuggled into his neck, tears of sadness in her eyes. 'Maybe you could talk to Albert, find out what's going on. I would hate to think that he would stop the girls from seeing their mother.

When Harry went round to see Albert a few days later, he too was greeted at the door by the ferocious Felicity.

'Go away Harry, before Albert sees you. He is furious with you for helping Nellie, he called you a traitor and said he no longer considers you a friend.' She slammed the door in his face.

Harry was just as stunned as Felicity had been, this was a side of Albert he had never seen before. They had never been exceptionally close but to be written off like that was something he wouldn't have expected. Still, he decided, if that's the way he wanted it to be, he wasn't going to pursue the matter.

Chapter Eighteen

Dunedin – June 1860

Nellie travelled down to Dunedin by coach to see about setting up a shop and find suitable accommodation. Dunedin was Harry's suggestion. He had visited many times and was impressed with the rapid growth in the area and felt it might be an ideal place for Nellie to become immersed in establishing a new shop. He didn't know what to make of Albert and the circumstances Nellie had now found herself in. He had a soft spot for Nellie and wanted to do whatever he could to help her readjust to her new life on her own. He knew she was strong enough but that didn't stop him from feeling concerned for her.

It was a long, but not unpleasant journey to Dunedin and Nellie allowed her mind to clear of all the worrisome thoughts that had been clogging her brain these past couple of weeks and enjoy the scenery that passed by her carriage window. Her confidence was buoyed by the fact that she now had more than enough money to set herself up and perhaps buy a house if she found something suitable. She was well aware of the fact that being on her own without a man to do her bidding was a disadvantage. She knew she may not be taken seriously by some people and would be a vulnerable target to someone wanting to dupe her out of her money if she was not vigilant.

The carriage pulled up outside the Provincial Hotel where her suitcases were handed down to a porter. Nellie followed the porter into the hotel lobby and signed the register, as Mrs Abernathy. On the trip down she had decided that if Albert had disowned her then it might be better all round if she used her maiden name. She had no idea if it should entail any legal procedure but that was not foremost in her mind right now, first she needed to find a new home.

Her hotel room was large and tastefully decorated, the centrepiece being the large comfortable bed with its frilled pillows and counterpane. She flopped down on the bed, kicked off her shoes and lay back, luxuriating in the softness. She dozed for a while then got up and ran herself a warm bath, adding some lavender water from a small blue glass bottle on the bathroom shelf, courtesy of the hotel. She sighed as she immersed her tired, aching body into the aromatic water and lay back with her head resting on the back of the tub until the water ran cold. She got out, dried herself, got dressed in one of her finest gowns and went downstairs to the dining room. This would be the first time she had dined alone in such an establishment, she felt very conspicuous and somewhat nervous.

'Are you meeting anyone?' asked the friendly maître d.

'No,' Nellie shook her head. 'I am dining alone tonight.'

The man nodded knowingly. 'In that case Miss …,'

'Mrs Abernathy,' she said quickly.

'Mrs Abernathy,' he smiled, 'in that case may I suggest a table over here by the window, where you can observe the activities on the street. These are our most popular tables.'

'Thank you,' said Nellie, as the maître d held a chair out for her.

Nellie placed her order, ate the meal without paying much attention to what it was or how it tasted, and left as soon as she could. Dining alone was not something she felt she would ever get used to.

Next morning, she was up bright and early, anxious to see what this new town had to offer. Her first stop was the bank, she needed to get her finances sorted before she did anything else.

She instinctively trusted the bank manager from the moment she sat down in his office, a kindly soul who reminded her very much of Uncle Silas.

'Well Mrs Abernathy, what is it that I can assist you with today?' he asked kindly, clasping his hands together on the top of his tidy desk.

Nellie shifted uncomfortably. 'It's a rather long story I'm afraid Mr Longman and I could do with some advice. I need an advisor, an agent, and you come highly recommended by Mr Harry Croxley, a dear friend of mine.'

'Ahh Mr Croxley, yes, I have had many dealings with him, I hold him in high regard. You are fortunate to have such a friend Mrs Abernathy. Now, how can I help?'

'Well, I would like to establish a business here in Dunedin and perhaps buy a boarding house. My husband and I are sadly no longer together and I do not wish to live alone so I suppose a boarding house would be more acceptable, would it not?'

'Indeed, Mrs Abernathy, indeed,' nodded Mr Longman thoughtfully. 'What type of business are you looking to establish may I ask?'

'A dress shop and haberdashery,' replied Nellie proudly.

'Have you any experience in this type of business, Mrs Abernathy?'

'Yes, I have owned two such businesses in the past twelve or thirteen years.'

'Capital, capital,' the bank manager said enthusiastically. 'It just so happens that I may have the perfect solution for you Mrs Abernathy, if you would just give me a moment to check on something first.'

Mr Longman walked out of the office leaving Nellie twisting her fingers nervously in her lap. She pondered over the wisdom of setting up a business on her own, it wouldn't be the same without Albert's support. A tear trickled down her cheek at the thought of him. She missed him and her beautiful girls dearly, she hadn't seen them for such a long time. She still could not believe that he would simply write off their marriage and stop her from seeing their lovely children without at least seeing her face to face. Then again, if he had listened to whatever venom Felicity might have poured out to him, she could understand his hurt, the wounding of his pride. If only she could talk to him, assure him that he was her only love now, that she and the girls were her life. But he had made it quite clear that he wanted nothing to do with her. At least that is the message Felicity portrayed. To see her shop all packed up and empty and no sign of Albert or the children for the past two weeks or so, led Nellie to believe that perhaps Felicity was right, Albert had moved on, perhaps he'd even found someone else. She quickly dried her tears when Mr Longman walked back into the office.

'I can confirm Mrs Abernathy that if it pleases you there is a delightful building just coming available to lease, or for purchase. It is close by if you would care to come and have a look at it.'

Nellie was surprised at the offer. 'Oh, I didn't expect to be looking at anything so soon.'

'Is that a problem Mrs Abernathy?' The bank manager's eyebrows arched quizzically.

'No, not at all, I am just a little taken aback, I really had no expectations further than a cursory meeting with you today. I have considerable funds that need to be transferred into an account with your bank and….'

'Let's talk about that when we have had a look at the property Mrs Abernathy. No sense in getting ahead of ourselves if you decide Dunedin is not the place for you, come along,' he said smiling as he opened the door for her.

Nellie smiled back at Mr Longman, gathered up her handbag and shawl and walked ahead of him out the door.

'This is a newly established side street directly off the main street. There are other businesses opening up, or have recently opened, which would work in well alongside your dress shop,' Mr Longman explained enthusiastically. 'One of my clients owns one of the buildings and is looking for a quick sale as he needs to get back to England to deal with family matters, he does not expect to return. Ahh, here it is. What do you think Mrs Abernathy, is it not a pretty shop frontage? There are also rooms upstairs with amenities that would serve as accommodation, if you decide that is what you would prefer, rather than a boarding house.'

Nellie stood in front of the new stone building, awed by its structural beauty and similarity to the buildings back home in London.

'It is, as you say, a very attractive building Mr Longman, it reminds me of home.'

Mr Longman smiled, 'Indeed it does,' he agreed, 'these buildings were designed along the same lines as those you might find in Edinburgh. I have the keys, would you like to take a look?'

'Yes please,' breathed Nellie. 'Is it vacant?'

'It is, Mr Reed is available at any time to discuss options. As I said, he is looking for a quick sale as his ship departs in two weeks' time.'

Nellie walked through the door and the tinkle of a wee bell above the door took her straight back to the shop she and Katherine had owned back in London. A tear formed in her eye and she hurriedly dabbed it away with her handkerchief. Her emotions were all over the place today.

'Is it not to your liking Mrs Abernathy, we do not need to go any further if...'

'No Mr Longman, it is very much to my liking, it's just that it reminds me of the shop I had in London.' She smiled at him and went to stand in front of the bay window with its many small wood framed panes. 'I would like to have a look upstairs, 'she said and looked around for the staircase.

Mr Longman led Nellie out to a small kitchenette and through into a larger room which would suit as a workroom. They went to the far end where a door was discreetly hidden behind a heavy drape. He drew the curtain back and ushered Nellie ahead of him up the stairs. The rooms at the top were bright and airy with large windows facing out on to the street allowing the morning sun to beam through, illuminating the dust mites floating in the disturbed air.

The small window at the back of the room above the kitchen sink looked out over the enclosed courtyard below with its outdoor privy and a clothesline.

'No room for a garden I'm afraid,' but then again you may not require a garden. There is plenty of fresh produce available just up the street.'

Nellie nodded and continued to explore one of the bedrooms. It was on the back wall of the building but it did have a small window which would catch the late afternoon sun. The second bedroom took Nellie's breath away, it was light and airy, just like the main room, and she could envisage it as her bedroom with pretty lace curtains and a big soft bed with a feather down quilt and bright coloured counterpane. She turned to the man standing patiently waiting in what would become her lounge.

'Mr Longman, I will take it. As you rightly say, this will be perfect for my venture and living up here would be a far better option than trying to manage a boarding house as well as a business. Thank you, you have been most helpful.'

'Are you sure Mrs Abernathy? We haven't even discussed the price yet.'

'I am happy to pay whatever Mr Reed is asking,' she smiled, excitement beginning to take hold as butterflies danced in her stomach.

It took several days for Nellie and Mr Longman to sort out Nellie's finances and set up her new account. Nellie had a large envelope of paperwork, given to her by her Solicitors' back in London. She also had a good deal of money she carried with her in a strongbox, which fitted discretely inside one of her suitcases. The bag was one she had purchased in London especially for that purpose. She smiled each time someone picked up the small suitcase not expecting it to be quite as heavy as it was. They would look at her quizzically but she would just smile back and shrug her shoulders. She had barely let that suitcase out of her sight since she left England. It was a huge relief to her now to be able to safely deposit the money in the bank.

Nellie wasted no time in setting up her shop and furnishing her new lodgings. She was happy and excited for the first time in a very long time. Harry, bless his heart, brought her trunks down by horse and cart and stayed with her for a few days to help her unpack. He was impressed with her purchase and pleased that she had something to set her mind to.

'Nellie, I recalled you telling me you sent some trunks over from France before you left. I took the liberty of checking with the warehouse and I am pleased to report they are there waiting for you. I can arrange for them to be brought down if you like.'

'Oh,' said Nellie, 'I thought perhaps they might have been given away too, along with all the other things from my shop. If you could make those arrangements for me Harry I would be so very grateful. What would I have done without you, how am I ever going to repay you for your kindness.'

'Well, there is one thing,' he said shyly, 'I would like to buy Agnes a new dress, perhaps you could design something nice for her.'

'Harry it would be my immense pleasure to make something special for Agnes and I will not have you paying for it, this will be my gift to you both for all you have done for me. Now, if you want it to be a surprise, may I suggest you purchase a fashion magazine, find out what takes her fancy and send me the picture. What is her favourite colour?'

'Bright colours,' he smiled, 'she loves bright cheerful colours.'

'I do believe I have the perfect fabrics and I have a fair idea of her size too, so it will be my very first order.' She leaned up and kissed Harry affectionately on the cheek. He blushed but she could tell he was pleased.

'Have you seen Albert?' she asked before he left.

Harry shook his head. 'I've not seen sight nor sound of him Nellie. Heaven only knows what is going on with him. If he no longer considers me a friend then who am I to contradict him,' he said sadly. 'It's not as if we were exceptionally close, but I did have a lot of respect for the man.'

'Do you know where he might have gone?' Nellie asked hopefully.

'Gone?'

'Yes, Felicity said he had packed up and moved away, taking the girls with him. He even packed up the shop.'

Harry was surprised. 'He never said anything to me about moving away. How did he know I was helping you if he is living somewhere else?'

'I suppose Felicity wrote and told him,' said Nellie.

Nellie put an advertisement in the window of the shop seeking a shop assistant and a seamstress. Several women applied giving Nellie the privilege of choosing the most suitable applicants rather than having to take on whoever applied. Victoria was a bright cheerful young woman who had recently left school and was eager to begin working. Being the eldest of seven children, she wasn't in any hurry to get married and start a family of her own. She wanted to spread her wings a little first and sewing and haberdashery was something that interested her. Gladys Longbottom was an older woman; her husband had been dead three years and her children were all grown up. She had been spending most of her time mending and sewing for her friends and neighbours but when someone told her about Nellie's advertisement, she hurried down to have a look for herself. Nellie warmed to Gladys immediately, she had a gentle, motherly personality which Nellie felt would be an advantage when it came to dealing with her more mature clients. Victoria, on the other hand, would bring some youthfulness to the business.

The two new staff members were eager to start straight away and jumped at the chance to help unpack the trunks and set up the shop. They were beside themselves with excitement as item after item was drawn carefully out of the over-stuffed packing boxes. The French laces and trims especially delighted Gladys. She had never seen such finery, most of the work she had done had been practical and sensible. She couldn't wait to start working with such treasures. And the fabrics, it was all Nellie could do to keep the two women unpacking as they stopped to admire each piece of material they took out.

It took a week longer than expected to set up the shop but Nellie was delighted with the result. Right at the very bottom of the last trunk, were six carefully wrapped bottles of French wine she had purchased from France, for special occasions. The three ladies stood in the centre of the shop now and raised their glasses in celebration. They all jumped with surprise when the doorbell rang behind them, it was Harry and Agnes.

'We've come to see how you are getting on,' said Harry. 'Agnes and I have been worried about you, you haven't answered our letter.'

Nellie grinned from ear to ear and hugged her dear friends warmly.

"Your timing couldn't be better,' she laughed, 'we have just this minute finished setting up the shop. Come, let's get you a glass of champagne, you can help us celebrate.'

'Champagne?' asked Harry, 'where on earth did you get champagne?'

'What is champagne?' asked Agnes.

'It's a delicious alcoholic drink with bubbles,' laughed Nellie. 'I bought some bottles in France and secretly packed them at the bottom of the trunks of fabrics.

Agnes took a sip from her glass, pulling back in surprise as bubbles tickled her nose.

'It's actually rather nice,' said Agnes, taking another sip. 'Mmmm I could get used to this.'

'I think the price of a bottle of champagne and the cost of sourcing it and getting it here would no doubt put you off, my dear,' smiled Harry.

It was a beautiful sunny Sunday morning and people were out and about walking. Several of them walking past the shop, stopped to peer in the windows and stare wide-eyed at the stunning gowns on display. Some of them smiled at the excited gathering inside, so Nellie decided to prop open the door and let them join in the fun.

Later that night, when everyone had gone and the shop had been closed up, Agnes, Harry and Nellie went upstairs to Nellie's newly furnished accommodation rooms to have something to eat and catch up on what had been happening since Nellie had left Christchurch, it had been six weeks.

'I'm sorry I didn't answer your letter,' Nellie apologised, 'but as you can see I have been very busy, and I'm sorry you were so concerned that you felt you needed to come down and check up on me, but I am glad you did, I appreciate you looking out for me. It does my heart good to know I have such lovely friends to call on.' She reached across the table and affectionately squeezed their hands. 'Any news of Albert and the girls,' she asked hesitantly.

'Sorry Nellie, I've not seen hide nor hair of Albert, or the girls for that matter. But then again, I have been travelling with my work and Agnes has been busy creating beautiful gardens in our yard. She is growing vegetables and we have even planted fruit trees, haven't we my love,' said Harry as he gazed lovingly at his beautiful red-haired wife.

'We have, and I must confess I have developed quite a fondness for this gardening malarky,' she laughed. 'It is a joy to be able to walk out to the garden and pick fresh vegetables for our dinner. The fruit trees haven't had time to bear any fruit yet but I am looking forward to being able to eat fresh fruit off the trees, and if there's an abundance, I can make preserves.'

'Where are you staying?' asked Nellie suddenly. 'You are welcome to stay here if you like, you can have my bed, I am happy to sleep in the spare room.'

'I always stay at the boarding house across the road when I am here in Dunedin,' explained Harry, 'we have a room there for the next two nights.'

The next morning, while Harry was off doing business in town, Agnes wandered across to the shop. Nellie asked her to choose some fabric and trim because she insisted her first garments would be a dress for her and a stylish shirt for Harry, gifts of gratitude for everything they had done for her. Agnes had a difficult time choosing but finally settled on one of two brightly coloured fabrics and matching trims. Nellie took note of the other fabric Agnes liked and decided that she would secretly make two dresses. Agnes had no use for fancy gowns but it didn't mean that she couldn't have two 'Sunday best' frocks for special occasions. Harry was also not one for fancy clothes so Nellie decided she would get Gladys to make up two plain but stylish shirts for Harry to wear on special occasions too.

Chapter Nineteen

Margaret – 1865

Over the next five years Nellie, and her business, thrived. Victoria and Gladys were still her valued and trusted employees, they worked remarkably well as a team with hardly a cross word said between them. Harry would call in to see Nellie at the shop every time he was in Dunedin on business. Since his visit four years ago, when he had reluctantly told Nellie he had seen Albert walking down the street with another woman on his arm, they had never spoken of Albert and the girls again. Nellie never stopped thinking of them of course, but her heart had been broken so many times during her lifetime she had become numb to her emotions. Although she displayed a bright and cheerful demeanour and seemed happy in her daily life, it was all on a surface level, she would not allow anything to touch her heart.

One afternoon a group of schoolgirls walked by Nellie's shop.

'Those uniforms look very smart, don't they?' Nellie commented to Victoria when she spotted them.

'Yes I think they might be from Christchurch, our girls wear a different coloured uniform. The fabric looks like it might have come from the Dunedin woollen mills though.'

One of the girls stopped and stared up at the name above the door. She seemed to be deep in thought for a few moments before deciding to open the door and step inside. When she did, she sucked in her breath when she saw Nellie standing there. Nellie thought the young girl looked very familiar, she stared at her and the young girl stared back.

'Mum, is that you?'

'Margaret? Oh my heavens, Margaret, I, how, what are you doing here? I never expected to...'

Margaret flew into her mother's arms.

'When did you get back?' she asked, her eyes swimming with tears

'Get back from where darling?'

'From England. Aunt Felicity said you were never coming back but here you are. I recognised the style of one of your gowns in the window, then I saw your name above the door. How long have you been back' she asked, accusingly?

'My beautiful dear girl, I have been back for several years.'

'Then why didn't you come home to us? Father was so very upset; he was terribly sad when you didn't come home.' Margaret was in tears.

'I did come back home my darling, but you had moved away.'

'Moved away? Mother we are still in the same house we have always been in. Who told you we had moved away?'

'When I came back, my shop was all packed up and closed and Aunt Felicity said you had gone away.'

Nellie drew Margaret out the back to the kitchen where they could both sit down.

'We did go to Wellington, but that was just for a few weeks to visit Grandma and Grandpa. Father was so upset after Aunt Felicity told him you weren't coming back, he just had to get away for a while. Aunt Felicity stayed behind and took care of the house. When we got home, she had packed up all your things and put them in storage. Father was furious with her.' Then realisation dawned on Margaret's young face. 'You have been back in New Zealand all this time?'

'Yes I have. I wrote to you all, every week, but I never received any letters in return. I suppose your father was so angry he didn't even want to read my letters or let me see you.'

'That can't be right,' wailed Margaret. 'Father was terribly sad when you didn't come back. We never saw any letters, I know Father would love to have heard from you but no letters came Mother, none at all. Aunt Felicity always collected the post and left it on the hall table but there were never any letters from you. I once heard her tell Father he should get a divorce and find another wife but he said NO. He does have another lady friend now though. Marigold and I don't like her one little bit, she is ever so bossy.'

Nellie stifled a smile. 'How is your sister? How are you both? Are you well and happy?' Nellie allowed the tears to stream down her face unchecked.

'Yes Mother, we are both well and healthy but we have never been truly happy since you left. We have missed you terribly.'

'Oh my dear child we have so much to catch up on. What are you doing in Dunedin? Is this a school trip?'

'Yes, we are here to visit the textile mills, we are studying textiles for our sewing class.'

'Do you like to sew?'

'I love to sew Mother, perhaps I get that from you. I cannot believe I am sitting here talking to you, this doesn't seem real, does it?'

'No it doesn't my darling. Where are you staying, can I come and see you this evening? Perhaps we could have dinner together before you go back to Christchurch.'

'We are staying in rooms at the boarding school but I am sure they wouldn't mind if I came and stayed with you. Can I come and stay here with you mother? Please, we have so much to talk about.'

Nellie gathered her daughter into a warm loving embrace and they both cried.

'Come on,' said Nellie grabbing her hat and coat, let's go and see your teacher, of course you can come and stay with me, I wouldn't have it any other way, not after all this time apart.'

When Margaret's teacher heard Nellie's story, she didn't hesitate to let Margaret go and stay with her long-lost mother. She suggested Margaret could stay with her mother until she was due to travel back to Christchurch with the rest of her class.

Margaret and Nellie had two glorious days together, they never stopped talking the whole time. They bared their hearts and souls to each other and shared absolutely everything about the years they were apart. There were many tears but there were also many smiles and lots and lots of hugs.

Nellie hated saying goodbye to Margaret when it came time for her to leave. She tucked a note in Margaret's pocket. 'This is my address, will you write to me?'

'Of course I will write Mother and Marigold will too.'

'Only if your father agrees though,' added Nellie thoughtfully. 'I do not want to incur his wrath, especially if he is planning on marrying again.'

'Heaven forbid Mother,' laughed Margaret, 'Marigold and I will not allow that to happen.'

Nellie smiled to herself. 'Atta girl,' she thought.

As soon as she got home, Margaret wasted no time in telling her father that she had seen her mother. She told him everything while her father paced the floor, head down, fuming at what he was hearing. He was furious when he learned that Nellie had been back in New Zealand for the past five years, he wanted answers and he wanted them now.

'Father are you angry with Mother?' Margaret started to cry.

Albert stopped pacing and faced his daughter.

'No Margaret, I am not angry with your mother,' he said through gritted teeth. 'I am angry at the situation. How could we not have known she was in the country for all these years? How is that possible? And how is it that we never saw her letters?' Then realisation dawned. 'Felicity!' he roared, 'Felicity, I want you in here right now. Margaret, you go up to your room and close the door, I don't want Marigold hearing any of this until I have had time to think it through.'

'Yes father,' she said obediently, and left the room, passing Felicity on the stairs.

Albert looked up as Felicity entered the room.

'Shut the door,' he demanded.

Felicity did as she was bid and turned to face her brother.

'What is it Albert, you seem upset.'

'Do you remember the time I took the girls and went to visit mother and father in Wellington?'

'Yes, of course, but that was years ago.'

'Five years to be exact. Five bloody years.'

'I don't understand Albert.'

'Oh, don't you,' he glared at her. 'Don't you have any idea, Felicity?'

'I'm quite sure I do not Albert, please enlighten me.' Felicity was beginning to feel a little uneasy.

'While we were in Wellington did you receive any visitors?'

'Visitors?'

'Yes, did anyone call here to see me?'

Felicity hesitated as Albert continued to glare unblinkingly at her, it was most unnerving.

'I, I, I'm not sure I remember Albert, we do get lots of callers you know.'

Albert lost his patience. 'I'm talking about Nellie, Felicity. You do remember Nellie, don't you? My wife, the girl's mother? She came back didn't she Felicity. She came back to us and you sent her away. All these years she has been living in Dunedin believing we no longer wanted to see her. And what about all the letters she wrote, what did you do with those?'

The blood drained from Felicity's face as she struggled to quickly come up with a plausible explanation.

'How could you even countenance such a thing Felicity? I have suffered your presence in my home all these years to appease our parents because you couldn't find anyone to marry you, and this is how you repay me.'

'I thought it was for the best Albert,' she said sullenly. 'She left you for that other man, she was unfaithful to you Albert, I felt it was best, I knew you and the girls would get over her sooner or later. I was here to help you and to take her place.'

'And there it is,' spat Albert. 'You wanted to take her place. You were always jealous of Nellie weren't you. I want you to leave this house, immediately. It's a pity our parents are dead or I would have sent you back to them. I don't want you here in my house any longer, and by the way, what did you do with all the items from Nellie's haberdashery?'

'I had them placed in storage.'

'Then before you leave here, I want you to write down exactly where I can find it all and leave a key, if there is one. Now get out of my sight, I don't care how well intentioned you thought you were being, I never want to see you again.'

Felicity wasn't upset, she was angry. Angry at being found out, angry at Nellie for being discovered and angry at Albert after all she had done for him and his girls. Someone would pay for this; it wasn't all her fault, someone would pay.

Albert arranged for his lady friend to watch the girls while he went down to Dunedin. He didn't tell her what it was about and he asked Margaret not to tell her either.

'It has been a long time since I last saw your mother, Margaret, I am not at all sure how things will go when I see her so I don't want to unsettle things here if there is no need, you do understand, don't you?'

'Yes Father, of course. I am so pleased you are going to see Mother, I think she will be pleased to see you.'

'Well, that remains to be seen,' he wasn't so confident.

Chapter Twenty

Albert and Nellie reunite - 1866

Nellie looked up as the bell above the door rang to indicate someone had entered the store. She drew a sharp intake of breath when she saw Albert standing there.

'Albert, oh goodness me, it really is you, after all these years, how well you look,' she smiled as her eyes filled with tears.

Albert stood and stared at her for a long moment.

'Nellie, it is so good to see you too, and you are looking well yourself. Is there somewhere we can talk? We have a lot of catching up to do I think.'

'Yes, we do. Victoria, will you mind the shop please, I will be back some time this afternoon.'

'Yes Mrs Abernathy,' replied the girl.

'Mrs Abernathy?' queried Albert as they walked down the street towards Nellie's favourite tea shop.

'Yes, I decided it was probably best, I didn't want to go back to England and I didn't want to cause any upheaval for you and the girls if you knew I was still here in New Zealand.'

Albert let out a long breath as if he had been holding it in forever.

'Nellie there is so much that needs to be talked about and rectified, that is, if rectification is even possible.'

They sat down at a corner table in the tea house and talked for the next two hours over endless cups of tea. They talked about the letters Albert never received, and what had happened when Nellie arrived home. They discussed the mischief making tales Felicity spun to Albert and Harry and the packing up of the shop. It seemed that Felicity was at the bottom of all of it.

'I want you to know that Felicity has gone,' said Albert seriously, 'I sent her packing. She is a nasty vindictive woman when she wants to be Nellie, but I suppose you have known that all along haven't you?'

'She was your sister, Albert, and in the early days she was relatively accommodating. Things only changed when we got married, she didn't seem to know where to fit in.'

'Don't you dare feel sorry for her Nellie. I knew her better than you ever did, remember we grew up together. I thought she would settle down in time, and as you rightly say, she did seem to accept you for a while. She certainly stepped up and took over your role as mother to our girls once she got back from her trip.' He saw the stricken look on Nellie's face and he reached out for her hand. 'I'm sorry Nellie but I believe it is best we lay everything out on the table now, no more lies or mixed messages between us. If we are to have a future together, we need to be totally honest with each other, don't you agree?'

'A future together? Do you really think we might have a future together Albert?'

'If that is what you want Nellie, then I would surely like to explore the possibility. Now, tell me about Nick, did he really survive the shipwreck? What happened over there Nellie, please feel free to tell me everything, I need to know.'

Nellie poured her heart out to Albert, she left nothing out, not even her bout of confusion, she felt she owed him that much. Then she went on to tell him about what drove Felicity home ahead of her.

'Because it was just the two of us on the trip, Felicity and I got along quite well, we looked out for each other and became quite close, or so I thought. Everything was going well until she saw Nick kiss me. She was so angry she boarded the first ship heading back to New Zealand before I even knew she had left. I sent a letter from France hoping that it would get to you before too much damage was done.'

'I never received any letters from you Nellie.'

'I wrote, often, now I know how Nick must have felt,' she sighed.

'Nick?'

'Yes, apparently he wrote to me after he got out of prison. He thought I must have given up on him when he didn't get a reply. All rather sad really isn't it, the things that are left to the imagination because of the lack of truthful information.'

Nellie went on to fill Albert in on all the remaining details of her stay in London, the trip home and being greeted at the door by Felicity. She then told him how Harry and Agnes had helped her through the worst of it and how Harry was instrumental in getting her to Dunedin where she was finally able to get herself settled and re-established as a respected dress designer and seamstress.

They both sat quietly for a time deep in their own thoughts.

Nellie's hand rested on the white tablecloth beside her cup and saucer, Albert placed one of his on top.

'Nellie, I know it is too early to make any plans, but do you think we could ever overcome these past five years apart and pick up the pieces of our lives again?'

'I thought you had someone else in your life now Albert. I do not hold anything against you for that, I would hardly have expected you to wait for me forever, especially given the information you were dealt.'

'If you are talking about Gertrude then yes, we have been seeing each other for a while but I am not in love with her. In fact, I am not sure how I really feel about her, perhaps she has just become more of a habit than a potential wife. I know Margaret doesn't like her very much and I don't think Marigold does either. While we are talking about other people, you haven't told me how you resolved things with Nick in the end. It must have come as quite a shock when you first found out he was still alive?'

Nellie dropped her head down and watched her shaking fingers twisting a ribbon on her gown.

'Shocked is one word for it,' she smiled ruefully. 'Felicity saw him kiss me after our first meeting and took it all the wrong way. She left before I could explain the situation to her. I don't deny there was a stirring of feelings on my part at the time, but they disappeared very quickly when I thought of you and the girls back home,' she said smiling up at Albert. I knew you would always be my future, and when I left England, I was in no doubt about that. Besides, it appears Nick was only interested in my inheritance,' she said ruefully. 'And that's another thing I would like to tell you about sometime, the sorting out of Uncle Silas's estate.

It was getting late so they decided to leave the tea house and head back to Nellie's place. Gladys and Victoria had locked up the shop and gone home, so Nellie invited Albert in. He sat at the table while she made him something to eat.

'Nellie I am so sorry things went the way they did, I am beyond livid at the damage Felicity has caused. I would like to come and visit and bring the girls with me if I may, I know they would love to spend some time with you, perhaps they could stay for the holidays?'

Nellie's eyes swam with tears.

'I would love that Albert, thank you. You have no idea how much I have missed you and our girls. Margaret has grown into a beautiful young woman and I am sure Marigold has too. You have done well by them.'

'Right then, let's write, keep in touch.'

He stood and reached out to Nellie for what he intended to be a light embrace, but once they were in each other's arms the embrace deepened. They held on to each other, melting away the years, until Albert drew gently away. Nellie looked up and saw the tears in her eyes reflected in his own, she squeezed his hand as she ushered him to the top of the stairs.

'I have enjoyed today Albert.' She kissed him lightly on the cheek and smiled as he blushed and quickly turned to make his way down the stairs. Nellie followed him down and shut and locked the door behind him. He would be leaving the hotel and heading straight back to Christchurch on the first coach in the morning so they wouldn't see each other until he returned.

Nellie went back upstairs. She was restless so she decided to sit down and write a letter to Katherine to tell her the wonderful news, that she had met up with Albert and Margaret.

Katherine and Benjamin had been devastated when they received Nellie's first letter five years ago, telling them about what had happened when she returned home. Nellie knew this letter would make them both very happy.

The next two weeks dragged by as Nellie eagerly waited to hear from Albert and the girls. Every day she watched for the post, her heart sinking each time a letter didn't arrive. Finally, the postman stopped and dropped some letters on Nellie's counter, she recognised Albert's handwriting on one of the letters and raced up stairs with it. She put the kettle on and while it heated up for her cup of tea, she ripped the letter open. There were seven pages written in three different hands, two pages from each of the girls and three from Albert. They "couldn't wait to come and visit", the girls said, and they wanted to know if they could stay for the Christmas holidays, four months away. Albert wrote of his delight at meeting up with Nellie again. He said he had told Gertrude he wanted to take the time to reacquaint himself with his wife. 'It had not gone well,' Albert wrote. 'Gertrude was very angry and has left, vowing never to return. She said she was not about to become second fiddle to my first wife.' As for Felicity, Albert wrote, she was packed and gone by the time he got back and he had no idea where she went. Initially he did not care so long as she left his house, but in hindsight he admitted he was becoming a bit concerned for her wellbeing. She was not used to having to fare for herself, their parents were dead and he was her only living relative. He made sure there were sufficient funds in her bank account to support a comfortable lifestyle, but beyond that he did not know what had become of her.

'All I can say Nellie, is that she was a very angry woman when she left. I have seen her angry before, I know she has a vindictive streak if she is crossed, but her demeanour was very ugly the last time I saw her.'

Chapter Twenty-One

Felicity -1866

Felicity watched from behind the curtains of her room at the lodging house right across the street from Nellie's dress shop. She had been furious to see Albert there two weeks ago. He and Nellie had seemed very friendly, too friendly for her liking, she was not about to let that tramp of a woman ruin the life she had so carefully set up for herself. She was perfectly happy being Albert's housekeeper and a mother to his girls. Now that despicable woman was ruining everything, again, something had to be done, and soon. She would be restored to her rightful place in Albert's home once Miss Abernathy was no longer on the scene, she would see to that. Gertrude might have treated her with indifference but at least she was not a threat to Felicity's place in the household, but Nellie was a different matter altogether.

'She's probably lied to you Albert,' she said, talking animatedly to herself. 'She's probably told you all kinds of terrible lies about me. She is evil, Albert, pure evil, you need to see that. I will make sure you don't get caught up in her trap again, I owe you that much my dear brother.' She smiled wickedly. If anyone had been watching her, they would have every reason to be concerned for her mental wellbeing.

Nellie waited until the weekend when the shop was closed, to post her letters to Albert and the girls. She wrote that she would love for them to come and stay for the Christmas holidays, for as long as they liked. She wrote a separate note to Albert inviting him to join them for all or part of the holidays as well.

'I will put twin beds in my spare room for the girls Albert, and you could perhaps take a room across the street at the lodging house.'

She popped the letters into three separate envelopes so that the girls would receive their very own letter and not one that was included with their father's. It was Saturday, she would go for her regular weekly walk, pass by the Post Office on the way and post the letters. She stepped out the front door pulling her shawl around her shoulders. It was late Spring but there was still a cold nip in the air. Blossoms were in full flower on the trees and sprigs of bright green appeared on the plants and trees lining the streets and in people's front gardens, a sheer delight after the drab coat of winter. She had a spring in her step, life was taking a turn for the better and for once in a very long time she was looking forward to Christmas.

Nellie walked quickly up the quiet side street towards the main street and turned left, the Post Office stood just a few yards down the road. She didn't normally come this way but it was a pleasant change and it gave her a chance to do a little window shopping along the way. She posted her letters and walked on to the next corner, turned left again and headed down towards the waterfront. She passed Custom House, a place she knew well with all her trading and importing of goods from France. Nellie left the road and made her way up to the top of a grassy hill, this was her favourite spot. She loved to watch the waves breaking on the rocks far below and feel the wind blowing through her hair. She untied her bonnet and taking out the pins, shook out her hair and allowed it to blow in the breeze. She took a deep breath and smiled broadly; the world was a much better place now, she was reuniting with her family again, at last.

She stood for some time just staring mindlessly down at the waves, she was totally lost in thought. Just as she was about to leave, she sensed someone behind her and turned to smile and say hello. A cry escaped her lips as she felt herself falling through space, then there was pain, excruciating pain, followed by nothingness.

Felicity turned and walked down off the hill as if she didn't have a care in the world.

'Well, that's taken care of that,' she smiled to herself, 'now all I have to do is wait until the time is right and Albert will be only too happy to take me back and install me in my rightful place in our home.'

She sauntered down the street towards the boarding house smiling at her clever plan to get rid of Nellie. She was oblivious to the man following her, she hadn't considered the fact that someone might have seen her push Nellie off the cliff. She entered the boarding house, mounted the stairs, fumbled for the room key in her drawstring purse, pushed it into the lock and turned the key. As she opened the door, she felt herself being pushed from behind. A hand was placed firmly across her mouth as she was bundled into the room. She heard the door close behind her and struggled for all she was worth, but gave up when she realised that she was no match for her assailant.

'I saw what you did,' the man snarled in her ear. She could smell his stale breath and body odour and grimaced. 'I saw you push that poor woman off the cliff. Now, I am going to take my hand from your mouth and you will be quiet, do you understand? If you make a sound, I will be marching you straight down to the police station, do you understand me!' he barked.

Felicity flinched and nodded. He pushed her to sit down on the bed. She stared up at the man standing over her, she felt intimidated, terrified.

'Wha... what do you want of me?' she stammered.

'As I said, lady, I saw what you just did, you pushed that poor woman off the cliff. You killed her, you are a murderer. Now I may not be the upper-class law-abiding type of gentleman you most likely mix with but I sure as hell am not a murderer. So, what am I to do with you?

Felicity, dumbstruck with fear, simply stared at the man.

'Mind if I sit down?' he said. He didn't wait for an answer, he plonked himself down beside her on the bed. She sat up straighter and pulled herself away from him, not taking her eyes off him, she was bewildered. Did he want money?

'You living here with anyone else? You expecting anyone?'

Felicity contemplated lying and saying she was expecting her husband at any time but realised it would soon prove to be a lie and she didn't want to think of the consequences so she simply shook her head.

'Good, that's good,' said the man. He sat for some time saying nothing but Felicity could see he was thinking things through.

'Right,' he said suddenly, causing Felicity to jump, 'here's what we are going to do. I am going to give you two options, either I take you down to the station, hand you over to the constabulary and tell them what I saw, or' he paused for a moment, Felicity's heart was racing, she couldn't imagine being locked up in a prison cell. 'Or,' continued the man, 'you come with me.'

'Where to?' asked Felicity, her heart in her mouth.

'I've got a run holding up in the mountains, I need a housekeeper. Look, I'm not really a bad person, I'm just trying to make a go of things.'

Felicity shook her head. 'You want me to go and live in the mountains with you?' she gasped.

'Why not? If you stay here, you will be locked up for murder because I will tell the Police what I saw. Like I say, I don't abide murderin'. I don't know what you had against that woman but I don't reckon it would have warranted you pushing her off the cliff and killing her like that.' He glanced at Felicity. Her mouth was set and, for the first time, he noticed her scars. If it wasn't for that, he considered she would be an attractive woman.

'If you come with me, no one need ever know it was you,' he continued. 'You could hide away with me and no one would ever find you. Now, I'm going to leave you to think about what you are going to do. What's your name anyways?'

'Fe, Felicity,' she stumbled.'

'My name's Jack. Right then, I will be back shortly.

Felicity nodded and Jack left the room. She allowed herself to collapse in a trembling heap on the bed as soon as he shut and locked the door.

'What on earth was going on?' she muttered to herself, 'this isn't how things were supposed to go.' She had planned on waiting until Nellie had been buried and the family were wallowing in their grief, then she would show up on the doorstep and they would welcome her back with open arms because they would need her and all would be forgiven and forgotten. She couldn't bear the thought of being taken to the Police station. She couldn't imagine herself being locked up in a cell with all those rough prisoners, she didn't think she could survive such an ordeal. She rolled over on to her back and allowed herself to consider Jack's offer. Would she be able to convince the Police that she didn't do it? After all it would be this man's word against hers and wouldn't they surely take her word against his? Then again, she thought, they would probably wonder what she was doing living in the lodgings opposite Nellie's shop, and they would most certainly find out that she had caused the demise of her brother's marriage. Perhaps, if she did go and hide away with this man for a while, she could eventually find her way back to Albert and the girls. Maybe it wasn't such a bad idea to be away and out of sight until things calmed down. If nobody else had seen her around and nobody saw her leave then why would they even connect her with Nellie's death? She didn't even put her real name on the lodge keeper's register.

By the time Jack came back half an hour later, Felicity had made up her mind.

'I will go with you,' she stated flatly, 'but not forever.'

'You will stay with me for as long as I need you Felicity, it will be my decision, not yours, do you understand that?'

Felicity nodded.

'Pack up your things, we leave as soon as it's dark. I have a horse and dray parked in the yard behind the Smithy's. Do you have any money on you?'

Felicity nodded. 'Yes, I withdrew all my funds this morning, I didn't want to be seen going into any banks for a few weeks.'

'Good, hand it over, I will go and get some supplies to take with us and pack them into the wagon. Give me a list of things you might need to take with you. It will be mighty cold in the winter, you will need warm clothing and your fancy dresses will be of no use to you up in the mountains.'

Felicity drew a wad of notes from her purse and handed them to Jack. He whistled when he saw how much there was.

'Is this all of it?' he asked. She nodded. She wasn't about to tell him about the notes she had sewn into the hems of her dresses.

Jack took the key off Felicity's nightstand and turned to her. 'Pack up all your things, I will be back for you as soon as it gets dark.'

After he left, Felicity burst into tears. She considered herself strong enough to handle most situations in life, she'd had to endure the constant taunts and sniggers she'd suffered at school because of her scars. When she became an adult, people tended to stare then quickly look away, embarrassed. Felicity was used to that, she had built up barriers against it, but now, this situation this was entirely different. She wasn't sure how she was going to deal with it. Going up into the mountains with a strange man, well, it was unheard of and most unacceptable in her societal world, whatever would people think? But then again, what people would she even encounter, up in the mountains. Were other people living up there? What type of people were they? What would they think of Jack bringing home a stranger, and a woman at that?

She pictured herself sitting in a cold damp prison cell in rags, her hair a knotted mess, and decided she really had no option but to go with this man to his mountain home. She just hoped and prayed that he wouldn't treat her too unkindly. She pulled herself up off the bed and began to pack up her belongings. She had left some of her hats and dresses in storage ready to be picked up when she returned home to Albert and the girls; they would have to stay there.

Meanwhile, Jack was setting up an alibi in case any suspicion was cast his way with regard to Felicity's whereabouts should anyone have seen him following her or going into the boarding house. He stocked up the wagon with supplies and tied the tarpaulin covers down tightly before securing the horses to the wagon and leaving them tethered there in the Smithy's yard. He stood and chatted with the Smithy and another customer as the blacksmith hammered out repairs on a horseshoe over a blazing fire. Both men, should they ever be approached by the Police, could rightly say that they had seen Jack Millward and that he had been alone.

As soon as the streets were dark, Jack made his way surreptitiously down the street to Felicity's boarding house hugging closely to the shop doorways and shying away from the pools of light under the streetlamps. He quietly opened the boarding house door and ventured up the stairs to Felicity's room. He unlocked the door and went in. She was ready and waiting with her luggage all packed. Jack was concerned at the volume of baggage Felicity had. How were they going to carry that through the streets without being noticed?

'Is there a back alley behind this building?' asked Jack.

'Yes, that's where the privy is,' responded Felicity. Then, with embarrassment, 'I would very much like to go to the privy please. You have kept me locked up in my room all this time without my being able to...'

'Yes, yes, of course,' mumbled Jack, embarrassed, 'I'm coming with you but we need to be very quiet, we can't be seen together.'

While Felicity went about her business, Jack took the opportunity to scout the access into the back alley. When Felicity emerged from the privy, he grabbed her arm and led her back up the stairs.

'Right, this is what we are going to do. I will go and get the horses and wagon and bring them around to the end of the alley where it opens out on to Edinburgh Street. Then I will come and get you and your things,' he glanced around the room, spotting the trunk sitting on the floor beside the door. 'That's definitely not going, you're going to have to leave it here,' he ordered.

Felicity nodded and sat back down on the bed. She watched Jack leave and heard him turn the key in the lock, she secretly hoped that he didn't return, that something dreadful would happen to him and he never came back. That would solve all her problems and she could get on with her plans to regain her rightful place in Albert's household. But she knew she was trapped, it was a no-win situation, it was either a prison cell or a mountain hideaway. She could certainly put on a good act if she put her mind to it and she knew she could probably plead her innocence to the police, but there was the added inconvenience of Nellie's dead body and the fact that she and Nellie had never really gotten along. Her anger flared. She had helped Albert to see the light, she had reminded him constantly that Nellie had betrayed him by kissing another man. This was all Nellie's fault, but it was she, Felicity, who was bearing the brunt of the whole ugly affair.

'Damn that woman for coming back into our lives, she should have stayed back in England where she belonged,' Felicity fumed as she paced the floor, hands clenched in tight fists. Would anyone believe she had Albert and the girls' best interests at heart? Would anyone believe that she wasn't the one who pushed Nellie off the cliff to her death? There was a witness who would say otherwise, Jack. Felicity's head swam as she tried to rationalise the swirling mass of thoughts cascading through her mind. She heard the key turn in the lock half an hour later and her heart stopped. She had hoped Jack might have changed his mind, but that hope had just died. Resignedly she picked up what she could carry and followed Jack down the stairs and out the back gate. She was trembling as they walked down the damp dark alley to where the horses and wagon were waiting. What would become of her? What was she doing? She had made the decision that running away with this stranger was less terrifying than going to jail, but now she wasn't so sure. At least

Albert would be able to visit her in jail. Jack heaved Felicity's bags onto the back of the wagon and turned to her.

'I need to make sure no one sees you so I am going to put you in the back of the wagon until we are safely out of sight, and if I hear one sound out of you, or you try to escape, I will tie you up and put a rag in your mouth. Do you understand me?' he hissed.

Felicity nodded, terror gripping her. Never in her life had anyone ever treated her this badly, she was mortified beyond belief, she wasn't even sure she would survive whatever it was that lay before her. She began to think that taking her chances with the police might have been a safer option. Jack saw her hesitation and asked again, 'do you understand me?'

Felicity nodded and meekly climbed into the back of the wagon. She lay down amongst the packages stacked in the wagon and made herself as comfortable as she could. Jack pulled the tarpaulin up over her but left a small gap by her head where she could see a bit of light and breathe some fresh air. It was claustrophobic under the cover and she had to fight down the feelings of panic that were beginning to stir. She knew she needed to stay as calm as she could, she certainly didn't want to be tied up and gagged.

The steady clip clop of the horses and the rolling of the wagon wheels across the uneven ground caused Felicity to feel a bit drowsy. She drifted off into a light fitful sleep only becoming fully wide awake and alert when the wagon came to a stop.

Jack ripped the tarpaulin cover back and suggested Felicity could ride up the front now that they were well out of town. He didn't like having to speak so harshly to the woman, or make her lie down in the back, it must have been very uncomfortable, but he needed her to co-operate and this was the only way he knew how. He had no idea how she would behave and he didn't want to take the chance of being caught with her in his company. He sure as hell didn't want to be accused of being complicit in what she had done. Then again, isn't that exactly what he was doing, involving himself? He had been wondering why he just didn't walk away, leave her to her own devices and hope that someone would eventually find out what she'd done, then it would be none of his business. But he had made it his business, on the spur of the moment. His mother always said his impulsiveness would get him into trouble one day.

'It's not far to the lake where we will set up camp for the rest of the night,' he explained as he helped Felicity out of the wagon. He picked her up and dumped her unceremoniously on the wooden bench seat and swung himself up beside her. He picked up the reins, clicking his tongue at the horses to get them moving again. There was an almost full moon so the track ahead was reasonably well lit.

Felicity gripped the sides of the rough wooden seat as the wagon rumbled over the uneven track. She had a hundred and one questions to ask this man sitting beside her but her teeth were clenched so tight she couldn't speak. She was afraid to speak. Maybe she didn't want to know the answers to her questions, the main ones being, where exactly was he taking her and how long will it take to get there? She took a deep breath and settled back on the seat. She had no idea where she was or even what direction they were going in. She could see mountain ranges straight ahead of them in the moonlight and figured they were probably heading west.

'I've got a spread up in the high country, it's a bit rugged but it was all I could afford and the sheep are doing well on it.'

'What's your homestead like?' Felicity didn't like the sound of what he was describing. High country, rugged, couldn't afford, sheep, these were unfamiliar words to her, they represented a life that was totally outside her comprehension. Now, it appeared, this would be her new reality.

'Homestead?' laughed Jack 'hardly call it a homestead. It's a shed with a window and a fireplace. Hopin' you can make something homely out of it.'

He glanced sideways at Felicity and caught his breath, she looked terrified. What the hell was he thinking? He'd basically kidnapped this poor woman and here he was, dragging her unwillingly up in to the mountains to be his housekeeper and skivvy. Then he reminded himself that he had witnessed her kill a woman, in cold blood. He straightened up in his seat. No, he thought, he was probably doing her a favour by saving her from a life in prison. She might still feel like a prisoner, but it would be a darned sight better than being locked up in a cell for the rest of her life. He tried to reassure himself he had done the right thing by her.

'With the money you gave me I bought some bedding and cooking utensils and crockery and knives and forks and things like that,' he said, hoping it would help settle the fear written on her face. 'I told the chap behind the counter that I was setting up a new home, so he helped me out with what he thought I might need. Right helpful he was too, he even wrote me up a grocery list. There should be enough provisions in the back of this wagon for you to make the place comfortable. I have plenty of food supplies to keep us going for a while and I can do another run to town before winter if needs be. Once winter sets in we won't be going anywhere for two or three months.'

'Why not?' asked Felicity, her mouth going dry.

'Because of the snow and the rivers. You've never seen anything so terrifying as a raging river through these mountains after heavy rain or when the snow starts to melt. I've heard a few heart-breaking stories over the years of people who have tried to cross the rivers in winter, very few succeed. The food will last if we are careful and there will always be plenty of mutton, it is a sheep farm after all,' Jack was still talking but she had tuned him out, she was calculating in her head.

Eight months until winter and then I will be trapped for another two or three months, that's almost a year. She didn't think she could wait a whole year to get back home, her mind was in overdrive. Perhaps she could make it so that he did have to go back to town before winter to get more food supplies, then she could go with him.

'You seem deep in thought, what are you thinking about?'

'I am just worried about what lies ahead for me,' Felicity said.

'I'm not sure I could last a whole year way out here. I need to get back to my family as soon as I can.'

Jack turned to look at Felicity. 'What you don't seem to understand is that if you want to avoid going to jail, you won't be going home for a very long time, if ever. Once they find that woman's body there will be a Police enquiry. They will be looking for her murderer, it could take years before you can safely go back.'

Felicity's eyes filled with tears, Jack felt awful, he hated to see a woman cry.

'I'm sorry to be so harsh, but you need to know what you are facing,' he tried to explain. 'You need to make the decision to either continue on with me or I can take you back to town tomorrow morning. Despite what has happened tonight, I will not hold you prisoner Felicity, but if I do take you back, I will be going to the police to tell them what I saw. My conscience wouldn't let me rest otherwise. As it is I am wrestling with my decision to offer you a way out, whether or not I am doing the right thing. I am aiding and abetting a murderer and that doesn't sit right with me, but there's nothing I can do for that poor dead woman and I would hate to think that I would be responsible for seeing you spend the rest of your life in a gaol cell. Damn, I wish I had never seen you do what you did, this is a complication I would never have foreseen happening in my life. Believe it or not I am a law-abiding citizen, I have never been in trouble with the law in my life, now here I am harbouring a criminal.'

He hated Felicity in that moment and she could sense it. She gritted her teeth and held on to the seat of the wagon so tightly her nails dug into the wood, her mind churning with his words.

They pulled up alongside the lake where they would make camp for the night. The sky under the full gaze of the moon was deep navy velvet scattered with stars that sparkled like diamonds as they reflected in the still water. Felicity gasped at the sight.

'I don't think I have ever seen anything quite as beautiful as this,' she said quietly, brushing aside all her troubled thoughts for a moment.

'Yes, that's one thing about living way out here, there is always something like this to take your breath away,' responded Jack.

In a clearing beside the lake Felicity could see that someone had already made a fire pit with rocks and a brace for hanging a pot over the fire.

'You wait here, I'm just going to gather some wood for the fire' he instructed.

She looked around her. 'Where's the privy?

'Squat down by the lake,' he said.

'I can't do that,' exclaimed Felicity in horror. 'I can't just squat like an animal.'

'Then you are going to be very uncomfortable because that is pretty much what you are going to have to do until I dig us a long drop,' he said as he marched off towards the nearby trees.

Felicity stared after him, the situation was getting worse by the minute. She needed to make a decision, tonight. Was she going to stay with this man or was she going to ask him to take her back to Dunedin in the morning. At least she had a choice, of sorts.

Jack gathered some firewood and returned to the camp site. He looked at Felicity as she sat on the wagon seat looking absolutely distraught and wondered if perhaps this woman was going to be more trouble than she was worth. If she decided she wanted to go back to town in the morning he would gladly take her. Maybe he would change his mind and make that decision for her, but could he report her to the police, could he really do that to the woman?

Chapter Twenty-Two

Learning Curves

Felicity barely slept, she had never had to sleep on the ground in her life, let alone out in the dark under the stars. It shocked her how many strange and disturbing noises there were in the night, noises she had never heard before. She got up to relieve herself behind the wagon, not sure she would ever get used to the indignity of such a necessary act. She was beginning to wonder again if prison might be a better option. She went down to the lake, cupped her hands in the ice-cold water and had a drink. It tasted good, she had another then washed her face, the cold sting of the water reviving her a little.

'Morning, see you've survived the night then, that's a good start,' said Jack rising from his bedroll scratching at his body parts.

Felicity averted her eyes and groaned.

'I'll get the fire going and we'll have a cuppa and something to eat before we decide which direction we will be going in this morning, either onwards to my place or back to town.'

Neither of them spoke for some time until Jack broke the silence.

'I'm in two minds about taking you back to town Felicity. On the one hand, I think you should be punished for what you did, but I don't want to be responsible for you spending the rest of your life in jail, I don't think I could live with myself if I did that. On the other hand, I don't want you to feel that I am holding you captive either. You are free to choose Felicity, right here, right now. Your future is in your hands, I will abide by your decision.'

Felicity stared at Jack as he spoke, she continued to stare at him for a while then looked away.

'I have obviously been giving it a lot of thought too. If I go back to Dunedin and go to prison, they might have mercy on me when they hear how that woman stole my life and give me a lighter sentence. Albert could come and visit me,' she brightened at the thought.

'Murder is murder, no matter what the circumstances,' Jack informed her. 'I wouldn't count on that scenario coming to pass.'

Felicity hung her head. Jack watched her as she wrung her hands in her lap. For the life of him he couldn't figure out what it was about this woman that caused him to act the way he had done. He felt the need to protect her somehow. Was it just her scars, did he feel sorry for her? When he first saw her face, he was shocked, but that wasn't enough to make him want to protect her. No, there was something else. He was not physically attracted to her, she was certainly not the kind of woman he would want to marry and have children with. No, there was no way he could commit this woman to a life locked in a prison cell, despite what she had done. He figured she must have had her reasons. He stood up and started packing up their camp.

'Right, I'm making the decision,' he said. 'Come on, we're going to carry on, I think you will be better off in the mountains with me for a while. It will give us time to think things through and if you still decide you want to go back to town after winter then I will take you back.'

Felicity nodded in agreement and stood listlessly by while Jack packed up. He hoisted her up on the wagon and she settled herself on the seat as best she could. She was still aching from yesterday's journey. The morning dragged on in silence, interspersed occasionally with bird song. They were heading through lush pastures now, some with sheep, some with cattle. Felicity could make out small white balls of movement high up on the hills and wondered what they might be but didn't ask. She didn't feel like talking and Jack seemed to be content to just ride along in silence as well.

As they got closer to the mountain ranges Felicity perked up a little.

'How long have you had this farm of yours?' she asked.

'About a year. I worked for a bloke on a nearby station for a couple of years, that's where I did most of my learning. When this property came up for lease, my boss encouraged me to take it. Now I make decisions for myself. It's a bit daunting, but I figured if you don't take the opportunities when they come along, they might never come again.'

'Do you really think I am a suitable person to be the type of companion you need?'

'Hell no,' Jack threw back his head and roared with laughter. 'You'd be the least likely candidate I reckon,' then his smile faded. 'I figured if you were the type of person who could push someone off a cliff like that then maybe you would be strong enough to survive in the mountains.' He was quiet for a moment then hesitantly he asked, 'why did you push that woman off the cliff? What did she do to you that was so dreadful that you felt you had to murder her?'

Felicity flinched at the word 'murder'. 'I just wanted her out of the way that's all. She wormed her way into my dear brother's life and then betrayed him, I will never forgive her for that. She is a thief and a cheat and she deserved to die.' Felicity spat out the last words. 'She has ruined my life, she has taken everything from me, my brother, my home, my two beautiful girls, everything.'

Jack was initially taken aback, then he reminded himself that after what he had seen Felicity do, nothing about her should surprise him.

'So how did you think you were going to get away with it?' Jack was curious.

'With what, pushing Nellie off a cliff? I don't know,' she shrugged. 'I didn't plan anything, it just happened. I didn't see anyone around when I pushed her. I didn't plan on how I was going to get rid of her I just knew that I needed to. I needed to get my life back and that wasn't going to happen while she was still around. I thought if she died, then I would just wait until after the funeral and go back to my brother's home, my home, and pick up where we left off.'

Jack's blood ran cold. This woman sounded like she might be a bit of a mental case and he wasn't sure how he was going to deal with that. Whatever the situation turned out to be, he was beginning to understand that it might not be as easy as he first thought.

It was late afternoon when Jack finally pulled up in front of his 'home'. Felicity sat and looked around. She had to admit, it was a beautiful setting. The hut was as basic as Jack had said it was, but at least he had bought new things for her to try and turn it into a home. She felt she might be able to endure some hardship for a short time, after all, the alternative was a cold gaol cell.

Jack reached up and lifted her down off the wagon. Her tired, aching legs buckled beneath her so he helped her over to sit on a wooden plank supported by two blocks of wood which served as a seat. It rested against the wall of the house under the overhanging eaves of the roof.

'Stay here while I tend to the animals and unpack the wagon,' he instructed, 'then we'll have something to eat.'

Felicity watched Jack for a while then, as the strength in her legs returned, she stood up and walked to the door. She pushed it open slowly and peered into the dim interior. One room, no interior walls, no privacy, just one big room with a stone fireplace at one end, a table and three old wooden chairs in the middle and a wooden bed frame built-in along the back wall. There was only one small window with no curtain, below which stood a bench with a couple of shelves underneath it. To top it all off, it had a dirt floor. Felicity leaned against the door frame as tears filled her eyes, how on earth was she going to turn this grubby little shed into a comfortable home? She'd seen bigger woodsheds behind some of the houses back home in Wellington. Home, she thought, this could never be home.

Jack called from the wagon. 'If you're up to it, you can give me a hand with these provisions. You can set the place up as you like, the house will be your domain, along with the cooking and cleaning.'

Jack had let the dogs off and they were now taking turns coming up to sniff her, trying to decide whether they liked her or not, they did not. One sniffed her skirts, tucked his tail between his legs and walked away glaring back at her over his shoulder, the other two growled deep in their throats and snarled.

'Give them time,' said Jack, 'they'll get used to you.' But he wasn't so sure, they were generally happy to greet strangers, he'd never seen them react this way before.

Felicity pulled herself together, pushed her emotions down and numbly set about helping Jack unload the wagon. By the time they stowed her luggage and the household goods inside the compact dwelling, there was not much room to move around.

'Once you get everything unpacked and put in its place there will be more space,' Jack said hopefully. 'Reckon you could fix this place up real nice.' He went back outside to stack the farm supplies into a small shed behind the house.

Felicity walked over to the fireplace, took a tin of matches from the roughhewn mantlepiece, got down on her knees and proceeded to coax the fire into life. She stood and looked around for a tap to fill the kettle then, realising there wasn't one, went outside to look for water.

'Rain barrel, round beside the house,' pointed Jack when he saw what she was looking for.

She filled the blackened kettle, took it back inside and set it on its hook above the steadily building fire. She searched through the pile of parcels until she found a box of tea leaves and another box labelled *Sugar*. While she waited for the water to boil, she stacked the boxes, jars, and cans of food on the shelves under the bench and propped the sacks of flour against the wall. She found a dusty old rag hanging on a hook at the side of the bench, took it outside and shook it vigorously then went back and wiped down the table, which was covered in a thick layer of dust. She wiped down the two wooden chairs then turned to check on the water. She was about to throw a handful of tea leaves into the boiling water when Jack walked in and stopped her.

'I bought you a teapot, I think it's in this box here, and there's a teacup and saucer for you too. I've already got my favourite mug,' he added, pointing to an old tea-stained enamel mug on a hook by the fire.

Felicity put a smaller quantity of the tea leaves into the teapot and, using the same cloth she'd wiped the table down with, picked up the kettle of boiling water and poured some into the teapot. She sank down on a chair and waited until the tea brewed to her liking. Jack noticed how tired and drawn she looked.

'Why don't I cook us some beans and bacon for our dinner eh, you look done in.'

"I am' Felicity admitted, 'I don't think I have ever been so tired in all my life.'

While the bacon fried in the pan and the beans heated up in the pot, Jack helped Felicity roll out the new mattress he'd bought and together they made up the bed. Felicity could hardly wait to fall into it and sleep. Then she came quickly awake and alert.

'Where are you going to sleep?' she asked, not sure she wanted to know the answer.

'I will sleep outside under the stars for a few days until we get a bit more used to each other. Then I would like to think we could share the bed. We can put some sort of barrier down between us if you like, a curtain perhaps. Believe me Felicity, I have no desire to bed you, all I want is someone to keep house and do the cooking, that's all.'

Felicity was so relieved she almost cried. She dreaded this man, any man, seeing her ugly scarred body. She knew that anyone seeing her scars would be repulsed and instantly turn away, she had suffered such experiences.

Felicity enjoyed her beans and bacon, she was so hungry she felt she could have eaten just about anything. They both washed up the dishes in a round basin and left them to dry on a tea towel Felicity had found in a brown paper parcel. It had also contained fresh white sheets for the bed and some towels. As soon as Jack had said goodnight and gone outside for the night, Felicity quickly washed as best she could and donned one of her nightgowns, luxuriating in its softness and the sweet smell of lavender. She went over to the bed, pulled the covers back and sank down into the mattress, enjoying the feel of fresh new linen. The pillow, with its lavender smelling pillowcase was also soft and comfortable. She was grateful to Jack for these provisions at least.

Birdsong woke Felicity the following morning, she had slept soundly right through the night. She sat up quickly, wondering where Jack was. She didn't want him to see her in her night attire so she quickly dressed in the clothes she had worn the day before, turning her nose up at the stale smell of them. There was a polite knock at the door and Jack peered in before stepping into the room.

'Morning Felicity, I trust you slept well?'

Felicity nodded. 'Yes I did, thank you.'

Jack went over and got the fire going then went outside to fill the kettle with water. When he returned, he looked Felicity up and down.

'When we've had breakfast, I will go and get the tin tub from around the back and fill it up so you can have a decent wash. You might want to check in those parcels over there for something more suitable to wear.'

Jack rummaged around and found some oats to make a pot of porridge. After they had finished eating, Felicity filled up the basin to do their dishes then left them to dry on the bench top. She was looking forward to having a much-needed soak in the tub, and as soon as the water boiled in the kettle, she added it to the cold-water Jack had half-filled the tub with. It was still only lukewarm but she sank gratefully into it and let out a satisfied sigh.

Jack rode off to check on the stock, leaving her time to bathe and get settled in. He also needed time to himself to get his thoughts around the events of the past few days, everything had happened so fast. He had hoped that Felicity might become a worthy companion and be able to help him run the farm. Then he frowned at the thought and decided he might also have to give up and take her back to town before long if she proved to be too much of a handful. He wondered if he should have just ignored what he had seen Felicity do on the cliff that day, but then again, he was a good person, an honest man, and it just did not sit right with him, knowing what he saw and doing nothing about it. As for the police, he knew Felicity would either end up in a gaol cell or a mental asylum and he wasn't sure he could have lived with that on his conscience. It was a beautiful day and he was enjoying being back out in the mountains, breathing the fresh air. Out here he could forget about Felicity for a while and think about more important things, like his stock and his farm, there was much to do before Autumn. He didn't want to think about the winter, when they would be trapped in the hut together for days and weeks on end. No, that didn't bear thinking about right now.

Felicity, meanwhile, had no such thoughts on her mind. In fact, as far as she was concerned each day was a step closer to her returning to her former life, in her rightful place, as head of Albert's household. She was now bathed, scented, and dressed in one of the plain shifts she had found in one of the parcels, it felt good to be wearing clean fresh clothes again. She decided that she might as well get on with her new life instead of fighting it, she needed to make the most of it, for now anyway. She brushed her hair until it shone, then tied it back out of the way with one of her ribbons. She emptied most of the water out of the tub using the washing up basin then dragged the tin tub back around to the back of the house. While she was there, she noticed some crude attempts had been made to start a vegetable garden at some stage. It was only growing weeds now, but Felicity thought it might be worth seeing if she could grow some vegetables. She was a good cook and had always loved making nutritious meals for the family. She hoped Jack had thought to buy some seeds. As she went through the last of the packages and boxes, she found an assortment of goods which would help to improve the interior of the hut. One large package revealed a bolt of plain brown heavy-duty fabric. Curtains, thought Felicity, perfect. She threw the bolt on the bed and continued to rummage. She discovered a black iron pot, which would replace the worn out one currently sitting beside the fire, two mixing bowls, kitchen utensils, tin plates and bowls, and some assorted knives, forks and spoons. Nothing fancy, just serviceable.

'Probably bought with my money,' she mumbled.

By the time Jack came back later that afternoon Felicity had put away most of the goods. The cutlery and crockery were stacked neatly on the shelf under the bench along with the kitchenware and utensils. She had made a crude shelving arrangement with the empty wooden crates and these now displayed the cans and packet goods. She moved the large bags of flour and sugar along the wall to the corner out of the way. Half a dozen dish towels and two clean fresh crisp linen tablecloths, one of which now adorned the table, were stacked neatly on one of the shelves. Jack was impressed.

'My, you have been busy, it looks more like a home now.'

'I need you to put a rope around the bed posts at the top and hang a curtain,' said Felicity without preamble. 'And I need another one put around under the bench to cover the shelves.'

'Right you are madam,' smiled Jack tipping his forefinger to his brow in mock salute. 'Anything else?'

'Yes, we need a safe to put our meat in to keep the flies out. And I could do with one or two shelves over there to put the tea and sugar bowl and milk jug and salt and pepper shakers on,' she demanded.

'I will get on to it as soon as I've had me cuppa then.'

Jack sat at the table and watched while Felicity set about

making the tea and buttering some bread. She had been surprised and delighted to discover some butter and jam amongst the supply of goods

'I will make us some scones tomorrow, you will like my scones, they are my speciality.'

'I must say Felicity, I had my doubts about your domestic abilities, but it appears I may have been wrong.'

'I can assure you I do rather well in the domestic department, when I've a mind to. Do you have a house cow?'

Jack was a bit taken aback. 'A house cow, what would you know about house cows?'

'A friend of my father's had a small farm just out of Wellington and he had a house cow. Mother and I would collect cream and milk from him and we would make our own butter,' she said proudly.

'Well then, perhaps I should look at purchasing a house cow. The neighbour to the south rears' calves, I will have a chat with him and see if we can't purchase a cow who is perhaps past her calving days.'

Over the next few weeks, Jack got on with his daily routine on the farm leaving Felicity to fend for herself during the day. He was still sleeping outside under the stars, or in the shed if it rained, but his patience was wearing thin. He had no intention of approaching Felicity physically, he just wanted to sleep in a comfortable bed. It was his house, the nights were getting cooler, and it was time he took a stand, so, one morning, after a particularly uncomfortable and chilly night, Jack got up, rolled up his swag and stormed inside.

'Felicity, I will be sleeping in that bed from now on. It's up to you as to whether you sleep in it with me, or make yourself a bed on the floor, I really don't care.' He was grumpy and he didn't try to hide it. Felicity's stricken face made him regret his outburst.

'Look, I'm sorry, I had a rough night last night, it's getting colder out there now and I miss my bed.'

Felicity nodded. 'Very well then Jack, but we have to make a barrier down the middle of the bed, I will not share it with you otherwise.'

'Fine by me,' he said, relieved that he didn't have to deal with a Felicity melt down. He had experienced one or two of those lately, when she was over-tired or something didn't work or go her way when she wanted it to. The outbursts that ensued were not something he wished to experience too often.

Jack nailed a piece of curtain to the roof and let it drop down through the centre of the bed forming two separate sides. Felicity loved it, she now had the wall on one side and a curtain on the other, her own private space. She also asked Jack to tie the bottom of the curtain to the base of the bed at the head and foot so the centre curtain stayed firmly in place. He was happy to oblige, he was finally getting his bed back, well half of it anyway. That first night did not go well for Felicity.

'You snored all night Jack,' she growled when she heard him get up to stoke the fire the next morning.

'Best sleep I've had in ages,' he said with a smile, 'you'll get used to it.'

Felicity got up and dressed herself in her new private cubicle. She felt comfortable and secure in there, it was her safe-haven.

Chapter Twenty-Three

Autumn 1867

As the months drifted slowly by, Felicity became bored with the daily routine of looking after Jack and his house. She slept fitfully because of his snoring, she wasn't used to sharing a bed with anyone and she hated it. She would lie awake in the dark gritting her teeth, willing him to shut up. Sometimes she would give up trying to sleep and sit by the fire watching the flames dancing silently on the last piece of wood he had placed there before he went to bed. The days were getting colder now, Felicity didn't mind the cold but then she had always lived in warm stately homes with fires in every room. Now she was living in a draughty wooden hut with a dirt floor. She had swept and swept and swept that floor, trying to get rid of as much loose dirt as possible, stomping around on it to try and flatten it down to make it look like a wooden floor. She didn't like the dirt and dust that seemed to gather every day, she did her best to keep things as clean and tidy as she possibly could. Jack might have thought she was doing it for him but nothing she did was ever for him, she did everything to suit herself, she always had.

Albert had always let his sister do whatever she wanted. He felt sorry for her after the accident that burned her so badly, he had become her protector then, and as far as she was concerned, he still was. After all, even though he had sent her away, he continued to pay money into her bank account. She was convinced he had only sent her away until he could sort things out with Nellie then everything could go back to the way it was. She was livid that day she saw Albert and Nellie together, it was all she could do not to scream out the window at them from her lodgings across the road. She had to do something to get Albert back on her side. She was convinced that now Nellie was dead, Albert would welcome her back with open arms. She gave no consideration as to how he and the girls might feel about Nellie's demise, after all she had been gone for five years and they had gotten along just fine without her.

As autumn took hold, Felicity couldn't help but notice how beautiful the changing colours of the trees had been. The days were getting chilly but the blue-sky days that followed the cool frosty mornings were breath-taking. She started to go for walks up a nearby hill which afforded views across to a large valley that ran down between two enormous mountain ranges. She could see a small hut halfway up a hill on the other side of the river and sheep further up on the mountainside. One day, as she was walking along the top of the hill, she could hear voices. People were calling out and whistling, dogs were barking. She looked around to see where all the noise was coming from and spotted small white blobs, sheep, on the mountainside as they began to move in a line, heading down towards the bottom of the range. She watched in fascination as several horses and riders came into view. She squinted her eyes against the sun and could make out several small objects running behind the mob of sheep. Dogs, lots of them.

'What on earth are they doing?' she wondered. She would make a point of asking Jack when he got back. 'Back from where though, where did he go each day, what did he do?' She had been so disinterested in the farm and Jack's activities that she'd never asked him what he did all day. He never talked about it either, he must have known she wasn't interested. Tonight, she would ask him to tell her about the farm, she was curious now.

When she got back from her walk, Felicity set about making a rich mutton stew for their dinner. Jack's face lit up when he walked in the door later that night and caught the aroma.

'Aahh mutton stew, smells good,' he said with a smile as

Felicity spooned the food onto their plates.

'I saw some people on horses with dogs across the river today,' said Felicity as she sat down opposite Jack at the table. 'What would they be doing?'

'Mustering,' said Jack taking a mouthful of the delicious stew.

'Mustering? What's that?'

'We let the sheep roam around the high country for the spring and summer months but as the weather gets colder, we bring them down before it snows. If we don't, they won't find much to eat and they could get covered in snow and die.'

'Oh,' said Felicity. 'Where are your sheep then? Are they still up in the hills?'

'Yep, boys have just about finished rounding up the mob from the neighbouring farms, it's our turn next,' he explained before shovelling in another mouthful.

'What boys are those then?'

'Musterers, a gang of horsemen who love to get up early and ride the ranges looking for sheep,' he laughed.

'Do you like to muster?'

'Sure do, I spend most of my days riding around the property, keeping an eye on the stock and the fences. I shot a couple of rabbits today, thought you might like to make a rabbit stew.'

Felicity screwed her face up at the thought. 'Ugh, disgusting little creatures, why would anyone want to eat them?'

'Lots of people do,' Jack mumbled through another mouthful. 'Poor people who don't have a choice. They eat what they can find. I guess you've never known what it's like to be poor have you Felicity.' If Jack thought Felicity might be offended by his remarks he was mistaken.

'No Jack, I haven't, and I don't ever intend to be.'

'Wait until the end of winter when our supplies are running low, then you might get a bit of an understanding of what it's like to live on meagre pickings.'

Felicity didn't respond and they spent the rest of the evening in silence.

As the nights got colder and the sun began to set a lot earlier, Jack tended to spend more time inside by the fire reading or just staring into the flames smoking his pipe. He and Felicity didn't have much in common, she didn't seem particularly interested in the farm and she wasn't terribly worldly-wise so there was little to talk about. Sometimes they played cards but Felicity didn't like to lose so Jack gave up on that idea. She had found some needles and thread in amongst the supplies and, at the time, had been rather surprised at Jack's thoughtfulness, then she remembered the shop keeper had helped him put together what he thought might be needed to set up a home, nonetheless she was pleased to have them. She didn't particularly like needlework but as the days grew colder and shorter, she decided that needlework might be a good distraction during their long winter evenings by the fire. She began working on a quilt using small squares she had cut from the gown she had been wearing when they left town. It had been one of her favourites but the trip into the mountains on the wagon and the few times she had worn it since, had made it quite shabby. Now it would become a bed cover, to remind her of home.

'Better carry on with the firewood,' Jack said as he rose from the breakfast table one morning. 'We need to stack as much as possible under the eaves by the door before we get snowed in.'

Felicity nodded, and once the breakfast things were cleared away and washed up, she took off her apron and went outside to help. She enjoyed the stunning cloudless skies that came with the cooler weather and she didn't mind the cold too much, she preferred it to the beating heat of summer. Jack had been thoughtful enough to buy her a warm, serviceable coat which she now grabbed off the peg behind the door. The dogs snarled at her as she stepped outside, they had never gotten used to her, and she didn't try to make friends with them either. They had been allowed to sleep inside in front of the fire before Felicity came along, but she made it very plain from the outset that she was not about to share her home with three stinking dogs.

Jack and the dogs were not impressed but at least Jack could understand Felicity's point of view. She had never had animals in her life and she clearly didn't like dogs, even the horses shied away from her.

'Animals can be a lifeline when you live in places like this,' Jack tried to explain to her. 'I don't know what I would do without my mates,' he said rubbing the horse's noses and patting the dogs. 'I suppose you won't be offering to milk the cow then,' he smiled at her. Felicity threw him a dour look and walked off. Jack had laughed but he was disappointed at her disdain for his furry mates, he'd never met anyone who didn't like animals.

Jack arrived home earlier than usual one day to tell Felicity that the musterers would be arriving in the morning, before daybreak.

'Arriving where, here?' she asked, feeling a little concerned.

'Yes, here at the house, first thing. They will want some breakfast. I suggest you cook up a big pot of oats, they will want lots of bread, and some stew wouldn't go amiss either.'

Felicity was stunned. 'You mean I have to feed them?'

'Yes, you have to feed them,' Jack said harshly, thinking Felicity was just being lazy not wanting to cook for the musterers.

'How, how many?' she stuttered.

'Six counting me.'

Felicity let herself slump down on the nearest chair, her heart was pounding. She had never been in the company of more than one man without Albert being there to protect her. Five strange men, in her house, and she had to feed them. She hoped Jack would protect her from them.

'I have killed a couple of the older sheep, there should be enough meat and bones to make a decent stew and some soup for a few days, and enough left over to feed their dogs as well.

'Dogs? More dogs?' Oh, this was getting to be too much, Jack was asking way too much of her, she didn't like his three dogs, let alone anyone else's.

'How many dogs?' he squeaked pitifully.

'Two a piece, maybe three.' Jack was watching Felicity closely. She appeared to be crumbling before his very eyes, he started to feel sorry for her.

'Look, I will do what I can to help, I've done it all before, everything will be fine.'

Felicity was visibly shaking, she didn't think she could even stand up, so she chose to sit and rest her head on her arms on the table. Jack decided it might be best to leave her alone for a while to come to terms with the situation. He figured she would sort herself out and everything would be fine. He went out and started packing up the gear he would need for the muster. As it was only a small run holding there was no need for the men to stay in the shepherds' huts, like they did on the bigger stations. They would return to Jack's house each night instead.

Felicity looked haggard and tired the next morning, with dark circles under her eyes. She hadn't slept a wink all night worrying about all those men and their dogs and horses, all of them here, in and around her tiny home. She was terrified, she needed Albert, he would know what to do, he would get her out of a situation like this, he always did.

'Felicity. Felicity!'

She jumped when Jack raised his voice. 'Pardon?'

'Are you going to be alright? You look dreadful.'

'I haven't slept all night, I have been so worried.'

'Felicity, all you have to do is prepare breakfast for us and pack bread and cold meat for our lunch. We won't be back until it's almost dark so you will have plenty of time to prepare an evening meal.'

'Tonight? Are they staying here tonight?'

'Yes, they will be here for at least two or three nights depending on how well the muster goes. I will light a fire out beside the hut to keep us warm and they will bunk down in the shed behind the house if it snows. They are used to sleeping rough,' he smiled.

Felicity did not smile back, in fact she thought she might be about to throw up so she raced outside and stood with her back to the wall against the side of the house. Her head was spinning. Never in her life had she ever had to deal with a difficult situation without her parents or Albert being there to protect her. Sailing back from England on her own when she went there with Nellie all those years ago was the only other time she could think of where she felt out of her depth. Fortunately, she had been taken under the wing of a lovely family she'd met on board and they had kept a watchful eye on her, she had felt safe with them. On one occasion one of the sailors had made some disparaging remarks about Felicity's scars and was quickly dealt to by the father of this family who reported the man's actions to the captain. The seaman was soundly disciplined, much to Felicity's satisfaction. Now, however, Felicity felt terribly alone, alone and frightened. Who was going to look out for her now, could she rely on Jack to protect her? He wasn't half the man her Albert was, could she trust him?

It was cold and dark outside. Felicity stoked up the fire and set about making a large pot of oat porridge. She had no idea what to expect of the next few hours, she was out of her depth now, not in control and she felt helpless and terrified. A sudden noise from outside made Felicity jump with fright. The noise grew louder, horses, dogs, creaking saddles, voices. The musterers had arrived.

Chapter Twenty-Four

The Musterers

Jack went outside to greet the musterers. Felicity could hear the men talking animatedly amongst themselves, greeting Jack like a long-lost friend. She knew nothing about these men and she didn't particularly want to know. All she wanted to do was to feed them and get them out of her house as quickly as possible.

'See you've got yourself a wee wifey since we were here last year Jacky,' laughed the first man through the door. Jack wasn't sure how to explain Felicity's existence in his hut so he decided not to contradict the man's assumption and let them all think she and Jack were married. It would be too complicated to explain otherwise.

'This is Felicity,' Jack introduced the men to her one by one. Felicity didn't like the way they were looking at her, she tried to hide her face as much as possible. She gave them a cursory nod and busied herself stirring the pot of oatmeal. Two of them had to eat out of the mixing bowls as there were only four cereal bowls and four plates. They seemed satisfied when they finally got up from the table and went outside to get ready to leave. While they were eating Felicity had drawn the curtains around the bed and had sat right up in the corner waiting for them to leave. Jack pulled the curtain back.

'We're off now Felicity, that wasn't so bad, was it? We'll be back around dusk.'

When Felicity didn't respond Jack dropped the curtain back and left. Felicity sat where she was until everything went quiet, no voices, no animal noises, nothing, just how she liked it. She crawled off the bed and set about clearing the dishes and doing the washing up. By the time she finished, the sun was creeping up from the horizon with the promise of another exquisite blue-sky day. This at least, lifted her spirits. She ventured outside to see if there was anything she could gather from the garden to add to the mutton stew she was planning to cook for the evening meal. Filling the bellies of six hungry men was going to be a challenge. Sadly, there was not much to be had in the garden, she would need to make some bread and dumplings to fill them up instead. There were a few potatoes still in the bag they brought with them but if she used them all on these men, they would run themselves out for the winter. She was extremely grateful when one of the musterer's had presented her with some freshly made cheese from the previous farm they'd stayed at, and a large pound cake. Felicity did what she used to do when she was running Albert's household, she sat down and made a list, drew up some recipes and checked her ingredients. Satisfied with her plan she began the preparations. By the time the men returned that night, the hut was warm and welcoming and filled with the delicious smell of mutton stew and fresh dumplings.

The men washed up outside in the trough behind the house and after setting up their bed rolls in the shed, came inside to eat. They were so engrossed in discussing the day's activities that they barely took any notice of Felicity, except to say thank you when she passed them a plate of food. Once again, she took her meal and sat quietly behind the curtains of her bed and listened to the conversations. She had no idea what they were talking about most of the time, she just wished they would hurry up and leave so she could clean up and do what she could to prepare for breakfast in the morning. The men were tired and after eating their fill, were happy to retire. Jack helped Felicity with the dishes before he too collapsed into his bed. So far, her fears of having to deal with six men hadn't been realised.

She was glad to see the riders off the next morning after a feed of oatmeal, toast with lard, and cups of tea. She had made several cold meat and cheese sandwiches and added some pieces of pound cake. She hoped the cheese and the cake would last. It would fill a gap and go down well with the cold tea they carried in their glass bottles. There were a few apples left in the barrel but Felicity decided to leave them until the last day. By the time the men were due to arrive back that night she was more prepared and less trepidatious than she had been the previous night. The second night, and breakfast the following morning, went pretty much the same as the day before, with Felicity still preferring to hide away behind the bedroom curtains while they were eating. The third night, however, would set off a chain of events that would prove to be Felicity's undoing.

The men arrived back a little earlier than expected. They were in high spirits; the mustering was over for another season. Jack's flock had been the last on their list and they had succeeded in bringing the whole lot down and settling them in to the lower pastures in good time. The snowy weather would be upon them any day now. The meal wasn't quite ready so four of the men, including Jack, sat around the table to play cards while the other two drew back the curtains and rudely set themselves up on the bed. Felicity was horrified. How dare they, that was her private domain, she was furious and she let Jack know it.

Jack wasn't sure how to deal with Felicity's outrage. He didn't want to exacerbate the situation nor did he want to appear weak in front of the musterers. Before he could say a word one of the younger men sitting on the bed spoke up.

'Come on missus, we don't mean any offence.'

Felicity glared at Jack. 'He's right Felicity, they don't mean any harm, just leave it be.'

Just leave it be, just leave it be! That was her private domain, how dare they sully it. She quietly seethed while she served up the meals then grabbing her coat, went outside to wait until they had finished. It was a cold night but she was too angry to notice. The sooner these men went on their merry way the better.

A beam of light shone out from the doorway as one of the men came out.

'Alright then Mrs? Bit cold to be sitting out here tonight, why don't you come back inside.'

Felicity ignored him. 'Suit yourself ya snooty little madam,' he huffed as he turned towards the long drop.

That was enough to ignite the fire that had been burning just below the surface. Felicity launched herself at the man, scratching and clawing at his face and kicking him.

'Whoa, steady on little lady,' he yelled, trying to fend her off.

Felicity hissed at him and continued her attack. Another of the men appeared from the doorway.

'Everything alright out here?' he asked. When he saw what was happening, he grabbed Felicity around the waist from behind and pulled her off his mate.

'No need to behave like that,' he growled in her ear.

Felicity let out a blood curdling scream and Jack came rushing out in time to see the musterer trying to hold on to an hysterical Felicity as she flailed her arms and legs about in an absolute fury.

'Put her down,' Jack ordered.

'Be it on your head if I do Jack, I'm warnin' ya she will attack again.'

'Let her go,' Jack repeated. The man shrugged and released Felicity. The minute he let go she turned around and launched an attack on the man who had been holding her. He took one look at Jack and said, 'Sorry mate but she deserves this,' he slapped her hard across the face. 'I've had to deal with hysterical women like this in my own household, this is the only way to calm them down and bring them in to line, believe me.'

'Jack didn't know what to do as he saw Felicity drop to her knees, hands held to the reddening skin on the side of her face, tears rolling down her cheeks. As the men stood around watching her, waiting to see what she would do next, she rose slowly to her feet. A deep growl bubbled up from deep down in her throat and erupted into the cold night air with such ear-piercing force all the men backed away, uncertain what she would do next. Once again Felicity launched herself in a blind rage at the man nearest to her, which happened to be Jack.

'Best thing you can do is restrain her till she's calmed down,' one of the men suggested.

Jack dragged Felicity, writhing and screaming, into the hut and threw her on the bed. One of the men brought in a rope and with the help of two others they were able to tie her hands together and tether her to one of the bed posts. Jack leaned over her, apologised, and tried to stroke her hair and soothe her but she spat at him and screamed like a she-devil, kicking out with her legs. Jack reluctantly tied a cloth around her mouth to silence her. He drew the curtains around the bed and went and got the whiskey keg from under the kitchen bench.

'Didn't know you had this stashed away Jacky boy, would have got into it from the first night,' laughed Sid, the eldest of the group.

'That's why I didn't let on I had it,' said Jack, wouldn't have got any work out of you then would I.'

He was worried about Felicity, he didn't quite know what else he could do for her except leave her to calm down. He distracted himself by entertaining the men, bringing out the playing cards and pouring them each a whiskey.

The men played cards late into the night, all the while devouring Jack's precious whiskey. They stoked up the fire as the temperature dropped, tiredness was beginning to set in, it had been a long season of mustering and now, with bellies full of food and liquor, along with the effects of the heat from the fire, they all dozed off right where they were, at the table or on the floor.

Felicity had given up struggling against her bonds and had eventually nodded off with her tears drying on her cheeks. In the early hours of the morning she was awakened by one of the men going outside to relieve himself, she hoped it was Jack. By the sounds of the snoring the rest were all still asleep. She heard him come back inside and hoped he was coming to untie her and take the filthy rag out of her mouth. She heard him place another log on the fire then felt movement on the bed. It was not Jack, she could tell by the bulk of the man, and the smell of him. Then she realised it was the man she had attacked earlier.

'Hello Felicity,' he whispered as he leaned over her. 'Time to teach you a lesson, I don't like being attacked like that.' With one hand he undid his trousers then pushed up her skirt and without preamble roughly entered her. She tried to scream but the gag in her mouth muffled the sounds coming from deep within her. She continued to squirm and cry out as he thrust harder and deeper into her. Tears streamed down her cheeks; the pain was excruciating. She had never been with a man before and if this was what it was like, she never would again. Finally, he shuddered and groaned and flopped down beside her. She felt sick, she could feel bile rising up in her throat, it had nowhere to go so she had to force it down again before she choked. With a grunt of satisfaction Felicity's attacker pulled himself up off the bed, pulled up his trousers and went back by the fire as if nothing had happened. Her head was spinning, her mind was reeling from the shock of what had just happened. She had a burning throbbing pain between her legs. Nobody had ever touched her down there before, her mother had never talked to her about men and marriage and those sorts of things because she never expected Felicity to get married. Felicity couldn't imagine why any woman would want to willingly allow a man to do what this man had just done to her. She wanted to kill him. If it wasn't for her bindings she would be up off the bed and attacking him again. She couldn't even scream out her rage. She lay wide awake, terrified, starting at every little sound and movement, fearful that he might come back and attack her again, or that one of the others might. She was trembling with fear, she'd wet herself and was beginning to lose consciousness, the gag was restricting her breathing.

The sun was well up before the rest of the men stirred. Jack was up first, he stoked the fire then went to check on Felicity. She was asleep so he decided not to disturb her and went to make breakfast. He pulled the curtains securely around the bed, roused all the men, got them up and fed and finally sent them on their way. When he went back to check on Felicity, he was surprised to find she was still asleep. He didn't know how she could have slept through all the noise. He quietly undid her ties and removed the rag from her mouth thinking she was probably well rested and calmed down by now. She still didn't stir. He called her name and shook her, no response. His heart started beating wildly, had he killed her? He pulled her up by her shoulders and shook her. She gasped suddenly and her eyes flew open. She stared at Jack and his mouth went dry when he saw the haunted look in her eyes. He'd seen that look before, his girlfriend had been raped when she was a teenager and she had had that same haunted look. He lay Felicity back down on the bed and gently lifted her skirts. Tears filled his eyes when he saw the blood and bruising on her body. He cursed out loud. If the men were still here, he would be trying to find the culprit and would have beaten him to within an inch of his life. He would not tolerate this behaviour from any man, and certainly not to a woman like Felicity who, he suspected, had been a virgin.

He picked her up and set her down gently by the fire. He slowly removed her soiled clothes, washed her bruised and bloodied body and redressed her, she barely acknowledged what was happening. Jack was becoming concerned. He left her sitting on the chair while he prepared something for her to eat. He made a bowl of runny oatmeal and tried to get her to eat but she turned her head away and refused the food. He gave her water, which she did accept. He washed the bedding and hung it out to dry, constantly coming in to check on Felicity. She just sat leaning on the table with her eyes closed. He cleaned up the breakfast dishes and the mess left over from the musterers' night of drinking and card playing. Once the bedding was dry later in the afternoon, Jack remade the bed and lay Felicity down on it. She turned her back to him and faced the wall without uttering a sound and closed her eyes. He tried to talk to her, asking her if she wanted anything to eat or drink, but she didn't answer him, she wouldn't open her eyes.

That night Jack decided to sleep on the floor by the fire and leave Felicity alone in the bed. He remembered his girlfriend becoming very withdrawn and distant from everyone for a while after her attack. He just hoped and prayed that Felicity would recover soon, if she didn't, what would he do with her?

Chapter Twenty-Five

Nellie - Summer 1866

Nellie could feel herself being drawn up towards a beautiful, bright light. It was so peaceful here, so beautiful and peaceful, she felt she never wanted to leave. Suddenly there were voices and pain, dreadful pain. She moved her lips to say something, to ask whoever it was to go away and leave her in peace. She felt a sharp sting in her arm and once again she fell into oblivion.

'Where did you say you found her?' asked the Police Sergeant. He sat opposite a young man, pale-faced and shaken. They were sitting in the hospital waiting room on hard wooden chairs. A nurse came along and offered them a cup of tea, they both accepted.

'As I told the other Policeman,' the young man said, 'I was clambering across the rocks as I do most weekends with my dog Rastas, and he raced off and started barking at something. I followed him and there on the beach was this lady. I mean, gee whizz Sergeant I didn't know if she was alive or dead, she looked like she was dead.'

'Then what did you do lad?'

'I didn't really know what to do at first. I told Rastas to stay, which he did, he's a really obedient dog you know.' The Sergeant nodded patiently. 'I climbed up the hill to see if anyone was up the top because I figured that's where she must have fallen from. I saw a woman in a blue dress way down the bottom of the hill but nobody else seemed to be around so I ran here to the hospital.'

'You did well son,' said the Sergeant kindly. 'If you hadn't found her when you did, she may well be dead by now.'

'Do you think she will be alright Sergeant?' The boy showed genuine concern for the woman.

'I hope so son, I sincerely hope so. Now, I have all your details, you go on home and rest up, you've had a nasty shock. Do you have anyone at home to look after you?'

'Yes, me Mum and Dad are waiting outside for me.'

'We will need to call on you again at some stage so please don't go leaving the area without letting us know.'

The boy nodded and made his way out to his anxious parents and beloved canine.

By Monday afternoon Nellie had not regained consciousness. Nobody recognised her until one of the nurses came on shift and said she thought it could be Nellie, from Nellie's dress shop. A constable was immediately despatched to Nellie's shop. He had to go around the back to gain entry by breaking the glass pane in the back door. He found the addresses of Albert and Harry written in a notebook on the dining room table upstairs and took it straight back to the Police Station where they set about trying to contact the two men. A telegram was sent to both addresses, Harry receiving his first. He had no idea that Nellie and Albert had been in touch so, thinking he might be the closest person Nellie had to a next of kin, he wasted no time in saddling up his horse and heading for Dunedin. It would take him almost two days of hard riding.

Albert in the meantime, had also received a telegram stating that one Miss Cordelia Abernathy was seriously ill in Dunedin hospital. He was grief stricken, he'd only just found her, surely he wasn't about to lose her all over again. He didn't feel it would be fair to leave the girls behind, in case their mother did not survive and they never got the chance to say goodbye, so he packed all three of them up and they caught the next stagecoach out of town, which would get them into Dunedin in about three days time, all going well. The coach driver, once apprised of the need for their journey, wasted no time in getting them there as quick as he possibly could. He had deliveries and pick-ups to make along the way but he didn't waste time on small talk at the stops. Albert was exhausted with sleeplessness and worry by the time they reached Dunedin. The girls were a little more resilient and seemed to have taken the journey in their stride. The coach driver kindly took them right to the doors of the hospital, unloaded their luggage for them and left it in safe hands at the hospital reception desk. Albert and the girls hurried down the corridor to the room indicated by the receptionist and they looked anxiously through the door window. Harry was sitting beside the bed looking at Nellie, a sad expression on his face. Albert asked the girls to wait in the corridor while he went in first to see how their mother was doing.

'All these years I've had to live without my mother and now it looks like she's dead,' wailed Marigold.

'Shush,' hissed Margaret, 'Mother is not dead, she's just very ill that's all. You wait and see, she will be better before we know it.'

The girls watched their father slip quietly into the darkened room.

'Harry,' he said, holding out his hand in greeting. 'What on earth brings you here?'

'I got a telegram Albert. I'm sorry I didn't mean to intrude, I didn't know how the land lay between you and Nellie, so I decided I had best come down and see to Nellie myself, just in case.'

'Thank you, you have been a good friend to Nellie over the years Harry and I am truly grateful. Nellie told me what you have done for her since she came back from England. We met up a couple of weeks ago and had a good long talk. There is so much you and I need to catch up on, it's been far too long.'

'That it has, Albert, that it has.'

'Nellie and I sorted out all the nonsense that happened because of Felicity and we were looking forward to spending some time together this Christmas.'

He looked down at Nellie lying deathly pale against the

white pillowcase and shook his head. Taking her hand in both of his he sat down in the chair Harry had vacated for him.

'Have they told you anything yet? About her condition I mean.'

'No,' said Harry sombrely, 'I am not legally next of kin, but no doubt they will be happy to talk with you. Are the girls with you?'

'Yes, I made them wait out in the hallway. I just wanted a minute with Nellie on my own before I let them come in.'

'I will sit with them if you like,' offered Harry, 'I haven't seen them for years, no doubt they have grown.'

'They certainly have,' Albert smiled weakly, focusing his attention on Nellie as Harry quietly left the room.

'My poor dear girl,' whispered Albert tearfully, 'after everything you have endured in your life and now this. What on earth has happened? I am here for you now, all three of us are, and we will stay with you until we can take you home.'

He took his handkerchief out and wiped his tears away. Just then the Doctor walked in.

'Ah, you must be the husband,' he assumed holding out his hand.

'I am, although we have been estranged for some time but we are together again now.'

It wasn't exactly true at this stage but Albert didn't feel the need to elaborate.

'Right then, said the Doctor, 'I don't know how much you have been told already, but Mrs Abernathy was found near-dead on the beach below the cliff a few days ago. We have ascertained that she has suffered severe bruising and abrasions to her head, back and legs. She has a concussion, the effects of which we will not know until she regains consciousness. We also don't know yet what damage has been done to her spinal cord and whether she has any feeling in her lower limbs. She suffered a broken arm which as you can see is in plaster and her right ankle has also been broken. All in all Mr Abernathy....'

'Ah, it's Fitzgerald, Albert Fitzgerald,' answered Albert,

slightly embarrassed, my wife reverted to her maiden name.'

'Ah, I see,' said the Doctor distractedly. 'As I was saying Mr Fitzgerald, I would say that Mrs Abernathy is very lucky to be alive and we won't know the full extent of the damage until she wakes up.'

'Do you have any idea how long that will take?' asked Albert, the shock of the extent of Nellie's injuries beginning to sink in.

'I'm afraid I don't, it is entirely up to Mrs Abernathy as to when she wakes up. Just be here with her, talk to her, hold her hand, that kind of thing, it might be just what she needs to bring her round. I'm happy to extend visiting hours for you and your family in this instance, I believe it might help in Mrs Abernathy's recovery.' With that he nodded at Albert and walked out the door.

Albert sat holding Nellie's hand, not sure what to say. After a few moments he went out into the corridor and called the girls in.

'Harry would you stay a while, I would like to have a word with you while the girls visit with their mother.'

Harry nodded and Albert led the girls to their mother's bedside.

'Don't be frightened,' he whispered, 'Mummy is only sleeping. She has got some nasty cuts and bruises and some broken bones so while they get better her body needs to rest.'

The girls nodded. Margaret leaned over and kissed her mother's cheek.

'Hello Mummy,' she said, 'please wake up soon, we have so much more to talk about and so many plans to make for Christmas.'

Marigold was standing motionless beside the bed. 'Aren't you going to say hello Marigold?' asked Margaret.

'Is that our Mummy? I haven't seen her for so long I hardly recognise her,' wailed Marigold. 'Do you remember her Margaret?' she asked her sister.

'Yes, I remember lots of things about her, don't you?'

'I think so, I was only six when she went to England, and you must have been eight. I am not sure what memories are real and what might be dreams.'

Marigold leaned down and kissed her mother's cheek. 'Uncle Harry said that it is good to talk because even though Mummy is asleep, he thinks she can still hear us. Shall we talk about what we remember about her?'

Albert smiled. 'That's a wonderful idea girls, I'm sure your mother would love to hear your voices and listen to what you remember about her. I am just stepping into the corridor to speak to Mr Croxley.'

Harry was pacing the corridor and came up to Albert immediately when he saw him coming out of Nellie's room. They both sat on the chairs in the corridor, Albert pulling his around so he could talk to Harry face to face.

'Harry what do you make of all this. Do you have any idea what happened?' Albert asked as he leaned forward with his elbows on his knees.

'All I know is that the Police are involved and they…?'

'The Police? Good heavens do they suspect foul play then?'

'Yes, I think they do Albert. It appears a young lad playing on the rocks with his dog found her lying on the beach but that is all I know at this stage. Look, I can stay around for a few days if you would like me to keep an eye on the girls while you talk with the Police.'

'Would you Harry, I would be most grateful. How are we ever going to repay you for all your kindness?'

'Think nothing of it Albert, I am happy to help.

'Where are you staying?'

'Just across the road from Nellie's place in a boarding house, I thought it might be wise to keep an eye on her place for the time being.'

'Yes, yes of course. I was thinking we might stay in her upstairs flat. Apparently, Nellie was setting up beds for the girls and I am sure she won't mind me sleeping in her bed for now, under the circumstances.'

'I'm sure, if she was awake, she would insist on it,' smiled

Harry.

'Let's all meet up for dinner this evening shall we. I will go and talk to the Police and see what I can find out, then I think we need to make some interim plans. This could be the start of a long journey.'

'Yes I think you might be right about that Albert. Might I suggest we meet at the hotel on the corner, it has a quiet dining room and they serve an excellent meal.'

Harry left and Albert went back in to Nellie's room to sit with the girls for a while. The long days of travelling and the distress of seeing their mother so ill was taking its toll on the girls so Albert decided to take them back to Nellie's rooms above the shop.

'We will come back in the morning girls,' he assured them. 'You will be able to visit with your mother every day and we will stay here until she wakes up, but right now I think you need to get some rest, it has been a very long and tiring three days.'

The girls were thrilled when they saw how their mother had decorated their bedroom. Nellie had welcomed the opportunity to play around with bedding and curtain fabrics, it had been a pleasant change from dressmaking. She chose bright yellow gingham for the curtains with a frill around the edges that framed the windows when the curtains were tied back during the day to let the sun pour in. The bed covers were plain bright lemon and the wallpaper was a white background covered in bright yellow sunflowers. Frilly white pillows adorned the beds and soft woollen blankets were folded neatly at the foot of each bed. A small white dressing table with a large mirror on top, stood between the beds and two white wicker chairs with blue and yellow cushions sat either side of the window. A white sheepskin rug nestled between the twin beds.

'Oh this is heavenly,' cried Margaret with delight. 'It's like walking into sunshine, what do you think Marigold?' she asked her sister.

'Yellow is not my favourite colour,' admitted Marigold, but

this is lovely and I do love that colour blue on the cushions. Oh, and those blue flowers in the vase on the dressing table, aren't they pretty?'

The girls set about putting their clothes away in the dresser drawers while their father settled his things in Nellie's room.

'What time are we going out to dinner Daddy?' Margaret called from the bedroom.

'Around six, I think. Uncle Harry is staying just across the street, he will come and get us when he's ready.'

'We haven't seen Uncle Harry for such a long time, is he really an uncle?'

'Not a real one, no. Your Mother's dearest friend, Aunt Katherine, married Uncle Harry's brother. Your mother and Katherine were, and probably still are, very close friends, more like sisters really. So, although they are not true relatives, we have always looked on the Croxley's as if they were part of our family. Besides, Uncle Harry sounds better than Mr Croxley, doesn't it? I know he would prefer to be called uncle.'

'I have sometimes seen him on my way to school. Why did he stop coming to visit?' asked Margaret.

I'm not sure,' said Albert thoughtfully, 'I suppose after your mother ...., well while your mother was gone, he wasn't sure whether to call on us or not. I suggest we put an end to that this evening and let him know that he is most welcome to be a part of our family again, how does that sound?' The girls nodded in agreement.

'Right then,' said Albert, go and have a rest before we get dressed for dinner, we are dining at the hotel tonight.'

The girls clapped their hands with glee and went back to their bedroom to lie on their new beds.

Harry let himself in through the back door of Nellie's shop a couple of hours later and made his way up the stairs. He was pleased to see that Albert and the girls had settled in well. They were all dressed and ready to go so he led them back down the stairs and out the front door. They walked along the quiet streets towards the hotel, the girls enjoying looking at the window displays along the way.

'It's nice here, this street,' commented Albert. 'I'm glad Nellie found somewhere pleasant to live, she seemed to be happy here.'

'She was,' agreed Harry, 'at least as happy as she could be under the circumstances.'

Albert hung his head. 'I still can't quite believe how it all happened Harry, even our estrangement, yours and mine, has been unnecessary. So much could have been revealed and sorted out long before now if only we had met up sooner.' He sighed and shook his head. 'The whole messy business is all down to my sister; I will never forgive her for what she has done.'

'Where is she now, I take it she is no longer living under your roof.'

'No, she certainly is not. I have no idea where she is and I hate to say it but I don't much care right now, I just want to concentrate on getting Nellie well again and back home.'

Once they were settled into their booth in the dining room and their orders placed Albert chatted with Harry while the girls took in their luxurious surroundings.

'Harry, how are your lodgings, are they comfortable, are there many other occupants staying there?'

'It is very comfortable thank you Albert, the room is well appointed and spotlessly clean. I think there are five rooms in all, not including the owner's quarters. There was only one room available so I was fortunate to secure it, the previous occupant left without word a few days ago, so the landlady said.'

'How about you young ladies, have you settled in?'

'Yes, our room is beautiful,' gushed Marigold

'It's a bit strange with Mummy not being there though,' said Margaret wistfully, 'but it is lovely. I especially love the shop downstairs with all the beautiful gowns mother has made and all the ribbons and laces and pretty things.'

'Your mother told me you like to sew Margaret, would you like to be a dressmaker like her?'

Margaret's eyes sparkled. 'Ooooh yes, it would be wonderful

to be able to sew like Mummy and to work with all those beautiful fabrics she gets from overseas.'

'And what about you Marigold, do you like to sew too?'

Albert chuckled, 'I'm afraid Marigold takes after me, she is an avid reader and a clever little scholar aren't you my dear?' Albert smiled across at his youngest daughter.

Marigold looked down shyly as her cheeks reddened, both with pleasure and embarrassment.

'Yes Daddy I do love my books but I don't yet know what I want to do with my life, not like Margaret does. I would like to visit England one day though.'

'Would you young lady, well maybe that could be arranged,' said a woman coming to stand beside their table.' Harry jumped to his feet.

'Katherine, oh my dear Lord is it really you, when did you arrive? Come, sit down. Albert stood and held out his hands to Katherine. She took them in both of hers and stood on tip toes to kiss him on the cheek.

'Albert, it has been such a long time, too long.' She turned to the two girls rising to their feet. 'My goodness, Margaret, Marigold, how you have grown, I would not have recognised you if you had not been here with your father.' She glanced around the room. 'What are you all doing here? Where is Nellie? I went by her shop today and it was all locked up, so I decided to check in here until I found out what was going on. She wasn't expecting me.'

Harry and Albert exchanged glances, Margaret looked down and fidgeted with her fingers and Marigold continued to gape at this friend of her mother's, whom she could barely remember.

'Katherine, sit down please,' Harry stood back to let her slide into the booth beside the girls. 'When did you last hear from Nellie?'

'I got a letter about three months ago asking if I would like to come and help her in the shop and perhaps start up another branch in Oamaru. Now that dear Benjamin has passed on, I decided there was nothing to keep me in England anymore, so I packed up and boarded the first ship out. Why, what has happened, is she alright?'

'Katherine,' Harry took her hand and turned her to face him. 'Nellie has had a dreadful fall off a hilltop onto some rocks and has not yet regained consciousness. Albert and I have only just caught up with each other today and learned the news together, so we are all still in shock and processing the situation.'

Katherine was stunned, it was the last thing she expected to hear. 'She fell off a cliff? That sounds rather absurd.'

'Yes we agree. It is believed she may have been pushed. It has become a police matter now.'

'Pushed? Deliberately?'

Albert caught Katherine's eye and tilted his head slightly towards the girls.

'Oh, I'm sorry girls, this is not the conversation to be having here right now. Harry, Albert, we will discuss this later, but for now let us all catch up, it has been far too many years since we were last all together as one big happy family. Now Marigold, I heard you say you wanted to go to London, tell me what it is that makes you want to go there, maybe I can answer any questions you might have.'

Thoughts of Nellie were on everyone's minds but were gently shelved while the group reconnected after years of separation. They even managed a few giggles occasionally.

Chapter Twenty-Six

Questions

The smell of burning toast filled Harry's nostrils as he climbed the stairs to the accommodation rooms above Nellie's shop the next morning. Marigold had rushed down the stairs to open the door for him and was racing back up again, leaving Harry to follow on behind.

'Papa is making breakfast, she called over her shoulder, 'but he's just burnt the toast.'

'Yes, I gathered that,' laughed Harry. 'Hope you have plenty of oatmeal, I'm famished.'

When he reached the top of the stairs Harry saw Margaret sitting patiently waiting for her breakfast. Albert was busily flapping a tea towel around the room trying to get rid of the smoke that lingered from the burnt toast and Marigold was pouring boiling water from the kettle into the teapot.

'Please sit down,' Uncle Harry,' she instructed. 'When Papa finally makes us some un-burnt toast, we can all have breakfast.'

Albert turned, smiling a little sheepishly at Harry.

'I'm not normally the one who makes breakfast in my household,' he explained.

'I gathered that much Albert,' Harry laughed heartily, winking at the girls. 'Tell me, does Nellie have any oatmeal in the cupboard, I am a dab hand at making porridge you know.'

'Yes she does,' said Margaret, excited at the prospect of a decent breakfast. She leapt up from the table and opened the large cupboard containing an array of containers filled with dried goods. 'Here it is,' she handed the container to Harry.

'Step aside my good man,' Harry nudged Albert out of the way, 'what we all need is a good solid hearty porridge to see us through whatever this day may bring. Right, Margaret, you can be my assistant, where is the milk and sugar.'

After they had all but licked their plates clean, the girls did the dishes while Harry and Albert talked about their plans for the day.

'What time are we meeting Katherine?' Harry asked.

'She asked that we call on her at the hotel this morning on our way to the Police Station, she would like to come with us.'

'After you and the girls left the hotel last night I sat with Katherine and filled her in on everything we have learned so far,' said Harry. 'I think having Katherine here will be a big help.'

I agree whole-heartedly,' said Albert, 'Nellie might respond to her voice.' He looked up to make sure the girls were out of earshot and leaned in to talk quietly to Harry. 'I have been giving this situation a lot of thought during the night Harry, and I have a bad feeling about the whole thing, something just doesn't feel right. Nellie is as sure footed and careful as anyone I know, I cannot imagine her either throwing herself off a cliff or getting so close as to fall off the edge, it just doesn't make sense. I would like to take a walk up that hill today and have a look for myself, do you want to come with me?'

'Most definitely old chap, most definitely, I am here to help as much as I can. We all love our Nellie and I'm sure we can all work together to get her back on her feet and get to the bottom of this whole thing.'

The Police Sergeant opened the door to his office and ushered Albert, Harry, Katherine and the girls in. He glanced at Margaret and Marigold then asked the woman secretary sitting in the office outside his door, to come in.

Daisy, it might be as well if you took the girls to the kitchen, I'm not sure they need to be here for these discussions.'

Margaret shot him a look of disappointment and stared at her father hoping he would disagree. He didn't, so she had no choice but to get up and follow the secretary out of the room. Marigold was eager to get out of having to sit and listen to adults talking about things she didn't fully understand. As soon as the door closed, the Sergeant turned to face the three adults standing in front of him.

'I am Sergeant Subritzky, everyone here calls me Sarge, I would be obliged if you would do the same.' He shook their hands and asked them to sit in the chairs in front of his large desk which was covered in folders and piles of paper. 'Now then first of all, how is Mrs Abernathy?'

'When we left her last night, she was still unconscious. The arrival of her good friend Mrs Croxley here is certain to bring her round though.' Albert smiled at Katherine.

'Good, that's good. No doubt you will be visiting her during visiting hours this afternoon?

'Yes, as soon as the doors open,' said Harry.

The Sergeant nodded and cleared his throat. 'I have been talking this situation over with my colleagues and we are not completely comfortable with this being an accidental fall. We have spent some time talking with the young man who found Mrs Abernathy, and we have also checked the spot where we thought she may have lost her footing, if that is indeed what has happened.'

'Yes, we thought we might take a walk up there this morning too,' offered Albert.

'I'm afraid you won't get very far Mr Fitzgerald, we have cordoned off the whole area for now, but you are welcome to go up and get as close as the cordon will allow. We will keep you informed of any information that comes to hand.'

'What is it that makes you think Nellie's fall was not accidental?' asked Katherine.

'For one thing, there is no sign of disturbance on the ground at the top of the cliff. There doesn't appear to be any sign of someone slipping or grabbing at grass or loose rocks showing signs of someone falling.'

'So, what does that mean? How could she have fallen without any sign of ground disturbance?' asked Albert.

'In theory, if someone is pushed hard enough, they will fall out away from the edge, which is what I suspect has happened to Mrs Abernathy. Fortunately, she fell far enough out that she didn't land on the main body of rocks directly below the cliff.'

Katherine shuddered. 'What a ghastly thing for someone to do. If Nellie was pushed, do you have any idea of who, or why someone would do such a thing? Has this happened before, is there a lunatic running around here pushing people off cliffs?'

'None that we are aware of Mrs Croxley, but we are not ruling out that possibility. Do you know if Mrs Abernathy had any enemies, business rivals perhaps? I understand she owns a very successful dress shop down on Manchester Lane.'

'Aye, she does,' said Harry, 'but I doubt she would have annoyed or rivalled anyone enough for them to want to see her off.'

'We have only recently reconnected with Nellie,' explained Albert, 'so I cannot honestly say if she has any enemies or not. All I do know is that Nellie is a sweet-natured woman who wouldn't hurt a fly.'

'I totally agree with Albert, Sergeant, Nellie and I have been in business together and I have known her since she was a young girl, we are as close as sisters and I can honestly say with my hand on my heart that if anyone has any angst against our Nellie it won't be of her making.'

The Sergeant sat back in his chair and stretched, putting his hands on his head with a sigh. Well, that looks like that theory can be crossed off the list then. Did she have any gentlemen callers perhaps?' He was reaching for clues.

'I'm sure she would have told me if she did,' offered Katherine. 'We wrote to each other regularly and I know she would have mentioned something like that, we are very close and we share everything with each other.' She looked across at Albert who was leaning forward looking down at the floor between his feet. He was uncomfortable with the question.

Another sigh from the Sergeant. 'That is narrowing things down somewhat but getting us no closer to solving the problem. Now the young man who found her, Sam Handley, said he looked up to the top of the cliff when he first saw Mrs Abernathy and he thought he saw someone there. He left his dog to watch over the woman while he ran for help and when he got to the top of the hill, he saw a woman wearing a blue dress at the bottom of the hill where it leads down to the Esplanade. It is possible this person might be able to help us with our enquiries if we can find her.'

'Was she wearing a hat?' asked Katherine

'Yes, I do believe she was, a large-brimmed hat, so the lad said. She had her back to him and he couldn't say how tall she might have been as she was too far away. He said he could see a bit of dark brown hair below the hat.'

'We will keep a lookout for anyone matching that description,' assured Harry. He shuddered, drawing Katherine's attention.

'What is it Harry, are you alright?'

He smiled sheepishly. 'Just someone walking over my grave' he said.

It was close to lunch time when they finally left the Police Station, Marigold was bored and frustrated at having to wait around for so long with nothing to do.

'Let's go down to the Esplanade and have some lunch at the tea house, then we can walk up the hill before we go to the hospital,' suggested Albert.

They placed their orders and sat in the sun-filled room which looked out across the sparkling water in the harbour.

'Can we go down to the water's edge please Papa?' pleaded Marigold. Albert nodded and the girls ran excitedly out the door, pleased to finally be able to run around freely.

'What do you make of the situation now that we have

talked with the Police Sergeant?' asked Albert of his two companions.

'I don't know what to think?' answered Harry.

'Albert, you don't think it could have been...'

'Felicity? Yes Katherine, that thought has crossed my mind. I hope with all my heart that she wasn't involved, I don't think I could bear the thought of my sister trying to kill my wife. Good grief it sounds like one of those penny-horrible mystery books,' Albert managed a weak smile.

Katherine smiled at him sympathetically. She already knew in her heart that it could well have been Felicity, but she wasn't about to say that out loud, Albert was distraught enough. When the girls came back all pink cheeked, sandy footed and flushed with excitement the conversation lightened and the matter of who caused Nellie's fall was dropped, for now.

Chapter Twenty-Seven

Revelations – November 1866

Katherine, Harry, Albert and the girls took turns sitting with Nellie, holding her hands, and talking with her. On the third day after Katherine had arrived in Dunedin, she was sitting beside Nellie's hospital bed talking to her about London and the new fashions when Nellie began to stir. Katherine raced out into the corridor to call for a nurse. Two nurses and a doctor came running down the hall into the room, the doctor pulling his stethoscope from around his neck to check on Nellie's heart and lungs while a nurse took her pulse. Her eyes flickered open and she stared up at the nursing staff. One of the nurses stood aside and let Katherine step forward.

'Nellie?' Katherine clutched at her dear friend's hand. 'Nellie, it's me, Katherine.'

Nellie stared up at her friend, a tear beginning to trickle from her eye.

'Katherine?' she asked hoarsely. 'Is it really you?'

'Yes, it is really me Nellie,' said Katherine letting the tears run unashamedly down her own cheeks. 'You have come back to us at last. Albert and the girls are here, and Harry, we are all here Nellie, we are here to help you get well again.'

'What happened?' asked Nellie, glancing up at the doctor.

'You've had a nasty fall Mrs Abernathy. You have some cuts and bruises and a couple of broken bones, all of which appear to be mending well. We will give you something to manage the pain, don't hesitate to ask if you need anything. You will need to keep your fluids up so let's get you started on some water.

Mrs Croxley, perhaps you would like to help Mrs Abernathy to take a drink, slowly mind, just a sip at a time.'

Katherine nodded and asked the nurse if she was able to get someone to send word to Albert and Harry to say that Nellie was awake and to come as quickly as they could.

Katherine took the opportunity to reconnect with Nellie before the rest of the family arrived. They hugged and cried and talked non-stop until there was a quiet knock at the door.

Nellie's face lit up when Albert and the girls walked in.

'Nellie, my beautiful Nellie, you've come back to us, thank God.' Albert didn't try to hide his emotions. The girls rushed around the other side of the bed and leaned over to kiss their mother. She smiled at Margaret and then looked long and hard at Marigold.

'Marigold, is that my Marigold,' she reached her hand out towards Marigold who eagerly took it, holding it against her tear-stained cheek.

'Hello mother,' she said sadly. 'I am so excited to see you after all this time, but I am also sad to see you like this. I have really missed you mama.'

'I have missed you girls more than you can ever know,' whispered Nellie. 'We have a lot of catching up to do, haven't we?' she said smiling up at them. They both nodded, smiling back through her tears.

The reunion was extremely emotional and very tiring for Nellie so Katherine and Harry took the girls back to Nellie's place leaving Albert to sit with Nellie for a while.

'The Doctor tells me my wounds and bones are healing nicely,' she said. 'I can't remember what happened but I am sure it will all come back to me in time.'

'There is no need for you to worry about anything other than getting your health back and getting back on your feet so we can take you home and look after you,' Albert assured her.

'Home? Home to my place or home to yours?' Nellie looked confused.

Albert was taken aback. 'Oh, I hadn't really thought about

that. I have been so focused on you waking up that I hadn't given the details any thought. There is no need to make any decisions right now Nellie, let's just concentrate on getting you well first, then you can take your time to think about where you might like to do your convalescing. There are several options open to you, it will be entirely your decision where you go from here. We will love and support you whatever you decide to do.

Nellie took a deep breath and sighed. 'Thank you, Albert, whatever I decide, I would like to think it includes you and the girls. I have never stopped loving you Albert,' she said quietly as she slipped into a slumber.

Over dinner that night, Albert came up with a plan to help Nellie with her recovery until she was well enough to come home.

'What I think we should do is take turns visiting Nellie. The hospital has agreed to let us visit from eleven o'clock in the morning until two in the afternoon so let's share that time amongst all of us, that way we get to spend time alone with her rather than overwhelming her with too many visitors at once. Margaret, Marigold, you can either go together or separately, you decide which days you would like to go and I will let Uncle Harry and Aunt Katherine know so they know what days they can visit. How would that be?'

The girls were thrilled. They needed to reconnect with their mother, the years had separated them unkindly for far too long.

Katherine gave Albert a nod of approval. 'Sounds like a good plan to me.'

Albert smiled back. 'I am so glad you are here Katherine, I hope you are here to stay.'

'I'm pleased I arrived when I did, I just wish it had been sooner, then none of this might have happened.'

'Don't blame yourself,' said Albert quickly, 'you are here now and that is all that matters. Nellie needs you now more than ever.'

'It counts both ways Albert, I am missing Benjamin terribly and being here with Nellie is helping me as well.'

Harry popped in to see how things were going and when Albert told him of his plans for the hospital visits, he replied that now Nellie was awake and in good hands, he planned to return home to Christchurch the following day.

'Of course,' said Albert, 'you have gone above and beyond the bounds of friendship Harry and we are all truly grateful. We must keep in touch when we are all back in Christchurch, it is wonderful that we are reunited again, and it must stay that way,' he smiled warmly at him.

'Agreed,' said Harry leaning down to kiss his sister-in-law on the cheek. 'It is wonderful to have you here Katherine, Agnes is so looking forward to seeing you. We have two babies to show off to you now.'

'Thank you Harry, I can't wait to meet your new family and yes, let's not ever let anything come between us again. I have no intention of going back to England now that Benjamin has gone and who knows what Nellie and I will get up to next,' she grinned mischievously across at Albert, 'at the very least, I know we will be working together again.'

The next two weeks saw Nellie's strength improve. With help, she was able to get out of bed and spend some time sitting in a comfortable chair by the window. It was at this point that Albert made the decision to head back to Christchurch.

'I need to get back to work,' he told Nellie, 'it is getting close to Christmas and they need me. The girls can stay here with Katherine though, school has finished for the year.'

Nellie was disappointed to see Albert go but pleased that she would still have Katherine and the girls visiting every day. Katherine had re-opened the shop and moved into Nellie's room after Albert left. There were no complaints from Margaret and Marigold, they loved their Aunt Katherine, and they loved helping out in the shop. The shop had been closed for several weeks so Victoria and Gladys were thrilled when Katherine called on them to introduce herself and let them know they were welcome to return to work. With Christmas coming, the orders for new gowns started coming in thick and fast as soon as the doors opened. Katherine didn't have to put an advertisement in the local bulletin, word of mouth spread faster than any newspaper. Margaret's skills were put to good use, stitching hems and helping Gladys with basic sewing tasks. Katherine got Marigold to help with measuring and cutting patterns and fabric, utilising her good head for numbers.

Meanwhile, the police continued with their enquiries into Nellie's fall. No further sightings had been made of the woman in the blue dress with the blue wide-brimmed hat and there was little else for the police to base their enquiries on at this stage.

Chapter Twenty-Eight

Felicity - 1867

Harry met up with Albert when he got back to Christchurch and said he had business to attend to in Dunedin and would be heading down that way the following week if there was anything he wanted taken down for Nellie and the girls. Albert gave Harry a few items that were small enough to pack into one of Harry's saddle-bags. 'Tell the girls I will be back before Christmas,' he said, 'and thank you Harry.'

When Harry got to Dunedin he took a room at the lodging house across the road from Nellie's shop. He was thrilled to see the shop open and thriving again. The bell above the door tinkled softly when he opened it, but he doubted it would have been heard above the excited babble of several women standing around discussing fabrics and fashions with Katherine anyway. She looked up and smiled when she spotted her brother-in-law.

'Excuse me a moment ladies, I will be back with you shortly. Go through these designs and let me know which ones suit and which ones you think you might like to make changes to. Harry, lovely to see you again, how are things back home?'

'Everything's going well,' he responded, 'it seems my employees barely missed me while I was away and they appear to do quite well without me. I guess I should be grateful for that as it does give me the freedom to come and go as I please.'

'Yes it does,' said Katherine, 'and it also shows what a good manager you must be to have put the right people in the right positions to carry out the work to your satisfaction.'

'Ah, the wise words of a seasoned businesswoman,' he smiled. He looked around the busy store and the noisy group of ladies, heads and hats bent over the counter in animated conversation. 'So how is business going here?'

'Nellie has a very loyal group of customers who are hell bent on making sure her business stays open and thrives,' laughed Katherine. 'They were thrilled to see the shop open again, I think Nellie will be pleased.'

'I'm sure she will be. How is she?'

'She is doing well, better than we hoped actually.'

'Can I go and see her today do you think?'

'Yes of course. As a matter of fact, it is my turn to visit after lunch today but as you can see, I have my hands full here. Margaret and Marigold visited with her this morning so why don't you take my turn this afternoon, I am sure she would love to see you.'

Nellie was thrilled to see Harry, she had always had a bit of a soft spot for him ever since she first set foot in New Zealand. He had never let her down, not once.

'Hello Harry, it is lovely to see you back so soon, thank you for coming, I know it can't be easy for you to get away from your business and the family.'

'Actually Nellie, I hate to admit it but it is easier than I thought it would be, my staff are coping admirably without me and Agnes and the kids are off visiting with her family up north,' he laughed.

'Good,' she said, 'then I won't feel guilty about you spending time here with me. Have you seen Albert?'

'Yes, I caught up with him just before I left. All is going well with him too, although he is missing you terribly and he's anxious to get back down here to see you. He loves you very much Nellie, you have no idea how much he regrets what has happened.'

Nellie smiled. 'So how are Agnes and the children?'

'Agnes is well, getting rounder by the day. I can't believe this will be our third child, another baby in the house, we are truly blessed. The other two are growing so quickly, I swear they grow an inch every day,' he laughed.

'I am so pleased for you Harry, Benjamin would have been thrilled to see you carrying on the Croxley name.'

'Yes, Katherine told me as much. It's funny you know, even though I didn't see much of my brother in our adult years, I miss him. It was a comfort to know I had family somewhere in the world.'

'And now you have Katherine and Agnes and two and a half children.'

Harry pulled himself out of his reverie and smiled at Nellie.

'How right you are,' he said, 'I should be counting my blessings shouldn't I. Now to more important matters, how are things with you, any progress?'

'Well, if you would like to hand me my dressing gown and turn your back for a moment I will show you,' she smiled gleefully.

Harry did as he was bid.

'You can look now.'

When Harry turned around Nellie was standing by her bed, a little shaky after having been lying down for so long but definitely looking much stronger than the last time he had seen her.

'Well would you look at that,' he laughed. 'That is wonderful Nellie, my goodness you will be out of here in no time.'

Harry offered Nellie his arm and gently helped her hobble around the room before she sank gratefully into the wicker chair by the window. He sat down in a chair beside her and they talked about Albert, the girls, news from Christchurch, how Dunedin was growing so quickly, but he didn't mention her shop, that was Katherine's news to share. Eventually, reluctantly, he left the hospital and made his way back to the boarding house, leaving Nellie sitting in her chair in the sun.

Albert arrived in Dunedin two weeks before Christmas and caught up with Harry and Katherine. He was delighted to see the girls so well and happy and obviously enjoying helping out in their mother's shop. They all gathered in Nellies flat above the shop for dinner on Albert's second night back and once the girls were both in bed, the conversation turned to the Police investigation.

'I stopped in at the Police Station to get an update on my way to visit Nellie today,' said Albert, 'unfortunately, they haven't been able to make much progress. They have put notices up with a description of the woman the young man saw walking down the hill, but so far no one has come forward. I'm afraid we may never know what happened, or who was involved,' Albert said sadly. 'I did say I would like to pay the young man who found Nellie, a sum of money for his troubles. Something to help with his education perhaps, Nellie may not be with us today if it wasn't for him.'

Katherine and Harry both agreed it was a lovely idea.

'What about Felicity, have you seen or heard anything of her?' asked Katherine.

'No, I haven't been able to track her down at all, nobody has seen or heard from her since she left Christchurch. I must admit I am getting a bit worried, I just hope she has been able to set herself up somewhere suitable, she certainly has enough money going into her account to keep her in the manner in which she is accustomed.' Albert hesitated for a moment. 'Her account, I haven't checked on that, although I have been putting money into it on a regular basis. I will call in to the bank when I get home and see if there have been any transactions that might give us a clue as to where she might be. I suppose she could have gone back to Wellington, even though Mum and Dad have gone, it might be familiar territory for her there. I just hope she hasn't been duped by some scoundrel who might take advantage of her if they knew she had money.'

'From what I know of Felicity, my sympathies would lie with the scoundrel,' laughed Harry. Katherine and Albert both laughed too. It was getting late so they bade each other goodnight, Katherine following the men downstairs to lock up behind them.

Albert could only stay for a few days so he spent every moment he could with Nellie during the day and spent the evenings with the girls. He hated leaving them behind when he had to go back to Christchurch, but he could see that they were all well cared for and that Nellie was well on her way to recovery.

The morning after Albert arrived back in Christchurch he went straight down to the bank when it opened at 9 o'clock and requested a meeting with the bank manager.

'As it happens Mr Fitzgerald, Mr Bayliss has had a cancellation this morning, I will check to see if he can see you right away.' The secretary walked briskly across the room to the manager's office, knocked on the door and went in. She came out again and beckoned Albert. He walked into the manager's office, shook hands with the bank manager and sat in the seat indicated to him.

'Mr Fitzgerald, Albert, good to see you again? How may I be of assistance?

'As you know, I have been paying monies into an account for my sister and as I haven't seen or heard anything from her since she left, I am anxious to know if she is still accessing her funds on a regular basis. I feel this would at least put my mind at ease that she is still alive and well.'

'Now, is this account in your name Mr Fitzgerald?'

'Actually, it is in both our names.'

'Very well then,' he said taking a sheet of paper from his drawer and removing the pen from its ink well. What is your sister's name?

'Felicity Fitzgerald.'

'The bank manager began writing and then paused,

replacing the pen in the ink well. 'Felicity Fitzgerald you say?'

'Yes, that's right.'

'Well, that is interesting, it so happens the bank manager in Dunedin, at Miss Fitzgerald's request, asked for all her funds to be transferred to an account at his branch down there.'

'And did you?' asked Albert, a bit bewildered.

'Yes, yes we did.'

'So, she must be living in that area then?' Albert mumbled.

The bank manager rose from his desk and called out through the open door to his secretary.

'Miss Lacey, will you bring me Miss Felicity Fitzgerald's account file please.' He returned to his desk. 'I see this has come as some surprise to you Mr Fitzgerald. I would have thought you would have been notified of the account change.'

'There may well be a letter waiting for me at home but I have not been very attentive to my affairs in recent weeks. My wife had a dreadful accident and all my attention has been focused on her.'

There was a light tap on the door and Miss Lacey brought a brown folder in and placed it on the desk in front of the manager.

'Right then, let's have a look shall we.' He ran his finger down the column of figures showing regular deposits and withdrawals. He stopped and looked up from one of the papers he was reading. There is a note here from the Dunedin bank to advise that after we sent the funds to the bank in Dunedin, Miss Felicity withdrew all the funds and asked for the account to be closed.

'What, all of it?'

'Yes, I'm afraid so, all £500.'

'I don't understand,' exclaimed Albert, 'are there any funds left in the account here?'

The bank manager glanced through the file again and nodded. Yes, it appears every deposit you have made since then is still here,' he said.

Albert sat back in his chair. 'Why on earth would she need

to take all that money out of the bank? What is that damn fool of a woman up to now?' Albert looked up and apologised for his outburst.

'I don't mean to be an alarmist Albert, but has it occurred to you that she might have been forced to withdraw the funds against her will?'

Albert was stunned. 'Against her will? No, I hadn't considered that. Do you really think that could be a possibility?'

The bank manager turned the ledger around so Albert could read it.

'You look through the file, I will get my secretary to send a telegram to Dunedin and see if anyone can remember serving Miss Fitzgerald the day she withdrew the funds.'

He left the room and Albert glanced down at the regular withdrawals, all similar amounts, all drawn on a Thursday, until the last withdrawal. He looked at the date and paled. The letter from the Dunedin bank stated that the £500 lump sum had been drawn out the day before Nellie's accident.

Albert wasted no time in heading back to Dunedin. He wasn't going to wait for a return telegram from the bank manager, he wanted to talk to anyone who might have seen Felicity on that day. He wanted to know why Felicity was in Dunedin the day before Nellie's demise. Did she draw the money out herself, did she seem upset, alarm bells were ringing, he wanted answers.

The Dunedin bank manager ushered Albert in as soon as his assistant mentioned his name.

'Come in Mr Fitzgerald. I understand from the telegram I received from Christchurch that you are worried about your sister, Miss Felicity Fitzgerald?'

'I am, yes,' said Albert. 'Does anyone remember her coming in to make that large withdrawal?'

'Yes, my junior clerk, Mr Jefferson, might be able to help us there.'

He left the office and came back with a young man in his mid-twenties.

'Sit down Mr Jefferson if you please, this is Mr Fitzgerald. Now, will you please tell him what you can remember of the interaction you had with Miss Fitzgerald on the day she withdrew £500.'

The teller looked decidedly uncomfortable. Albert assured him he was not in any trouble so the man began to speak.

'It was around 3 o'clock, I remember the time because I was waiting for my tea break,' he said glancing at his boss. 'This lady, Miss Fitzgerald came in, I remember her because of the,' he pointed to the side of his face.'

'The scars, yes, please continue Mr Jefferson,' urged Albert. 'Did she seem distressed in any way?'

'Oh no, quite the contrary sir, she seemed really happy, she was smiling the whole time.'

'Were you not concerned about her taking all the money out of her account at once?' asked the bank manager.

The teller hung his head. 'Sorry sir, I know we are supposed to report large withdrawals to you but she asked me not to. She said she was buying a business and wanted to keep it quiet until the sale was complete.'

The bank manager sighed. 'Very well Mr Jefferson, is there anything else you can tell us?'

'No Sir.'

'You may go back to work. Oh, by the way, have you seen Miss Fitzgerald since that day?'

'No sir I haven't.'

'Well, there you have it Mr Fitzgerald, your sister seems to have purchased herself a business hereabouts.'

'Maybe you're right,' said Albert, 'but I can't for the life of me imagine what sort of business my sister would be interested in, it just doesn't make any sense.'

Later that evening when Albert relayed his findings to Katherine and Harry, they agreed it was not what they would have expected to hear but if she seemed happy and excited then who were they to question her decision.

'No doubt I will hear from her when she needs more funds,' grumbled Albert.

Chapter Twenty Nine

Going home

The family gathered in Nellie's upstairs rooms eagerly awaiting her arrival home. She had been in hospital for six weeks, but finally the doctors deemed her strong enough to leave the convalescent ward she had been recovering in. They decided that it would be best if Albert picked Nellie up from the hospital on his own while the rest of them waited for her at home.

Margaret let out a squeal of delight as she leaned halfway out the window.

'They're here, they're here.'

'Hush now girls, remember your mother is still not fully recovered yet, we must be careful not to overwhelm her or tire her out with loud noise and incessant chatter,' scolded Katherine.

'Sorry Aunt Katherine,' they chorused.

Katherine drew both girls into a hug. 'Don't worry, we will soon settle into a comfortable routine and I know you will help your mother as much as you can won't you.'

They both nodded, 'yes.'

They could hear giggling downstairs as Albert and Nellie were deciding how best to get Nellie up the stairs. Eventually Albert simply picked Nellie up and carried her. She was laughing as he deposited her safely in one of the comfortable chairs by the window. She smiled broadly as she looked around the bright cheerful room and its happy inhabitants, Margaret, Marigold, Katherine and Harry.

'Oh what a lovely homecoming,' she said softly, tears

welling in her eyes. 'You have no idea how good it is to be out of that hospital. As wonderful and caring as they were, there is simply no place like home. Now that I am home at last, perhaps we can have Christmas all over again,' she giggled. 'It wasn't much fun having to spend it in hospital.'

'Agreed,' they all cried in unison. 'We could combine your homecoming and a second Christmas celebration into one,' suggested Katherine.

On the table beneath the window, bathed in warm golden sunlight was the most beautiful vase of sunflowers Nellie had ever seen.

'These are beautiful,' she turned and looked at Katherine.

'Don't look at me, the girls are responsible for those.'

'We were walking past the flower stall and saw them and we both said at the same time, wouldn't mother love those,' the girls giggled.

'And you are so right, thank you girls and thank you for all your lovely visits, it has meant so much to me, getting to know you both again.'

The girls ran to their mother's side and put their arms around her, all three allowing their tears to flow unchecked.

'Come on now, this is a day for celebration, let's eat, lunch is ready,' said Katherine.

Albert and Harry decided to go down to the men's club after lunch for a drink and leave the girls to catch up. While Katherine cleared the table and started on the dishes, Margaret and Marigold sat and talked with their mother. As the subject rolled around to what they might like to do when they left school, Margaret got up and went into the bedroom, returning with a hard covered notebook.

'What have you got there Margaret?'

'I have been sketching some dress designs, just like you and Aunt Katherine do.'

'Really?' Nellie was intrigued, 'let me see. Margaret, these are wonderful, have you seen these Katherine?'

Katherine stood behind Nellie, looking over her shoulder.

'What a clever little thing you are,' smiled Katherine, I had no idea you had such a talent.'

'Neither did I,' remarked Nellie as she flipped through the pages. Margaret these are really good, and I am not just saying that because I am your mother. I think we should look at making up some of these designs for our young lady customers, what do you think Katherine?'

'What a wonderful idea, yes of course we must. We could start a whole new line for young misses,' she beamed at Margaret.

Margaret smiled shyly back at both of them. 'Do you really think they are that good?' she asked.

'Yes of course we do, we wouldn't say so if it weren't true.'

Marigold, feeling a little left out said, 'What about me, what am I good at?'

'Marigold, my darling, you have your father's head for figures and accounting, perhaps you could help with the bookkeeping and accounts, that way we can all work together as a team.'

'I suppose now is as good a time as any to tell you about the surprise I brought with me from London,' said Katherine. 'I have been waiting for the right moment, and I think that moment might be now.'

'Is it more fabrics and patterns? I would love to see what's new in the fashion world,' Nellie asked excitedly.

'Well, yes, there is quite a bit of fabric, and some laces, ribbons, buttons and decorative trims. But the best part is, I have brought a sewing machine.'

'A sewing machine?' chorused the girls. 'What does it look like?'

'Well, once the men get back, I will get them to help me unpack it from the crate downstairs, it's in the back room.

The women were in high spirits by the time the men returned.

'What on earth is all this racket about?' asked Albert, 'we could hear you from down on the street.'

'We have formed a new company called 'Young Misses', beamed Nellie proudly 'thanks to Margaret and her dress designs and Marigold and her bookkeeping prowess.'

'What about your schoolwork, will it not interfere with that? You know how I feel about your education girls,' Albert said sternly.

'Don't worry Albert,' soothed Nellie, we can work on this at the weekends and during the school holidays. Katherine and I can run it in between times and once the girls leave school they can carry on and make a career out of it if they want to.'

'You have it all worked out it seems,' Albert said, softening.

Nellie smiled at him. 'Yes, we have.' There was nothing more to be said on the matter. 'Now if you don't mind, Katherine has a task for you men.'

'Oh no,' groaned Harry, 'not a dreaded task, I don't like the sound of this Albert,' he chuckled as they followed Katherine down the stairs.

They opened the large box and gently manoeuvred the solid black treadle machine out of its wrappings. As they went to lift it Albert winced.

'This jolly thing weighs a ton,' he remarked, 'what on earth is it anyway?'

'It's a sewing machine Albert, it will revolutionise the business. Sewing seams will take a fraction of the time it takes for a seamstress to hand stitch them.'

'Is that right?' he said inspecting the complicated looking contraption. 'That's marvellous, what a wonderful invention. I deal with machinery and new inventions all the time but I have never seen anything like this.'

'Neither have I,' marvelled Harry, 'very impressive indeed.'

Nellie was standing at the top of the stairs listening to the conversation below.

'Can someone please come and help me down so I can see it too,' she pleaded.

As Albert set her down beside the machine, Nellie's eyes flew open in astonishment.

'Katherine, this is marvellous, how clever and generous of you to do this, thank you.' She hugged her friend and whispered, 'we have so much to look forward to, haven't we.'

'Yes,' confirmed Katherine, 'we certainly have.'

Katherine moved into the lodging house across the road from the shop so that Nellie could have her own room back. The girls were firmly ensconced in their shared bedroom and although they squabbled from time to time, by and large everyone was settled and happy. Nellie ventured downstairs from time to time to sit out the back of the shop and talk with Gladys, Katherine and Victoria. She had taught herself how to use the new sewing machine, with the help of the detailed instruction manual that came with it, and now she was teaching Margaret how to use it. The machine had certainly speeded up the stitching of seams and hems, leaving Gladys and Katherine to do the more detailed hand stitching and finishing touches. Their customers were amazed to see how precise and uniform the stitching on their gowns was, and the speed with which their orders were being filled, it was a marvel. Nellie got Margaret working on men's shirts before starting on her own line of 'junior ladies' dresses.

'When you have mastered the machine and you can turn out a faultless shirt, then we will start your new line, my darling,' Nellie had explained encouragingly to Margaret. 'I know Aunt Katherine has taught you and Marigold how to cut patterns, this is the next phase of your apprenticeship. I learnt to sew at the orphanage mending children's clothing long before Aunt Katherine would let me start cutting patterns and making new clothes, and I am pleased she did. One must learn the basics first.

As January drew to a close, the discussion needed to be had about what would happen after the holidays when the girls had to go back to school. Did they all move to Dunedin or should they move back to Christchurch? The girls had been asking Nellie if they could stay but she didn't want to make any decisions without talking to Albert first. Until now, they had discussed nothing further than working towards her full recovery. When he came down the following week, Nellie said she would like to talk with him, alone.

Katherine called out to the girls to put on their hats and then took them off for a walk down by the water.

Nellie sat awkwardly across the table from Albert, fidgeting with her handkerchief.

'Albert, where do we go from here?' she asked nervously, 'we haven't really spoken about it.'

'I haven't wanted to push you Nellie, I wanted to make sure you got back to good health before I made any suggestions. Now it seems the time has come for us to look towards the future.' He got down on one knee beside Nellie's chair, took both her hands in his and looked imploringly into her eyes.'

Nellie Abernathy Fitzgerald, would you do me the great honour of becoming my wife, again, and moving back to Christchurch with me. Your shop is still there, we could.....'

'Yes,' whispered Nellie softly, 'yes Albert, yes, yes, yes. She stood and brought Albert up to stand before her as she put her arms around his neck and kissed him squarely on the lips.'

Albert laughed and picking her up, twirled her around the room. He put her down and drew back so he could look into her eyes. 'Are you really sure about this Nellie?'

'There is not a doubt in my mind Albert.'

Albert leaned down and kissed her slowly, deliberately, longingly. 'God I have missed you Nellie, so many endless nights I have lain awake longing for you,' his voice was husky.

On impulse, Nellie led him towards her bedroom.

Albert was a little surprised, excited, but surprised at what Nellie was offering.

'Are you sure?' he asked. 'I mean, we aren't married yet,' he was grinning from ear to ear.

'I cannot wait another minute my darling, let's make the most of this time alone and renew our love in the way only you and I know how.'

Albert and Nellie were glowing and smiling from ear to ear when Katherine and the girls returned from their walk. Katherine was thrilled, she had her suspicions about what they might have been up to and it warmed her heart. Unsurprisingly, the girls were beyond excited to hear that their parents were going to be married again, and that their mother would be moving back home to live with them in Christchurch.

A 'renewal of vows' ceremony was held in the same gardens that Nellie and Albert had been married in all those years ago. The girls took on the roles of bridesmaids while Katherine, once again, was matron of honour. The girls, having designed and made their own gowns, were an absolute picture but nobody could have outshone the bride on her special day, and the smile on Albert's face could have lit up a Christmas tree. Harry, and a very pregnant Agnes were also in attendance, Agnes having not been around for the first nuptials. Their children were running amok in the gardens but Harry soon brought them under control and sat with them to keep them quiet until the ceremony was over. There wasn't a dry eye in the house, even the Minister was misty eyed. He was the one who had officiated at their first nuptials. The reception, back at the same hotel as the first wedding reception, was a wonderful blend of good food, fine wine and lots of laughter.

Nellie, Albert and the girls quickly settled into their renewed family life, almost as if they had never been apart, only this time there was more love, more laughter and no Felicity.

In the end Katherine opted to stay on in Dunedin to keep Nellie's shop going for the time being. She liked Dunedin, she enjoyed working in the shop, and she also wanted to give Nellie and Albert some time alone together. She had moved into the flat above the shop and was loving it, especially the quiet times in the evenings when she could read or just sit and stare out the window at the busy little street below and think of Benjamin. She and Nellie had agreed to give it a year, to see if Katherine wanted to stay on in Dunedin and run the shop there, or whether she would rather move up to Christchurch and go back to working with Nellie in the shop they had initially opened together. Felicity's old room had been completely redecorated and it was there waiting for Katherine.

Chapter Thirty

Asylum – Summer 1867

Albert set down his pipe and newspaper, rose from his chair by the fire, and went to answer the front door. He swung it open and stared at the man standing on his doorstep.

'Yes, can I help you?' he asked.

'Mr Fitzgerald, Mr Albert Fitzgerald?'

'Yes, that's me, and who might you be sir?'

'Mr Fitzgerald, do you by any chance have a sister named Felicity.

'I do, yes,' answered Albert.

'In that case, I come bearing news about your sister Mr Fitzgerald, may I come in?'

Albert was stunned for a moment. Felicity? He hadn't seen or heard from her since he found out she had withdrawn all the money from her account almost a year ago.

'My name is Tom Scofield, Mr Fitzgerald. I am the Superintendent of the general hospital here in Christchurch.'

'Hospital?' Albert said with alarm.

'Yes, we have a young woman recently come to our facility who had a note in her pocket saying she was Felicity Fitzgerald. We haven't been able to get anything out of her I'm afraid, she is in a bit of a state.'

'What sort of state is she in?'

'To put it bluntly Mr Fitzgerald, she is in a secure wing of the mental ward.'

'Mental ward? Good grief. How did she get there?' 'Someone has obviously brought her in?'

'We don't know any more than that, we were hoping you might be able to shine some light on the situation.'

'No, I haven't seen or heard from her in quite some time. She caused me a great deal of grief and I sent her packing and haven't seen or heard from her since.' Albert hung his head in despair. 'Lord forgive me if I have had anything to do with her demise,' he muttered.

'One of the nurses said she saw a man walking away from the hospital grounds shortly after Felicity was found on the doorstep. We wondered if it might have been a member of her family, perhaps a bit too embarrassed to be seen at the asylum.'

'No, no it certainly wasn't me and I am her only family,' said Albert a little bewildered. 'Is she going to be alright, can we go and see her?'

'To the second question, yes of course you may visit during visiting hours, any day except Sunday. As to the first question, we have assessed her mental wellbeing and have come to the conclusion that she is best kept in the mental ward for the time being as she does not seem to be in full control of her faculties. She does not speak, she eats very little, and she shies away from being touched. Although she does not eat much, her health is not our main concern right now. She will not allow us to physically examine her so we are not sure if she has any illness or has suffered any accident or trauma to the body, anything that might help us to determine what may have caused her mental instability. During her struggles we noticed a wound on her lower leg, it looked like a dog bite. It doesn't appear to be infected so we are ruling out rabies at this juncture.' The Superintendent stood to leave. 'I am sorry to bring this to bear on you Mr Fitzgerald, if you care to come to my office on Monday morning, perhaps we could discuss your sister's ongoing care.'

'Yes, yes of course, I will be there at nine o'clock if that suits.'

The Superintendent nodded and Albert escorted him to the door. 'Thank you for taking the trouble to find me Mr Scofield, I do appreciate it.'

On Monday morning Albert was shown into Felicity's room. He was shocked to see the state she was in, pale faced, hair all wild and unkempt and seemingly lifeless.

'Felicity,' he called softly. 'Felicity, it's me, Albert.'

Felicity turned her head to look at her brother. Her eyes widened as recognition dawned. She slowly sat up on the bed and focused on Albert.

'Albert? Is that really you?' she croaked, 'you have come, at last you have come to take me home, oh Albert I knew you would, I knew you would find me. I have missed you so, you must miss having me to look after you since....'

Her voice trailed off when she heard the voices of two women talking in the corridor outside her room.

'Thank you Sister,' said one of the women, then Nellie appeared in the doorway and stood beside Albert.

'Hello Felicity,' Nellie said gently.

Felicity's mouth dropped open, her eyes widened and she let out a blood curdling scream as she leapt off the bed reaching for Nellie. Nellie was shocked and stepped back behind Albert. Felicity reached around and grabbed a handful of Nellie's hair, yanking it hard and pulling her down to the ground. Nellie was also screaming by now, in pain. Felicity stood over her and slapped her hard across the face before Albert grabbed her around the waist and threw her on the bed. Felicity turned and glared at Nellie as she kneeled on the floor with tears streaming down her cheeks and a look of horror and disbelief on her face.

Felicity was screaming at Nellie. 'You should be dead, why are you not dead?' I... I...'

'You what Felicity? Why do you think Nellie should be dead?' Albert's head was spinning.

'Because I pushed her off the cliff,' she spat, glaring at Nellie with such hatred it made Albert shudder. 'You should be dead, Albert belongs to me, you ruined everything, you should never have come back.'

Her screaming and vile outburst increased in volume

bringing two male orderlies and a nurse running into the room. They roughly grabbed Felicity and pinned her to the bed as the nurse inserted a needle into Felicity's arm slowly rendering her unconscious.

Nellie burst into tears. 'I was ever hopeful that it wasn't her. Oh Albert I am so sorry, I always prayed it wasn't her.'

Albert was trembling with shock, he felt sick. He gently pulled Nellie to her feet and held her tight as he led her back out into the corridor.

'Deep down I always feared that it might have been her,' he said, 'but I was reluctant to think that a sister of mine, someone I once cared deeply about, would ever do something so despicable. It beggars' belief, it really does, and she doesn't appear to be in the least bit remorseful, that's the part that bothers me most. There is no way on earth I will ever allow her to roam free again.'

Nellie was shocked, but not surprised, at the depth of Albert's hurt and anger. He had devoted his whole life from a very young age, to looking after his sister, especially after she got burned. Now, after all the terrible hurt and misery she had caused in the past, she had betrayed him once again by trying to murder his wife. It was bad enough that Felicity had orchestrated the demise of their marriage and had denied him and his two beautiful girls five years of growing up with their mother. They would have been very happy and fulfilling years, he knew that, just as the previous years had been.

'Come on,' he said gruffly, 'let's get out of here.' He stopped in to see the Superintendent on his way out.

'I will pay for my sister's keep,' he said without preamble. 'She will never be welcome in my home again so I am happy to leave her future care in your hands, I accept that it may well be long term. If you do think at some future point in time that she is fit enough to leave this facility I would be obliged if you would inform me as I will need to discuss her future with the legal authorities, since she has just admitted to trying to murder my wife.'

The Superintendent was shocked at the revelation and

concerned to see the state Nellie was in and the abject despair written on Albert's face. 'Would you both like to take a seat for a moment, I could get someone to bring you some water, a cup of tea perhaps?'

'No thank you, I just want to get out of here, I need to get Nellie home.'

Nellie was shaking uncontrollably by the time they arrived home. Albert's shock had given way to rage. He was desperately trying not to let Nellie see how angry he was, she was in an awful state, he needed to take care of her. He sat her down in her armchair, and went to make a cup of tea.

'What are we going to tell the girls Albert, they will need to know. Word will eventually get out about Felicity being in the asylum, the gossip is bound to catch up with them at some stage.'

'Yes, we will discuss it with them as soon as they get home, I guess they are old enough now to make up their own minds about how to deal with the situation.'

Nellie wrote to Katherine straight away to tell her about Felicity and what had happened at the hospital. That night she and Albert sat down with the girls and told them about their Aunt Felicity, where she was and what she had done.

'We never really liked Aunt Felicity, did we Margaret,' admitted Marigold petulantly. 'If she is the one who tried to kill you mama, then I hope I never see her again, I hate her.' She burst into tears and ran upstairs.

'I'll go and talk to her,' said Margaret, seemingly wise beyond her years. 'and no, we didn't like Aunt Felicity all that much, I agree with Marigold, I hope I never see her again either.'

Chapter Thirty-One

Bank notes and Letters

On hearing the rattle of the mail slot in the front door, Nellie went into the hallway and picked the letters up off the floor, there was one from the Asylum. She took it back to the kitchen where she was preparing a pot of tea before heading out to join the girls in the shop. She usually started around 10 o'clock and would take fresh baked goods for their morning tea. She sat down at the table and slit the letter open.

'*Dear Mr Fitzgerald,*' it started, '*I write to update you first and foremost on the condition of your sister, Miss Felicity Fitzgerald. Unfortunately, we have not made a lot of progress with her, she seems to be in a deep state of melancholy and will not interact or speak to any of the staff or other patients in the asylum. If anyone other than staff get too close to her, she is apt to erupt into hysterics requiring her to be put under sedation.*

There is, however, one bit of news which I think you might find interesting. Miss Fitzgerald had a visitor yesterday, a male visitor. He wouldn't leave his name and Miss Fitzgerald did not appear to recognise him or interact with him in any way. I just thought it worth mentioning. If he calls again, may I pass on your address in case he may wish to visit and talk with you. Perhaps he might be able to shed some light on what has happened with Miss Fitzgerald.

Please feel free to call on me at my office any day of the week between the hours of 10am and 3pm. I await your further instructions.

Yours sincerely,

Tom Scofield
Superintendent
Christchurch Hospital

Nellie gulped down the last of her tea, donned her hat and coat and walked briskly down to see Albert at his office.

'I wonder who her mystery visitor might have been?' Nellie queried as Albert read the letter. 'You don't suppose Harry might have gone to see her do you?'

'Harry? No, I doubt he'd want to visit her after what she did to you.'

Albert looked up as his office door flew open.

'Oh, good, I'm pleased you are both here,' said Margaret looking decidedly flustered. 'I went out the back door of the shop to throw out the dregs from the teapot and almost tripped over a suitcase and a carpet bag on the back step. Will you come and have a look, I don't know whether they belong to us or whether they have been left there by mistake. There doesn't seem to be any notes or names attached.'

Nellie and Albert hurried back up the street with Margaret. When they saw the suitcase and carpet bag, Albert gasped.

'I recognise those,' he said, 'they are Felicity's.' Albert picked up the carpet bag, placed it on the table and opened it. He pulled out item after item, some bits of clothing he recognised, others he didn't. It was the same with the suitcase.

'Some of these garments are rather plain, I would not have thought Felicity would choose to wear anything like this.'

'They are rather cheaply made and not of good quality,' said Nellie examining the garments closely.

'I wonder who could have left them here, I wonder if it was the same man who left Felicity at the hospital?' Albert addressed his query to Nellie.

Nellie picked up another one of Felicity's dresses, shook it out and laid it on top of the cases.

'I remember seeing her wearing this one,' she said. 'She had it with her when we went to England all those years ago, it was one of her favourites.' She checked the seams of the gown out of habit then stopped and let out a small gasp.

'What is it Nellie?' asked Albert, coming to stand beside her.

'Look,' she said, 'there's something sewn into the seam, and here, and here too. Hand me the sharp pointed scissors will you Margaret.'

Margaret quickly returned with the scissors and gave them to Nellie who went to work undoing one of the seams. There in the fold was a tightly rolled bank note. She quickly checked the rest of the gown and when she was sure she had found every one of the secured notes she unrolled them and put them on the table. Marigold took a warm iron from the stove and gently ironed them all flat between two pieces of fabric.

'Good heavens,' said Albert, 'there's over £100 here, why on earth would she feel the need to secrete money into her clothing like that, what on earth has the woman been up to? And who has left the bags here I wonder?'

Nellie and the girls rifled through the rest of the clothes in the bags and searched all the dresses, uncovering a further £100. Albert gathered up the notes and took them straight down to the bank.

'Don't do anything until I get back,' he instructed.

Margaret put the kettle on the stove to make a cup of tea and sat down with Nellie at the table. The doorbell tinkled and Marigold jumped to her feet.

'I'll go,' she said. Margaret and Nellie heard her let out a shriek and hurried out to see what was happening. 'It's Aunt Katherine,' she squealed, hugging her beloved aunt.

Katherine sat down with Nellie and the girls and caught up on the news. When the girls went out to the shop front to deal with customers, Nellie took Katherine back to the house.

'It's so good to see you Nellie, I have really missed you, that's why I am here. I have decided I would like to come 'home', that's if you will all have me,' she smiled.

Nellie was beside herself. 'Do you even need to ask,' she laughed, hugging her dearest friend. 'Everyone will be thrilled to have you home with us.'

Katherine opened her purse and brought out the letter Nellie had sent her. 'I think we need to talk about this. What on earth has happened?'

'There's a lot more than what I put in the letter,' admitted Nellie.

'It sounds like you had better tell me the story from the start then,' said Katherine.

Nellie filled Katherine in on how they'd had a visit from the hospital Superintendent and what happened when they went to see Felicity.

Katherine was horrified. 'I just knew in my bones that it had to have been Felicity. Like you, I was hoping it wasn't her, that she didn't have it in her to do something so cruel and nasty, but you say she admitted it?'

'You should have seen her Katherine. The hatred and malice pouring out of her made my blood run cold; I couldn't believe it, I never dreamed she hated me so much.'

Katherine leaned over and took Nellie's hand when she saw her eyes fill with tears.

'I suspect she is not of sound mind, to be able to do something that evil. You said she is in the hospital, is she in the asylum part?'

'Yes, they have her locked up thank goodness. If she was allowed to roam free, I would certainly live in fear for my life after what I witnessed. We don't know where she has been since Albert sent her away, there was just a note in her pocket with her name on it when they found her. Then we received a letter from the Superintendent this morning to say that she'd had a visitor, a man, and now her belongings turn up on the doorstep of the shop. It's all very strange don't you think?

Albert turned up at that point so Nellie went to make a fresh pot of tea leaving Katherine and Albert to catch up with each other's news.

'You've been gone a while,' Nellie said to Albert when she came back into the room

'I've had an interesting discussion with the bank manager,' he replied. 'As you may have noticed, the bank notes we found in Felicity's clothing were numbered and in sequence. By coincidence, when I took my shop banking in yesterday, there were two bank notes from the same number sequence. A stolen note was used to pay for goods from the store a couple of years ago and since then I have recorded the numbers and denominations of all the bank notes that come through,' he explained. 'It appears someone came into the store yesterday and purchased items, paying with the same notes that Felicity withdrew from the bank a year ago.'

'Do you know who it might have been? Did you have many customers in yesterday?' asked Katherine.

Albert smiled ruefully. 'Yes, it was a very busy day as we had a sale on stock feed. I will head off to the store shortly and have a talk with the staff, see if we can't shed some light on it. If we can find the person who handed over the bank notes, then we might find the same person who took Felicity to the hospital. Whoever it was, it might be the same person who dropped her belongings off to the dress shop as well. I am curious to know what she has been up to and I hope to heaven she hasn't done anything further to cause us or anyone else more pain and embarrassment.'

Albert finished the last of his cup of tea and left the house, deep in thought.

'When Albert gets a notion about something, he doesn't stop until he has it all figured out,' smiled Nellie 'best we just leave him to it. Now, on to more important things, where do you and I go from here? Should we leave the shop open in Dunedin and put a manageress in to run it do you think?'

'Let's leave all that for now Nellie, I think we have enough excitement going on, we can talk about our plans tomorrow. I'd like to go and see what you have done with the new haberdashery.'

Albert checked to see that there were no customers waiting

at the counter before asking his two shop assistants to step into his office with their docket books. The office had windows facing out to the store so they would be able to see if anyone came in.

'Now then gentlemen,' he began, 'I am looking to track down a customer who came into the store yesterday. I need you to cast your eye over your docket books and see if you can recall someone coming in and paying for their goods with a £10 bank note.'

He gave the men a moment or two to flick through their dockets.

'It would have to be yesterday,' sighed young Simon, 'it was a very busy day as you well know Mr Fitzgerald.'

'Yes, I do know Simon, and I...'

'Here,' jumped in Leslie, 'this one, it could be this man, Mr J. Millward. Most of my customers yesterday either charged their goods to their accounts or paid with coins but this one paid with a bank note. I remember because I gave him £5 in change.'

'Excellent. Does he give an address?'

'No,' Leslie shook his head. 'I did ask but he said he came from Dunedin and was just visiting.'

'Do you by chance, remember what he looked like?' asked Albert hopefully.

'Yes I do. I had been looking out for him to come back and pick up his goods so I saw him twice. He would be about five feet nine inches tall, about my height. He had brown curly hair, not sure what colour his eyes were, I wasn't looking,' he chuckled. 'Now if it had been a young lady.'

'Just get on with it Leslie, was he thickset or thin?' demanded Albert impatiently.

'He was thin built and he looked like any other farmer who comes in here, light brown trousers, grey shirt and a sweat stained stockman's hat.'

'How old would you say he was?'

'At a guess I would say around thirty something.'

'Thank you Leslie, you have been most helpful. Now, I have several things to do today but I will check in before closing.'

Albert headed straight back to see Nellie and Katherine at the shop, they were busy stocking shelves. He told them what he had learned from his staff.

'I am taking this information to the Police Station,' he informed them, 'it is high time we sorted this mess out. There seems to be a lot we don't know about my sister, and I want to find out what it is. Furthermore, I believe that somewhere, we will find that damned blue dress Felicity was wearing the day she... the day she...' he choked up.

Nellie reached out and took his hand. 'It's alright Albert, it was a while ago and I am recovered now.'

'It is not that long ago in my mind Nellie and I will never forgive her. You will never be physically one hundred percent again and it was she who tore us apart for all those precious years we could have had together, you and our darling girls, it is quite unforgiveable.' He squeezed her hand and took a deep breath. 'I have decided to take the coach down to Dunedin and visit with Sergeant Subritzky. I need to inform him of Felicity's confession and tell him about these new developments.'

'Why don't you just go to the police here and get them to pass it on?' asked Nellie.

'No, I feel I need to be down in Dunedin, where it all happened. There are still some pieces missing from the puzzle and I might be able to help the police further if I am down there.'

'Ah Mr Fitzgerald, Albert, it has been a while since we last spoke. How is your lovely wife?' asked Sergeant Subritzky as Albert walked into his office.

'She will always walk with a slight limp and she tires easily but other than that I am pleased to say she is doing well.'

'Glad to hear it, take a seat.'

Albert filled the Sergeant in on what had been happening, beginning with the hospital Superintendent's visit.

'Well, it seems we do have quite a mystery on our hands,' mused Subritzky. 'You say your sister has confessed to being the one who pushed your wife off the cliff?'

'Yes, I am sorry to say that is true. I was planning on coming to you with this information only if Felicity was ever deemed fit enough to leave the infirmary, but now, in light of what has been happening, I have decided we need to bring everything out in the open.'

'Indeed we do, Albert, indeed we do. I will pass this description of Mr Millward on to my constables and see if they can find out if he is known hereabouts, perhaps we can track his movements. Thank you for coming all this way to bring this to me Albert, it is a case which has bothered me somewhat, I would dearly like to rule a line under it and put it to rest. Now that we have talked this through, I would be obliged if you would inform the Sergeant in Christchurch of any further developments. Nelson is his name, Geoffrey Nelson, nice fellow. I will get in touch with him myself to familiarise him with the case and between us we will keep you abreast of anything that comes to light. We will check the hotels and lodging houses in the area and see if anyone knows of this Mr Millward. Perhaps we should also enquire further about any earlier sightings of Miss Fitzgerald while we are at it, maybe we missed something first time around. I will be in touch as soon as we find anything out. Oh, and Albert,' Albert was standing ready to leave, 'thank you again for bringing this to me, I know it can't have been easy for you.'

Albert nodded and left. He turned right outside the gaol and walked back down to the lodging house across the road from Nellie's dress shop. Albert was pleased to hear that Katherine wanted to come back to Christchurch, he knew Nellie missed her, and so did the girls.

The landlady at the lodging house asked Albert if he would like to join herself and two other lodgers for dinner that evening. As Albert had nothing else planned, he accepted. The dining room was beautifully set out with crystal glasses glistening under the chandelier hanging low over the table. The silverware also sparkled as it lay set out perfectly beside the white dinner plates sitting empty waiting for dinner to be served. During the course of the evening's conversation, the landlady, Morag Moore, asked Albert what had brought him back to Dunedin. She remembered he had stayed at her boarding house some time ago. He explained about Nellie owning the shop across the road, to which Morag replied, 'Nellie, oh yes, I remember her well, lovely lady she is. Wasn't it her who fell off the cliff, what was it, a year or so ago?'

'Yes, that was her,' answered Albert. 'And before you ask, she is well and happy and has another shop in Christchurch.' He didn't wish to divulge any more personal information.

'It was a strange time back then,' said Morag, very strange indeed. I remember I had a young woman staying here at the time, Mrs Fletcher I think her name was. She stayed in one of the upstairs rooms for a while, then all of a sudden she up and left without a word. Even left some of her belongings behind.'

Albert was thoughtful for a moment. 'She didn't happen to have a scar on the side of her face did she, this Mrs Fetcher?'

'Why yes she did, as I recall, a nasty looking scar it was too, poor lass.'

Albert almost choked on his dinner. He said nothing more until the other two guests had left the table and retired to their rooms. He turned to Morag.

'Morag, that the woman you spoke of earlier, Mrs Fletcher, I think it might have been my sister Felicity, she disappeared around that time, we are very concerned for her,' he lied, 'do you still have the belongings she left behind? They may offer us a clue as to her whereabouts.'

'I do, Mr Fitzgerald, yes, I put them up in the attic thinking that she might come back for them some day. I had forgotten all about them until this evening, shall I go and get them for you?'

'Yes please. May I come and help you?'

'Yes that would be helpful, the cases are quite heavy if I remember rightly.'

Together they hauled the trunk, a suitcase and two hat boxes from the attic and set them down in the lounge. Albert wasted no time in opening them up and there, right on the top of the trunk, was the blue dress Felicity had been wearing the day she pushed Nellie off the cliff. He sat down on the nearest chair with the dress crumpled in his lap. He would take it down to the Police Station in the morning so the young lad who had seen the woman in the blue dress and hat could identify it if he was able. Also, among Felicity's things, he found her pocketbook with details of a storage facility in Christchurch where he was sure he would find more of her belongings.

Albert helped the coachman load Felicity's trunk and suitcase on to the luggage rack on the roof of the coach, hopped inside, and sat back ready to face the long ride home. The Police Sergeant had been surprised to see the dress and hat Albert dropped off to him. He said he would get the young lad to come in and see if he could remember if this was the dress he saw the woman wearing that day and if it was, then they had a confession, evidence and an eyewitness to present before the judge, Felicity's fate was sealed. What would her sentence be, Albert pondered sadly?

Albert left Felicity's trunk and case at the coach depot and walked down to the hospital to fill the Superintendent in on what had been happening since they last spoke.

'Call me Tom, and if I may, can I call you Albert. I feel we are familiar enough with each other now to be on a first name basis,' said Tom offering his hand.

Albert shook the outstretched hand and agreed.

'Tom, there has been another development which I have every reason to believe will lead us to the identity of the man who brought Felicity in that night. This is his description. We believe his name is Millward, that's if we have the right man of course, I am only going by the observations of one of my staff. If he turns up again to visit Felicity, would you please ask if he is in fact the man we are looking for? I would very much like to talk with him about Felicity. I don't hold anything against the man, I have seen Felicity at her worst and she has not always been an easy person to get along with. In fact,' he smiled ruefully, 'I would congratulate the man on lasting this long with her. I will go into more detail with you regarding the police enquiry at a later date, but right now I am very weary and I would like to get home to my family.'

Albert left the hospital feeling a little brighter. He made no attempt to enquire after Felicity or to go and visit her, he was tired and just wanted to get home to Nellie and the girls. The delicious smell of roast mutton assailed his nostrils as he walked through the door where he was warmly greeted by Nellie and the girls.

'I know you will be tired Albert but we just can't wait to hear how your trip went,' gushed Nellie.

Albert hung his hat and coat on the coat stand and followed the family into the lounge, sinking gratefully into his chair by the fireplace. Nellie sat opposite him, Katherine pulled up a chair between them and the girls sat at Albert's feet.

'Where to begin,' he said 'firstly, you will no doubt be as surprised and alarmed as I was to hear that Felicity had been staying in the lodging house across the road from your shop in Dunedin,' he glanced at Nellie and Katherine in turn. 'It appears she disappeared the same night she pushed you off the cliff, from there we have no idea where she went. The Police are going to redouble their efforts to see if they can trace her movements and those of Mr Millward's. They suspect he may have been in Dunedin at the same time.'

The conversation continued all through dinner and late into the evening. Everyone had a theory, some more farfetched than others. Margaret and Marigold let their imaginations run away with them, as they tended to do, but this only succeeded in adding some levity to an otherwise disturbing situation. Other than Felicity's guilty conscience possibly driving her insane, nobody could guess what might have happened to cause her current demise. Albert didn't for one minute believe that Felicity even had a conscience, let alone a guilty one.

None of them slept well that night, each having dreams conjured up from the evening's conversation. They were all bleary eyed the next morning and grateful that it was Saturday and they didn't have to open the shop. They decided to have a quiet day at home. Margaret and Marigold asked if they could unpack their Aunt Felicity's trunk, to which Albert replied, 'suit yourselves, I want none of it.'

'That reminds me,' Albert said to Nellie, there is a note in the trunk from the warehouse down the road listing some items Felicity has stored there, remind me tomorrow morning to go and get them. No doubt the storage fees are well overdue by now.

Just as they were sitting down to their midday meal, there was a knock at the door.

'Yes?' said Albert, acknowledging the man standing on his doorstep.

'Mr Fitzgerald, Mr Albert Fitzgerald?'

'Yes, that's me.'

'I believe you might be looking for me sir, my name is Jack Millward.

Chapter Thirty-Two

Secrets unearthed

Albert invited the man standing hat in hand on his doorstep, to come inside, he was clearly nervous.

'The Superintendent at the hospital told me you wanted to see me and gave me your address. I do hope I have not come at an inopportune time.'

'We are just about to have lunch, would you care to join us?'

Jack was taken aback. 'I, er, well...'

'Come on man, you can meet Felicity's family and then you and I have much to talk about I think.'

'We do indeed,' said Jack humbly.

The conversation at the table was stilted as nobody knew what to say to this man, who had just appeared on their doorstep. He was quite possibly the only person who knew where Felicity had been for the past year. He was prepared to reveal everything right there and then at the dinner table but Albert asked that they please just enjoy the meal for now, they could talk about the situation after lunch. He wanted to talk to the man in private, to vet what he had to say before allowing the rest of his family to hear it.

After the table was cleared, Margaret and Marigold were put on dishes duty while Nellie and Katherine took a stroll in the garden. Once they were alone, Jack began to speak.

'I must apologise for what has happened to your sister Mr Fitzgerald, I meant her no harm. In fact, we got along very well, I have become very fond of her. I mean, I have not had relations with her or anything like that, I have treated her with the utmost respect.'

'Call me Albert and if I may, I will call you Jack. So, let's start at the beginning, when did you first meet Felicity and do you know what she has done?'

'Yes, I am aware of the terrible thing she has done to your wife, she did tell me. We spent many months together in a small hut in the mountains and ......

'She's been living in a hut in the mountains?' sputtered Albert, interrupting Jack midstream. He could barely control his laughter. 'Now that I would love to have seen.'

Jack smiled back, 'yes, it must have been quite a shock to her I suspect, and certainly a far cry from what she was used to but to be honest, she didn't have much of a choice.'

'What do you mean?' asked Albert.

'Look, I'm not proud of what I've done Albert, in fact I question myself everyday about my actions. If I had done things differently....'

'I am not here to judge you Jack, I know my sister, I know what a handful she can be. If you have survived living in a small hut in the mountains with her for the past twelve months or so, then I take my hat off to you. All I want is the truth.'

Jack nodded and looked down at his hands clasped tightly between his knees as his mind went back to the day he first saw Felicity.

'I was walking along the street when I thought I heard someone scream. I looked up just in time to see Felicity standing watching a woman falling off the cliff. She turned and walked down the hill towards me so I hid in a doorway and then followed her. I was so incensed by what I had seen I didn't quite know what to do. I knew my conscience wouldn't allow me to just walk away, I couldn't live with myself if I did that.'

Albert nodded his understanding. 'So, what did you do?'

'I followed her to the lodging house and when she opened the door, I pushed her in and shut the door behind me. I was angry, you see. As I followed her, I became more and more angry that she didn't seem to have a care in the world. She had just pushed someone off a cliff to her death and here she was walking down the street twirling her fancy umbrella as if nothing was amiss. It made my blood boil.'

'Yes, I think I would probably feel the same way Jack. So, what did you decide to do?'

'I had no idea what I was going to do, I just knew that I had to do something. When I confronted her I saw fear in her eyes, she seemed to be terrified of me. When she took her hat off, I saw the scars on her face and for some reason I began to feel sorry for her. I was torn between wanting to drag her off down to the police station and just walking away and leaving her there, but I felt I could do neither, I needed to come up with another option. That's when I cracked on to the idea of taking her back to my place up in the mountains. It would give us both time to think things through. In the end I gave her a choice, either she could come with me and be my housekeeper for a while until things died down back here, or I would take her to the police station and tell them what I saw her do. Obviously, she chose the former option.'

'So, Felicity rode on a wagon all the way across to the mountains and lived in a hut with you for a year?' Albert was still incredulous; he just couldn't picture Felicity living in a hut. 'How did she fare? Obviously not all that well considering where she has ended up.'

'To be honest with you Albert, she coped better than you might think. She did adapt to mountain life to a certain extent. I took some of her money and bought a wagon load of goods to take with us so that she would have some home comforts to make her life a little easier. My basic hut and meagre lifestyle were certainly not fit for a lady,' he smiled.

'So how did she spend her days, was she helpful at all? I can't imagine her being a farmer's housekeeper.'

'She did well enough,' said Jack thoughtfully. 'Of course, I have no idea what her life was like before I met her, although she did share a little bit about it from time to time. She told me about her childhood, how she got the scars and all that. She also told me, endlessly, how much she loved you and how you were always her saviour, her protector. She seemed to think that everything was perfect before you met your wife. She said she felt that Nellie had stolen you from her and that she had cheated on you and tried to ruin your life, that's why she did what she did. She wanted things to go back to the way they were when she ran the household and looked after the children, as if they were her own. Might I say, I am mightily relieved to see that your wife is still alive. You have no idea what a weight that has lifted off my shoulders Albert, I really mean that. All this time thinking she was dead has weighed heavily on me. Felicity must be relieved as well, I guess. She doesn't acknowledge me when I visit her,' he said sadly, 'so I have no idea what she is thinking.'

'She has seen Nellie,' said Albert, and she was none too pleased, I can tell you that much. In fact, it sent her further into despair than she was when you brought her to the hospital.'

'Ah,' said Jack, 'one of the nurses did say she had gotten worse.

'You seem upset, how can you care about a woman who does such heinous things to another human being. She has always been a jealous and conniving woman but I never in my wildest dreams thought she could commit such a hateful act.'

Jack shrugged his shoulders. 'I don't know,' he said, 'I.., there's just something about her. At first I just felt sorry for her but during the time we spent together I have become quite fond of her. But then she changed, after the attack.'

'What attack?' asked Albert.

'There were five musterers staying at the hut for two nights. Felicity didn't cope at all well with that situation. She tried to attack a couple of the men and we had to ahh, we had to restrain her.' Jack looked at Albert apologetically.

'I've seen Felicity in a rage Jack, believe me if I could have, I would have restrained her too. Carry on.'

We started drinking whiskey after dinner and eventually we all fell asleep inside the hut. It appears that during the night, while Felicity was still tied to the bed, one of the musterers raped her. I honestly didn't see or hear anything of the attack and neither did any of the others, nobody said anything before they left in the morning. I checked on her when I got up and she appeared to be asleep so I left her. When I came back, she seemed to be still asleep so I took off her gag and undid her bindings. It took a bit to bring her round but when I did, I could tell by the look in her eyes that something bad had happened, I'd seen that look once before. I checked her over and that's when I realised what had happened, when I saw the blood and the bruising.'

Albert flinched. 'Good God, I would never have wished that on her.' He could see Jack was struggling with this part of the story too so he got up and poured them both a brandy.

'That's when everything changed for the worse,' Jack continued. 'If I ever find out who it was, I will swing for him, I swear I will. From then on, she seemed to be in a trance, no emotions, nothing. We were trapped in the mountains for two months after that, because of the snow. I took care of her the best I could. The only time she reacted to anything was when one of the dogs bit her on the leg, boy did she yelp and scream and perform at that. She had kicked out at the dog as she walked past and the dog had bitten her in defence. It was all I could do to stop her tearing the poor animal limb from limb, I had to restrain her again until she calmed down. She seemed to go even further downhill after that. In the end I decided she needed to go to hospital, there was nothing else I could do for her and I was getting really worried. I was hoping that by bringing her here to Christchurch she would get better and perhaps reconnect with her family. I wanted her family to know what had become of her, but I didn't know how to go about that without landing myself in trouble.

Albert nodded, 'I am very grateful you have come forward Jack, that took courage. It has put my mind at ease to know that apart from that awful attack Felicity was well taken care of, thank you.'

'Albert, I know you are extremely angry with Felicity but if I may, I'd just like to say something in her defence.' Albert

267

nodded so Jack continued, 'I am not making excuses for what she has done, but have you considered that she might be mentally unwell to have done the things she has done? I mean, she is obviously ill now, but I mean before all this happened. Did it all start when she got burnt perhaps? I only ask because I have seen a similar situation with a member of my family. My cousin was a bright cheerful lad as a boy, we grew up together, then he suffered horrendous burns in a house fire and was never really the same after that. He went on to end up in gaol himself, he just seemed to go off the rails, if you know what I mean.'

Albert was thoughtful for a while then glancing across at Jack he said, 'You know, you might be on to something there. Felicity was a happy little girl until then. She did become very quiet and moody after the accident and we just thought it was because she was shy about her scars but perhaps the trauma of it all affected her more than we thought. Maybe I should be a little more tolerant and understanding.' He smiled, 'more like my beautiful soft-hearted wife perhaps. Anyway, that's enough about us,' he said, wanting to change the subject, 'tell me about yourself? What is your background? When did you arrive in New Zealand?'

'I was born here,' Jack said. 'I am ashamed to admit it, but I am illegitimate. My mother was a secretary for a member of Parliament in Wellington, they had an affair and I am the result of that affair. My mother went on to marry a coal merchant after I was born and he became my stepfather. He was a very good father figure I might add and I have a half-sister living in Wellington.'

'You say you own the sheep station you are living on?'

'Yes, my real father did at least acknowledge my existence and bestowed upon my mother the princely sum of £1000 which she invested for me until I came of age at twenty-one. I worked as a stockman and farm labourer until five years ago, that's when I decided to lease my own property, so that money has served me well.'

'My father was a member of Parliament in Wellington,' said

Albert. 'I remember he had a secretary, what was her name, Mary, yes that was it.' He looked up and was surprised to see Jack had turned quite pale.

'Are you unwell Jack, you seem to have lost all your colour.'

'My mother's name was Mary,' he whispered, 'she was secretary to a man named George, she would never tell me his surname, or why.'

Now it was Albert's turn to go pale. 'My father's name was George. What year did you say that money was given to your mother?'

'The year I was born, 1826.'

Albert leapt to his feet and left the room returning with a journal. This is a record of my father's accounts from that year.' He flicked through it, ran his hand down one of the pages, stopped and turned to Jack.

'Good God man, it appears you are my half-brother.'

Epilogue

After Albert's revelation, Jack went to visit his mother in Wellington to get answers, and if possible, a copy of his birth certificate. Sure enough, the name of the father on his birth certificate was one George Fitzgerald. He couldn't wait to get back to tell Albert.

Albert and the rest of his family welcomed this new-found 'brother' into the fold with open arms. The two men got along famously and over the ensuing years would become almost inseparable, they had a lot of ground to make up.

Jack let go of the lease on his property in the mountains and got a job in Christchurch as a Stock and Station Agent, that way he could still spend some time in the mountains when he visited his clients, he considered he had the best of both worlds. Albert helped him to build a nice house close by and Jack is engaged to a lovely young lady, the daughter of one of his clients, whom he visits more often than he needs to.

Albert and Jack both visited Felicity on a regular basis. Understandably Nellie never did. Felicity barely responded to either of the men but Jack was forever hopeful that she might 'come good' one day. Albert, on the other hand, held out no such hope and over the years he did soften just a little towards his sister, although he never forgave her.

Felicity never left the asylum, she simply wasted away over the years and died almost ten years to the day after she pushed Nellie off that cliff.

Katherine fell head over heels in love with the Postmaster about a year after she moved back to Christchurch. He is an attractive, jovial chap and fell head over heels in love with Katherine too. They got married in the Spring with Nellie, Margaret and Marigold as her attendants. She now lives and works with her husband in the Post Office.

Margaret and Marigold left school and took over the running of Nellie's Dress Shop and added a 'Junior Misses' range. They work well together, despite their differences, but perhaps that's what makes their partnership successful. Both of them are being courted by 'very nice, presentable, young men,' so Nellie and Albert are looking forward to weddings and grandchildren.

Nellie took Margaret and Marigold to France to introduce them to her contacts and to give them the opportunity to see the latest fashions and bring back some fresh ideas for the shop. Needless to say the girls have never stopped talking about it since.

Once Nellie felt confident enough to hand the business over to the girls, she was happy to walk away and leave them to it. She tires easily and isn't as agile as she used to be, even though she isn't yet fifty. Albert brought in a housekeeper, not that Nellie complained, she never was much of a domestic, but she enjoys the beautiful gardens she and Katherine created over the years and spends most of her time there.

Nellie and Albert have barely had a cross word between them since they remarried, they simply cherish every blessed day God grants them, taking nothing for granted.

Midday Sunday roast dinners at the Fitzgerald household have become something of a tradition now. It is a time for the extended family to catch up with each other. Albert had to buy a new, extendable, dining room table to accommodate the growing family, not that he complained mind you, he loved Sundays with his family, which now consisted of himself and Nellie, Margaret, Marigold, and sometimes their suitors, Katherine and her husband, Jack and his wife and of course Harry, Agnes and their four children.

This is Nellie's favourite day of the week, she adores her family and friends and cherishes every moment with them. Every now and then though, she reaches up and touches the wee silver heart hanging around her neck on a silver chain, and thinks about her parents and her sister Emilyn.

The End